He was looking drawn and weary. Inexorably, the Noss Head negotiations had begun on schedule. By day Cramer was sitting in the chair that everybody had expected to see occupied by Davidson Wylie. By night he haunted Scotland Yard, seeking the latest information.

"On the practical level, it means we have no place to start. Black Tuesday has no known supporters or known locations. But even more important, it means we have no idea what they're interested in. They probably don't have members already in prison, so it would have to be a political issue."

"Look, they've already gotten their money, and you don't think it's prisoners. What else could it be?"

The detective looked grim. "I just hope we don't have a terrorist group with its eye on North Sea oil."

"Oh, my God!"

P9-CRZ-137

Books by Emma Lathen

Accounting for Murder*
Ashes to Ashes*
Banking on Death*
By Hook or By Crook*
Come to Dust
Death Shall Overcome*
Double, Double, Oil and Trouble*
The Longer the Thread*
Murder Against the Grain*
Murder Makes the Wheels Go 'Round*
Murder to Go*
Pick Up Sticks*
A Place for Murder*
A Stitch in Time*
Sweet and Low*

*Published by POCKET BOOKS

EMMA LATHEN

A JOHN PUTNAM THATCHER MYSTERY

DOUBLE, DOUBLE, OIL AND TROUBLE

PUBLISHED BY POCKET BOOKS NEW YORK

POCKET BOOKS, a Simon & Schuster division of
GULF & WESTERN CORPORATION
1230 Avenue of the Americas, New York, N.Y. 10020

Published by arrangement with Simon and Schuster
Library of Congress Catalog Card Number: 78-5151

ISBN: 0-671-82125-3

First Pocket Books printing August, 1980

10 9 8 7 6 5 4 3 2 1

Contents

1. RAISING THE RIG   7
2. EXPLORATORY DRILLING   15
3. PIPELINES   26
4. ENERGY COSTS   36
5. DRY WELL   44
6. DEPLETION ALLOWANCE   56
7. FOREIGN AND DOMESTIC FIELDS   66
8. KNOWN RESERVES   78
9. TEXAS TOWERS   89
10. BOOMTOWN!   105
11. OFFSHORE OPERATIONS   115
12. PUMPING STATIONS   122
13. FREEZING IN THE DARK   134
14. SECONDARY RECOVERY   146
15. PETRODOLLARS   153
16. BLOWOUT   167
17. THE INDEPENDENTS   177
18. OIL SLICK   186
19. WILDCATTING   196
20. TWIN GUSHERS   206
21. CAPPING THE WELL   215
22. REFINING THE CRUDE   224

1 · Raising the Rig

On Wall Street, grief does not drape city lampposts in black. Joy can reign without leaving rose petals and laurel leaves for the Sanitation Department. In the financial community the emotions may be the same, but the symbols are different. One omitted dividend beats all the sackcloth and ashes in the world. Frequently it rivals suttee.

Thus, whatever happens to Dow Jones, wreaths do not appear on the steps of the Federal Reserve, where they would not only be inappropriate, they would be misplaced. Because Wall Street transcends the short, narrow thoroughfare in the Borough of Manhattan. Wall Street is a creed, linking true believers on the Rue de la Bourse and the Paseo de la Castellana. Every non-collective onion sold in Moscow proves that the Real Presence can materialize anywhere.

John Putnam Thatcher of the Sloan Guaranty Trust knew this very well. Unlike many people, he also knew that the best place to exploit his knowledge was on Wall Street proper, the Borough of Manhattan, the City of New York.

But senior vice presidents are fair game. Important events demand important men. Let Australia expand her nickel capacity and Thatcher would find himself on Macquarie Street, Sydney. If Battle Creek planned to saturate Scandinavia with cornflakes, Thatcher would get to Copenhagen before the cereal salesmen.

It was inevitable, therefore, when the Sloan decided on a major reshuffling of its European credits, that John Thatcher, supported by his second-in-command, Charlie Trinkam, should expect to spend several weeks on one of the most heavily trafficked extensions of Wall Street—the Bahnhofstrasse in Zurich, Switzerland.

This expectation did not include being awakened in the middle of the night in his comfortable bedroom at the Baur au Lac by a transatlantic call from the Sloan's chairman of the board.

"John! Thank God! I was afraid you might be out."

Thatcher stared at the phone. Voice, action, and words all suggested that in New York, George Lancer, that bulwark of respectability, was roaring drunk.

"George, it's three o'clock in the morning here. Why should I be out?"

"Never mind. Just listen to me. It's another terrorist kidnapping."

Thatcher automatically ran down the list of Sloan employees in South America. "Which one?" he asked tightly.

"Oh my God, I never thought of that! It's not one of ours. You remember I'm on the board at Macklin?"

"Calm down, George." Thatcher could think and speak more freely now that the victim was not someone he knew. "All right, you're on Macklin's board of directors. I suppose it's one of theirs."

"Their European manager was kidnapped in Istanbul yesterday by some splinter group called Black Tuesday. They want a million and a half in bills deposited in a numbered account in Zurich tomorrow."

Thatcher could already foresee his distasteful role in this melodrama.

"Macklin's paying, I take it?"

8

"We're all down here at the Sloan, counting the money out. It's going with a courier on the next plane to Zurich. He'll give it to you, together with the kidnappers' instructions and the number of the account. John, you won't like some of the details these SOB's insist on."

"What do you mean, some of them? The whole thing turns my stomach. What bank is the account at?"

"Union Suisse."

"Wonderful!" Thatcher had left the executive offices of Union Suisse a bare nine hours ago. "Has anybody warned Grimm?"

"John, I wanted to get you first. As soon as I hang up, I have to call Grimm—" Lancer paused painfully "—and then the television stations."

"Oh, my God!"

Thatcher had long since accepted the fact that doing business abroad separated him from his well-appointed office at the Sloan, from his invaluable Miss Corsa, and from all the other comforts of home.

"But this takes the cake," said Charlie Trinkam the next day.

He and Thatcher, each carrying two large briefcases, were proceeding up the Bahnhofstrasse.

"It is unusual, I grant you," said Thatcher. "And I, for one, refuse to say that it's all in a day's work." He had not turned his head. Without looking, he knew that Trinkam was scowling darkly. But there was another departure from normalcy. "Why are you talking out of the corner of your mouth, Charlie?"

Charlie did not relax his precautions. "Lipreaders," he said lopsidedly.

Still progressing, Thatcher considered this. "I doubt if anybody cares what we're saying. It's what we're delivering that counts."

Charlie could hardly disagree. In the four bags were enough small unmarked bills to make up the ransom.

Bad as this was, it was not the worst. Trained upon

them as they traversed the final block of the Bahnhofstrasse were television cameras from the BBC, Télévision Française, and CBS. Clattering overhead was a helicopter hired by *Paris Soir,* intent on an aerial view of this episode of history-in-the-making.

"Goddamned bunch of nuts," Charlie snarled.

"Look on it as a tribute," said Thatcher, shifting his burden as they finally neared the end of their ordeal by camera. "This whole absurd scenario is a compliment from some primitive minds."

Just ahead, a policeman was pulling open the great brass door of Union Suisse. Blinking unhappily, Leopold Grimm emerged, flinched visibly at the firing squad of photographers, then peered past the barricades in their direction.

"Try selling Grimm that line," Charlie replied with a resurgence of his usual irreverence. "You know, I've never seen him in broad daylight before. Terrible sight, isn't he?"

"He's suffering," said John Thatcher charitably.

"Look at him! You'd think he'd had to hoof it three blocks, like us," said Charlie.

With the witching hour at hand, Thatcher ignored this complaint by a confirmed taxi-taker. In seconds, one and a half million dollars were going to be off the Sloan's hands.

"Good morning, Leopold," he said soberly.

Just then *Paris Soir,* coming in for a close-up, filled the heavens.

"Such stupidity," Grimm retorted, bobbing his head in truncated greeting. With a glare at the helicopter, he hurried Trinkam and Thatcher indoors. "I must apologize. They insisted on a camera in the lobby. But in my office we will be safe."

When they reached this sanctuary, Leopold Grimm's agitation fell away to reveal the true man. He was cold, formidable, and angry.

"So!" he grunted, waving Thatcher and Trinkam to chairs. "Games for children! Evil children!"

Rescuing Davidson Wylie, Macklin's European manager, was an international exercise in fury. Across the Atlantic, the Sloan and the U.S. Treasury growled and rumbled. Here, authorities of the Canton of Zurich and the Republic of Switzerland cursed in four languages. No doubt the Turks were fulminating all over Asia Minor.

Thatcher himself resented force under duress.

Charlie Trinkam could always tell when it was time for him to pick up the ball: "Here is one and a half million dollars in small bills, Herr Grimm," he said formally, depositing his share on Grimm's desk and stooping for Thatcher's. Straightening, he tried to relieve the tension. "You'd better count it, Leopold."

This mild pleasantry nearly tripped them up. Grimm had to force a smile. "Somebody will certainly count it, Herr Trinkam," he said, training a crisp flow of German at his intercom. "We, meanwhile, will drink something."

By the time various minions had removed the ransom and provided coffee, brandy, and a pastry tray, the atmosphere had improved. But no amount of strudel makes an obligatory hour less tedious.

Grimm was aware of this. "Again, I apologize. But Hummel says that it will take at least an hour."

Hummel was the Zurich police. Thatcher had dealt with him at the Hotel Baur au Lac before he and Charlie set forth. Here at the other end, Hummel was still stage-managing. But the script had been written by others.

"Have we covered the points in the ransom note?" Thatcher asked, pulling out his copy and adding a final tick mark.

American exploiters of the emergent world!
Take warning! Today we have seized a prisoner of war from the Macklin Company. He will be executed unless you follow these instructions.

1. A restitution of $1.5 million must be made to us. You will assemble this sum in small unmarked bills at the Sloan Guaranty Trust in New York.

2. An officer of the Sloan will carry the money into the main office of Union Suisse in Zurich on

11

Wednesday, July 22. There will be live coverage by CBS, BBC and Télévision Française.

3. The money will be deposited in account numbered: 703 1218 of Union Suisse.

4. There will be no police surveillance of any person leaving Union Suisse on July 22.

If these instructions are followed, clemency will be granted and the prisoner released within thirty-six hours.

By order of
BLACK TUESDAY

"Now it's up to them," Thatcher concluded.

During the next few hours, somebody would enter the Union Suisse and leave with $1.5 million in cash.

"With 'no surveillance,'" Grimm quoted scornfully. "That was a condition. Switzerland has solemnly promised not to interfere."

"There's another tribute for you, John," said Charlie.

"Exactly," Thatcher replied. "Black Tuesday certainly trusts the Swiss."

Grimm was unmoved by the compliment. "They are right to do so. They will not be shot down like dogs the minute they appear. We will cooperate fully to regain your Davidson Wylie. But then, we will teach this Black Tuesday a little lesson."

Thatcher could only hope that Switzerland would succeed.

"We will provide an example to would-be kidnappers," continued Grimm with steely satisfaction. "No, they will not enjoy this ransom!"

"Money isn't everything," Charlie said heretically. "I'd put my marbles on Turkish justice. That is, I would with garden-variety crooks. With loonies like Black Tuesday, you never can tell."

The idiom puzzled Grimm, but he grasped the thrust of Charlie's argument. "You mean that the terrorists ignore deterrents? I agree. To stamp out this scourge, we should refuse to deal with such scum, no matter what they threaten!"

If the three of them had not been sitting in Grimm's office, obeying the kidnappers to the letter, this martial pronouncement would have sounded better.

"But it is a difficult decision," Grimm conceded to the unvoiced rebuttal. "I can comprehend Macklin's policy. It would not be easy for them to say, 'Do what you will! We do not pay!' "

"In addition, I understand they really need Wylie," said Thatcher. "Macklin hasn't done much building in Europe and Wylie is their expert."

"North Sea oil," said Grimm, knowledgeably. "Macklin is one of the construction firms bidding on the tanker farm off Noss Head. I remember now."

Repressing a smile, Thatcher nodded. The billion-dollar facility in north Scotland would involve tanker berths, onshore pumping stations, and pipelines to out-run the imagination of man. The British Department of Energy had received bids from German firms, Swedish firms, Japanese firms, and Macklin. Behind every bidder was bedrock engineering expertise—and a powerful bank. Somewhere, somehow, Leopold Grimm and Union Suisse were deeply involved.

"So Davidson Wylie is worth far more than one and a half million dollars, if he can get Noss Head for Macklin." Grimm was reassessing the whole situation.

"That certainly entered their calculations," said Thatcher. "In principle, Macklin and the U.S. govern-ment—and the Sloan, I might add—agree with you about terrorists completely."

With a tidy gesture, Grimm waved principle away. "Still it would be satisfying to capture these kidnap-pers."

"For all of us," said Thatcher truthfully.

Yet he could not help a selfish sense of relief that Davidson Wylie's fate was no longer in his hands. With luck, he and Trinkam could return to their in-tensive scrutiny of foreign-exchange desks.

Charlie was not superstitious about putting optimism into words.

"Well, it could have been worse," he said, checking his watch. "Getting up the cash was no real problem.

13

What if these clowns had wanted us to empty Sing Sing? Just as long as they deliver Wylie safe and sound."

"I am sure they will," said Grimm quickly.

The automatic reassurance amused Thatcher. The kidnappers trusted Swiss banks and vice versa.

He did not ruffle Grimm by saying as much, but followed Charlie's lead. "Your people must be just about through, Leopold. We leave Davidson Wylie in your capable hands," he said.

In the larger sense he was premature, as the weeks and months to come would prove. In the smaller sense, he was corrected immediately.

After a perfunctory buzz, a trim competent woman entered Grimm's office, notebook in hand. Out of deference to the visitors, Fräulein Leutenegger, a spiritual sister to Miss Corsa if Thatcher had ever seen one, made her report in serviceable English. Like Miss Corsa, she planted her darts with no visible emotion.

"We have completed the tally, Herr Grimm. I am afraid that the money brought by Herr Thatcher and Herr Trinkam—" here Fräulein Leutenegger glanced briefly at them "—is exactly seventeen dollars short."

Instinctively, two bankers thought about reprimands for cashier's desks and supervisory personnel. The third thought about escape.

"Leopold," said Charlie Trinkam, "will you take a personal check?"

2 · Exploratory Drilling

Following his appearance on world television, Thatcher was delighted to retire to private life or, in this case, the Hotel Baur au Lac. The service was excellent, the view was breathtaking and, best of all, there was not a camera in sight. After the Bahnhofstrasse, it was a haven.

But only for a very short time. Thatcher was relaxing with Charlie over a well-earned drink when he idly noticed a latecomer haranguing the headwaiter. Since the altercation was in rapid-fire French, his attention would have shifted if the dispute had not headed his way.

"Mr. Thatcher, this gentleman desires to speak with you," said the waiter, disassociating himself from any consequences.

His catch was nothing to fill any maître d'hôtel with pride. The young man's clothes, hair, and chinline all gave evidence of neglect. He did not believe in wasting time on niceties either. Speaking in unmistakably American accents, he sank into a spare chair and blurted:

"Did it go all right? Did Black Tuesday get their money?"

Charlie Trinkam had already been interviewed by too many people. "Why didn't you watch it on television?" he retorted. "Everyone else did."

"I just got off the plane," the young man explained earnestly. "It took hours to get cleared out of Istanbul."

"Istanbul?" Charlie repeated, while John Thatcher frowned.

There was a harsh laugh. "Talk about locking the stable door too late! The terrorists have got Dave somewhere right under the noses of the Turkish police, and the cops give *me* a hard time about going to Switzerland. Then I got tangled up with some kind of rock festival at the Zurich airport. There are thousands of longhairs—"

"Just a minute," Thatcher interrupted. "Exactly who are you?"

Their visitor gaped. "I'm Paul Volpe!" he started to protest before stopping in midflight. Then he produced a shamefaced grimace. "Look, I guess I began the wrong way. It never occurred to me you wouldn't know who I am. And the truth is, I've been spinning my wheels so much this past couple of days, I don't know which end is up anymore. But somebody at Macklin must have mentioned me. And I can prove that I'm Paul Volpe. God knows, if I could satisfy the Turkish police, I can satisfy anyone. See, here's my passport and my Italian residence permit and my driver's license."

"What do you think we are? The CIA? The next thing, you'll be giving us a password."

But even as Charlie recoiled from these hints of cloak and dagger, Thatcher stretched out a hand and began to leaf through Volpe's passport, studying exit and entry stamps.

"Yes," he murmured thoughtfully, "I believe Lancer did tell me about you."

Charlie's memory was also stirring to life. "Say, didn't the papers say you were in Istanbul when

16

Wylie was snatched? You work for Macklin, too."

"I wasn't just in Istanbul. I was looking down the barrel of the same gun."

Thatcher had no intention of encouraging more dramatics. "Well, you didn't get shot. And this morning, we delivered the ransom." He then undid the effect of this dash of cold water by succumbing to curiosity. "What exactly has been happening in Istanbul? I gather you've been there until today?"

"God, yes. You know, I still can't take it in. Poor Dave! They've got half of Turkey mobilized, but if you ask me they don't know where to start. It's the awful helplessness that gets to you. You keep thinking you should be doing something. But when you get right down to it, what is there to do but yell at someone?"

The monotonic chant alerted Thatcher. At his best Paul Volpe was probably not a robust figure. Short and slight, he had a pale complexion and long, nervous fingers. But now the white blotches of skin visible between the dark circles under his eyes and the dark shadow of his jaw were waxen, his fingers obsessively kneaded a corner of the tablecloth, and a tic just under one earlobe throbbed remorselessly. Emotional strain was bad enough. But Thatcher had a hunch that this young fool had compounded it.

"I'm sure you've done everything that could be done in this situation," Thatcher said dispassionately. "And as you probably haven't eaten in some time, perhaps we should defer our discussion. Trinkam and I were about to order."

As he half-expected, Paul Volpe reacted with impatience.

"No, no. You go ahead," he said. "I couldn't eat a thing . . ."

One hour later Volpe had demolished a steak, a large platter of fried potatoes and a mountain of salad. He still looked like the wrath of God, but his speech assumed a new coherence. The tic had subsided altogether.

"We dealt directly with the president of the bank," Thatcher told him. "The deposit was entered into the numbered account a full two hours before the deadline. What's more, the whole performance was televised, so the kidnappers could watch it."

"Then Dave should be all right. They promised they'd let him go within thirty-six hours of getting the money." Volpe's brow creased as a new worry emerged. "They won't have any trouble emptying the account, will they? Nobody's going to interfere with them?"

"Certainly not." Thatcher decided not to expound on Swiss attitudes. On the other hand he did not wish to raise false hopes. "The money will go through, but that does not guarantee Wylie's safety. After all, there is a real possibility that his abductors will not leave a witness to testify against them."

Volpe shook his head. "I don't see why not. Everyone in the restaurant saw as much of them as Dave did. If Black Tuesday lets Dave loose someplace off the beaten track, they can probably be on their way back to Libya, or Syria, or wherever they come from, before he gets to a main highway."

"Is that what they said they'd do?"

"They didn't say anything to me. They just left that damned note. Maybe I'd better tell you how it happened."

Charlie primed him. "Let's see, you were in Turkey before Wylie, weren't you?"

"Oh, I'd been there for three months. You know I'm working on the Aegean offshore oil situation. Under Dave, of course. When I finished up in Athens, he came down and checked out what I'd done. He was going to do the same thing in Istanbul. He got there Monday morning, and we spent the day going around to some of the Ministry officials. Then when dinner time came, he said he'd heard about this little place up the coast that specialized in fish. God, it never occurred to me that it might be dangerous to take him out of the city. I never thought twice about it."

"Why should you?" demanded Charlie. "You didn't expect terrorists to come crawling out of the woodwork. Nobody's blaming you."

"I'll bet that isn't how they see it in Houston." Volpe was kneading his napkin this time. "They've been so indoctrinated by years in South America and the Middle East that they take precautions unconsciously. They'll wonder why I didn't."

John Thatcher had just invested an hour bringing his guest to some measure of rationality. The good work was not going to be swamped by a tide of self-accusation.

"Nonsense!" he said bracingly. "Macklin is very much aware that conditions in Europe are unlike those elsewhere. Lancer tells me that's why they didn't assign one of their own people to set up a European office. They didn't have the right background."

"It's true that's why they hired Dave." Volpe's face cleared. "He's been doing business in Europe for over fifteen years."

Charlie Trinkam had some worldly wisdom to contribute. "And so long as Wylie was your boss, you were going to end up eating where he wanted. It didn't make any difference whether it was the Hilton, or some out-of-the-way gourmet spot the tourists haven't discovered yet."

"Well, this place sure hasn't been discovered." Volpe produced his first grin, shaky but genuine. "It's a ramshackle mom-and-pop operation with about ten or twelve tables. You know, the kind where they have the shellfish and squid and eels lying on a slab. After you pick out what you want, the owner does it for you right there. Hell, for all I know, the food is wonderful. I never got to taste it."

"You mean they were waiting for you?"

"No, things didn't happen that fast. I figure they must have been following us. Anyway, at first we were the only people there, but we were awfully early by Turkish standards, so that didn't surprise me. Another couple came in while we were choosing our dinner. Then we had a drink and the old man began

19

grilling our fish. The old lady had tossed together a plate of tidbits as appetizers. She was just putting them down when the door burst open, and these two guys came in. They had sten guns aimed at us and ski masks hiding their faces. I tell you, for a minute or two, I had a hard time taking it in. It was like something you see in the movies."

Thatcher decided that, by now, a measure of sympathy could do no harm.

"It must have been a shock," he murmured. "What did they say?"

"Not much. I suppose it was a real professional operation. They were in and out of there in less time than it takes to describe. They just barked a few orders in broken English about not moving and keeping our hands in sight. But they made Dave get up and one of them marched him out with a gun in his back. The other one waited until there was a whistle from the front and then started to back out. Just before he cleared the door he took an envelope out of his pocket and rammed it at the old man. The next thing we heard was a motor revving and tires screeching. So I ran to my car, but it wouldn't start. Later on the police showed me how the distributor cap had been taken off."

Charlie Trinkam occasionally fell into the error of admiring competence no matter how improperly applied. "Stands to reason," he said approvingly. "They would have immobilized all the transport before they came in. Only sensible thing to do."

Paul Volpe resented this detachment. "Oh, they were great," he said shortly. "Maybe you think I was lucky to deal with such efficient gunmen. As far as I'm concerned, my only stroke of luck was that the restaurant had a phone. When I went back in, the old man was already talking to the cops. I don't know what he told them, but he must have pressed the right button. Because the bigwigs arrived less than ten minutes after the locals. And I'll say one thing for them, they didn't waste any time once they read the ransom note. They were calling Macklin headquarters in Houston and alerting the border points before you could catch your breath."

Thatcher could well imagine how the letter had galvanized the Turkish authorities. "The police realized that Black Tuesday's schedule wasn't leaving much leeway," he remarked.

"I didn't know that then," Volpe answered. "It was damned frustrating. The envelope was addressed to Manager of Operations at the Macklin Company, but the police brass acted like it was none of my business. I do know that they read the ransom note over the phone to Hugo Cramer so he could get started. Then, after they photographed it and dusted it for fingerprints and all that jazz, they sent it on to him in Houston by the first plane." Volpe took a deep breath to continue loudly: "And I still say we were damn lucky to have the cops get cracking that fast."

Charlie was struck by this defensiveness. "Who says you weren't?"

"Hugo Cramer, for openers," snapped Volpe. "He gave me a lot of flak about how I should have kept the police out of it until we got Dave back. Christ! There were four other witnesses. Did he expect me to throttle them?"

Thatcher shook his head at this evidence of panic at Macklin's headquarters. "This Cramer of yours must have temporarily lost his head," he reasoned. "Terrorists aren't like ordinary kidnappers. They revel in publicity. And this particular group was demanding worldwide television coverage. I shouldn't let Cramer's outburst bother you. He's probably forgotten all about it by now."

But Paul Volpe's grievance against his home office covered more than a blast of criticism.

"They act as if having the police in on this doesn't matter one way or another. But if Captain Harbak hadn't got right on the stick, Black Tuesday could have Dave anywhere in the Middle East by now. At least we know he's still in Turkey."

"You mean because they alerted the border cross-ings?" Charlie was frankly dubious. "That's always being done, but it doesn't always work. Look at the number of American radicals who ended up in Algiers. Hell, Turkey has a damn long coast. They could have taken Wylie out in a dinghy for a rendezvous with a big boat."

Now, however, they were on Paul Volpe's ground—he knew the territory. "It's been clear as a bell the last two nights and they've been patrolling the coast from the air. Sure, they could have missed the dinghy, but not the big boat."

"Well, what about a land route?" suggested Charlie, dusting off his dim memories of Turkish geography. "Haven't I heard about smuggling between Iran and Turkey?"

Volpe was unimpressed. "You mean Kurdistan? The mountains there are ten thousand feet high. Besides, that area is seven hundred miles from Istanbul. They never could have gotten through the roadblocks to get to the foothills."

"Exactly so," said Thatcher decisively, closing the speculation. He knew nothing about Kurdistan and he rather suspected that neither did the terrorists. "The odds are that Wylie is being held in downtown Istanbul, just as you said earlier. But what interests me in your account of the kidnapping is that the envelope was already addressed. Black Tuesday was not simply cruising around looking for the most important American businessman they could find."

"Not on your life. The letter was centered around Macklin, too. There was nothing random about it."

Thatcher thought Volpe was missing the point. "Then who knew Wylie was going to be in Istanbul? Many people?"

Clearly this had not occurred to Volpe. He hesitated. "Some people, but not all that many. I had to make appointments for him at the Ministries. He was only going to be in town for a couple of days."

"Then the chances of his leaving downtown Istanbul were quite remote. It makes him an odd choice of victim."

Charlie had no trouble following the drift of Thatcher's argument. "So," he said turning to Volpe, "what's really interesting is that the note never mentioned Davidson Wylie specifically."

"I don't see what you're getting at."

"Maybe Wylie was an unexpected bonus." Charlie sounded amused. "You were the one who'd been around for months. Maybe they were planning to snatch you."

Volpe goggled. He was speechless for several seconds, then spoke without thinking. "Then it's a damned good thing they took Dave instead of me!"

"Self! . . . self!" Charlie chided him.

"That's not what I meant. Nobody would pay a million dollars for me. I'm not doing anything special. But with the Noss Head negotiations starting next week, Macklin doesn't have any choice about Dave. Nobody in Houston is prepared to make that kind of presentation to the British government. No matter what it costs them, Macklin has got to have Dave sitting at that table in London by Tuesday."

"Let's hope they do," said Thatcher gravely as he signaled for the check.

Charlie Trinkam could see another possibility.

"Volpe says he's going on to London to hold the fort," he said later. "Do you think he's hoping to step into his boss's shoes?"

Tolerantly Thatcher shook his head. "Oh, there's no doubt the boy is genuinely horrified at Wylie's plight. But he's human too. He wants to show how well he can pinch-hit in an emergency."

"Maybe," Charlie conceded. "But he sure has convinced himself that nobody in Houston is capable of operating in Europe."

"There, I think he may be unduly optimistic."

"And what was Wylie doing down in Turkey anyway? I thought he was their North Sea specialist."

Thatcher reminded himself that Macklin had never been one of Charlie's accounts. "It's a good deal more complicated than that. You know that Macklin has been doing heavy construction for the oil companies since before World War II?"

"God, have they been around that long? I think of them as a postwar phenomenon."

"It was after the war that they moved out of Texas and California onto the international scene." Thatcher mentally reviewed the far-flung arenas of Macklin's enterprises. "You could say that they spent the last thirty years working everywhere in the world except Europe. And, as they believe in bringing up people within the organization, the front office now has the same experience as the company at large. Then, when offshore oil became economically viable, Europe suddenly became part of the world oil scene. At that time Macklin didn't even have an office in Europe. They looked around and found Wylie, an American businessman with years of experience in Europe. They hired him to open a European office and to stay on top of the whole offshore oil picture. That was about three years ago and he has, in fact, already gotten a few small subcontracts in Germany. Then the big one came along."

Charlie had found his footing. "The British North Sea operation."

"Yes. The oil companies of course got the contracts for drilling rights long ago. The exploratory work is now far enough along so that commercial drilling at certain sites has begun. Six months ago the British government announced an invitation for bids as prime contractor on all the land work at Noss Head in northeast Scotland—dockage, storage, and pumping facilities."

"Big business," said Charlie appreciatively.

"Very big, indeed."

"And construction companies came rushing from the four corners of the globe." By now Charlie was right at home.

"And who can blame them?" Thatcher retorted. "There then began the endless process of negotiating with the British Department of Energy for deviations from the specifications, demanding clarifications,

24

putting in sliding scales, coping with the fluctuations in the pound, forging compromises with the trade unions. Finally it was all done."

"And the small fry had been shaken out."

"Considerably more than the small fry. The only ones left, even formally, are two American companies, two Scandinavian companies, and one German company. Next Tuesday is the starting date for the final presentations."

Charlie never bothered with mere formal contenders. "And what does the smart money say?"

"That it's neck-and-neck between Macklin and the German company. And Davidson Wylie is the man who has been the Macklin Company in the eyes of the British government. He's done all the bargaining in the last three months."

"Boy, what a time for him to be snatched." Charlie was rueful. "Do you think Wylie's really that essential?"

"Macklin doesn't want to find out the hard way." Thatcher raised two fingers to illustrate his points. "First of all, they know the contest between themselves and the Germans is extraordinarily evenly balanced. They don't want to lose a feather of their fighting weight. Second, there is some truth in the claims of young Volpe. Macklin doesn't have any seasoned European personnel. So, in Wylie's absence, they would not only have to send in a newcomer unfamiliar with these particular negotiations, but one unfamiliar with general practices in the area."

Charlie grinned. "They could get in real hot water trying some of their Venezuelan tricks over here."

"Precisely. Wylie himself regarded his presence as essential every minute of the next two weeks. That's why he checked out any problems in Scandinavia and then completed his circuit down to the Aegean. He didn't intend even to take a phone call from the Continent until this contract was awarded."

"Well, you've convinced me of one thing. That kid wasn't talking through his hat. Macklin has to have Wylie in London by next Tuesday."

3 · Pipelines

"It's over four days, and there's been no word of Wylie. What do you think now, Hugo?"

Shouldering the phone, Hugo Cramer thrust a fistful of silver at the bellboy. "Here, just dump them there, will you?"

"The closet is here, sir—"

"Fine," said Cramer, with a large impatient gesture that sped the London Hilton staff on its way. His briskness on the phone was not so impersonal. "My thinking's the same as it was when I got on the plane this morning, Arthur. What did you expect? Hell, I haven't unpacked yet."

This irritability did not deflect Arthur Shute back in Houston. Macklin's new president was not part of the tough, stubborn world of field engineers with their battered, expensive leather luggage. He was a nationally known executive who had scored successes in both the public and private sectors. In Texas he had revealed another gift; he could hold his own with old hands like Cramer, his vice president of operations.

"Now that Black Tuesday has reneged on its promise to release Wylie," he said as if Cramer had not spoken, "Macklin is in a ticklish predicament. I have Phil and Jensen here with me and we all agree that from now on we're going to have to play it by ear. Macklin won't spare any effort to get Wylie back safely, as I don't have to tell you. At the same time, we've got to be realistic. The Noss Head negotiations are supposed to start tomorrow. I've just come from a board meeting, and there was a consensus—"

"Arthur," said Cramer heavily, "save your speeches for the board, huh? And since we're on the subject, hold your committee meeting after I'm off the line."

At Macklin, Arthur Shute and Hugo Cramer ran the show. Their division of labor, like their mutual respect—if not liking—was complete. Out of committee, Shute became less of a politician and Cramer less of a rough diamond. Phil and Jensen were asked to leave.

"Has the London office heard anything new?" Shute demanded.

"I already told you." Cramer planted himself on the bed with a thump that made the springs protest. "They met me at Heathrow and said Dave was still missing. What more is there to hear?"

In spite of himself, Shute lowered his voice. "You know I told PR to keep on top of the press coverage? Well, so far there hasn't been anything in the papers tying Dave to Noss Head."

For a moment, Cramer did not see what he was driving at. "So?" he asked impatiently.

"But what if Black Tuesday knows anyhow? What if they figure that they're onto something better than they hoped. They could be hanging on to Wylie for a second installment."

"Don't go off half-cocked. It's a possibility, but it's an outside chance."

Shute continued to gnaw his bone. "They could really put us through the wringer."

"Yeah, but I don't remember terrorists ever playing that game." Cramer plucked thoughtfully at his lower lip. "Look, Macklin's bid for Noss Head isn't exactly front-page news. Black Tuesday probably never heard of it."

"I'd like to believe that."

"What the hell's gotten into you, Arthur? If they want more money, they've got to ask someone for it. There hasn't been a sound at Houston, there hasn't been a sound here in London. Who else are they going to talk to?"

Arthur Shute was too accustomed to Cramer's manner to be offended.

"Hugo, I realize everything's landing on you. You're going to have to ask the British if they're willing to grant a delay—"

"And a fat chance I've got there," Cramer interrupted, renewing an old argument.

Shute pushed on. "You're going to have to do Dave's job if he doesn't turn up. But there's one possibility about Black Tuesday that's occurred to me. They might have contacted Mrs. Wylie."

"Francesca?" Cramer said blankly.

"Why not? They might be afraid our offices are knee deep in police by now. And they could count on her being frightened enough about Wylie to do whatever they ordered."

"But . . ." Slowly Cramer closed his mouth and suppressed the remark he had been about to make. Instead, he said, after a pause: "All right, I suppose it's worth checking out."

Even as he spoke, he was shaking his head dubiously.

Any American man who spends his entire adult life on the Continent is likely to have a European wife. Hugo Cramer appreciated that fact, but he knew in his bones that it was going to make this interview more difficult. His previous acquaintance with Francesca Ercoli Wylie had been limited to her fleeting trips to Houston. It had never occurred to him, in those happier days, that he might have to deal with her alone.

"This must be a hard time for you, Francesca. I want

you to know that we'll do anything we can to help," he began.

"Of course, I am very anxious about David's welfare," she said gravely. "Like all his friends, I hoped he would be released immediately after the ransom payment. Now I do not know what to think. I can only hope that he is safe."

Her formal declaration of concern was as good as a six-foot wall between them. Grimly Cramer tried to effect a breach.

"Look," he said awkwardly, "I know you and Dave haven't been hitting it off lately."

Francesca's eyebrows rose. "Do you mean that David told you I have filed for divorce?"

"No, I didn't know it had gone that far."

"Perhaps he thought it was none of your business," Francesca said evenly.

Cramer reddened. "I'm not trying to butt into your affairs. But if Macklin didn't know about your divorce, maybe Black Tuesday doesn't either. In which case, you'd be a natural person to contact."

With complete self-possession Francesca responded: "Yes, I follow your reasoning. But, Hugo, I think you must have forgotten that this is not a private kidnapping. Terrorists always make their communications as public as possible. And if they want more money, they are thinking in terms of a sum that they know I could never amass."

Cramer set his jaw. "Look, Francesca, I'm not trying to swap theories with you. I'm asking you flat out. Have you heard from Dave or anyone who says they've got him? And for God's sake, don't clam up on me. If you don't want me to go to the cops, I won't. But I've got to know."

"I have heard nothing. But perhaps you should know that I have been in Germany. I only returned home this morning."

"You mean you've been away?" Cramer made it into an accusation. "They could have been trying to get you for days and we wouldn't even know!"

Francesca saw no need to apologize. "It is unfortunate, but it was business."

"Great!" Cramer stubbed out his cigarette and glanced at his hostess.

Francesca Wylie was an attractive woman, built on Rubenesque lines, who wielded her considerable sexuality with skill and composure. None of this bothered Cramer who had a wide experience of mature Venezuelan sirens. What jarred him was the fatal word *business*. He was dimly aware that whenever a German or Swedish film was dubbed into Italian, the dulcet Tuscan accents of the heroine were likely to be those of Francesca Wylie. But he had grown up in a different world. He knew he was hopelessly old-fashioned and that today younger Macklin wives were probably talking about their own advertising agencies or their own law practices. Christ, the wife of one of the accountants was even an oil engineer for Texaco! This self-knowledge did not reconcile him to Francesca's life-style; it did make him aware of the need for conciliation.

"Well, I suppose it can't be helped," he admitted. "I'm sorry if I sound tense, but this is a tough time for Dave to go missing."

"Of course." Francesca nodded to herself. "The Noss Head contract is about to be awarded."

Cramer frowned at her suspiciously. How did she know that? Dave had moved out of this Kensington apartment three months ago. Could Francesca have been . . . ? Suddenly Cramer remembered some gossip he had overheard.

"I forgot," he said sourly. "You've got your own sources."

Francesca laughed outright. "Surely that is irrelevant. Even before David left here, he was busy ingratiating himself with the entire British government. There is little likelihood that I could have avoided knowing about Noss Head."

"You make it sound as if he was groveling on his knees. He was trying to find out what problems were really worrying the Department of Energy so we could come up with solutions."

"Very well then. Call it what you will." Francesca shrugged away these distinctions. "I only know that it required my attendance at innumerable restaurants and clubs."

Actually, Cramer would have called it pressing the flesh, but he wanted Francesca's cooperation.

"I know that kind of thing can be a drag," he said in mollifying tones, "but we're past that stage now. With the timetable so critical, you'll understand we don't want any delay in communications. So if you hear anything about Dave, you'll let me know right away, won't you?"

"I shall." She spoke more to herself than to Cramer. "We all have our own timetables and to each of us, they are critical."

"And if there's anything we can do for you," said Cramer, returning full circle to his starting point.

"But there is." She caught at his sleeve as he rose to go. "We must make it a fair exchange. Promise to call me—immediately—if you at Macklin hear any news at all."

"You can depend on it," he assured her. "Whatever—and whenever—we hear about Dave, we'll be in touch with you."

She dropped her eyes. "Thank you, Hugo. You must imagine how difficult this is for me. This waiting—it is not easy."

North Sea oil, on the other hand, could wait for no man. Simon Livermore, a senior civil servant in the Department of Energy, was making this plain to Hugo Cramer the following morning.

"In view of the very unusual circumstances, I have already raised the possibility of a delay with my minister. He feels that the presentations must take place as originally scheduled, although he is naturally shocked and appalled by this latest terrorist outrage."

Indeed the minister was so moved he had dispatched his own personal assistant to be present and express his concern directly.

"I have been asked to assure you, Mr. Cramer, that we are keeping abreast of the entire situation," the assistant said resonantly.

Cramer's acknowledgment of this civility was a grunt. "That kind of knocks the pins from under me," he confessed. "I was going to ask if there was any chance for a delay."

The personal assistant produced a regretful smile. "I'm afraid not. But we are receiving daily reports from Istanbul and we will know as soon as there is any news. The Turkish police are being most cooperative."

Hugo Cramer might lack polish but he had long ago learned to distinguish the important man in any team huddle. He kept his eyes firmly fixed on Simon Livermore. "Sure, everyone's cooperative and concerned—until it comes to the crunch. Then it's business as usual, even if Macklin is crippled without Dave."

"No, you mustn't think of it that way, Mr. Cramer." Simon Livermore's tailoring was a shade less expensive than the assistant's, his neatly slicked hair was not as modish, his accent a trifle less clipped, but he was not parroting somebody else's words. "We will be going ahead exactly as planned on the basis of the preliminaries already completed by Mr. Wylie. That, as we both know, is half the battle. And should Mr. Wylie's absence continue, you as his superior will be able to make the presentation in his place."

It was as magnanimous a statement as one could ask from a bureaucrat. Cramer was fully aware of this.

"Yes, of course I'll stand in for Dave." Nonetheless he sighed heavily. "But I still don't like it."

Simon Livermore became even more human.

"Neither do I."

Macklin's misfortune had moved Simon Livermore a centimeter or so toward a show of sympathy. Four hours later it was the competition's chance. They, too, managed to edge him toward a display of emotion. But this time it was not sympathy. And the minister had not felt it necessary to send an emissary.

"It is always a pleasure to see you, Herr Engelhart. I am sorry I have so little time available this afternoon."

Under the rules governing this type of exchange, it was now the turn of Klaus Engelhart, marketing manager for Norddeutsche Werke GmbH of Hamburg, to apologize for demanding the meeting at a moment's notice. Without warning he departed from protocol.

"I must tell you, Mr. Livermore, that it is a surprise and disappointment to my firm to learn that secret negotiations between Macklin and the Department of Energy to delay the Noss Head award are now in progress."

Livermore was rigid with disapproval. "It is certainly true that Macklin requested such a delay. I fail to understand your characterization of this request as a secret negotiation."

Klaus Engelhart was a good ten years younger than any of the other principals clustering around the North Sea bonanza, and he looked like the kind of young man who moves ahead rapidly. Short and stocky, with a gleaming bald pate, he narrowed his eyes behind thick glasses as he continued heatedly: "You cannot deny that NDW has an interest—a vital interest—in this issue. With your experience of complex undertakings, you could scarcely expect such a maneuver by Macklin to remain concealed from us for long."

"If you will allow me to continue," Livermore said with reproof, "Macklin requested a delay. The request was denied. We are, therefore, proceeding as planned. No interests, except possibly those of Macklin, have been affected."

"Nonetheless, we should have been informed," Engelhart insisted. "What if there had been any doubt as to your decision? It would have been only correct that the minister hear NDW's views . . . and those of the other bidders, too, of course."

Livermore hid a smile at this reluctant recognition of the other formal contenders still in the race with Macklin and NDW. "If there had been any question of change, *all* those concerned would have been given such an opportunity. And in view of the worldwide publicity attaching to this latest outrage, I cannot believe any of them would have been surprised at Macklin's request."

"My company disapproves of these terrorists as much as everyone else. But Macklin cannot expect the world to stand still because of their difficulties." Engelhart shrugged. "After all, contracts are awarded on the basis of proposals, not of personalities. We are not to blame for Davidson Wylie's tragedy because our proposal is best."

It was common knowledge in certain parts of London that Klaus Engelhart firmly believed NDW's bid had a technical edge over that of Macklin. He was, however, uneasily aware that Wylie had been more resourceful in producing modifications tailormade to conform to British desires. More disinterested observers considered the two rivals as running neck-and-neck technically, with Wylie displaying more flexibility in his approach to the Ministry.

"Leaving aside the question of which bid will be most acceptable to my government," Livermore said smoothly, "we still have a problem. The minister is naturally concerned lest Mr. Wylie's enforced absence turn into a windfall for his competitors. On the other hand it is inconceivable that the deliberations of my government should be dictated by a band of terrorists."

Engelhart nodded too eagerly. "Very true."

Remembering what had just been said about the impossibility of maintaining secrets, Livermore decided to indulge himself by revealing one.

"As a matter of fact, I advised a delay," he admitted. "But my superiors overruled me. So we go on, as planned. And I suppose that is defensible. The development of Noss Head is, after all, more important than any one company—or any one man."

The British had already written off Davidson Wylie.

Not so Engelhart, to whom he was still real, dangerous, and very much in the running.

"Far more important," he agreed somberly. "But I hope, in the pressure of business, you will not forget that I look forward to having you and Mrs. Livermore as my guests some evening in the near future."

"Indeed I have not," answered Livermore, relieved to have an excuse at hand, "but my wife has extended her stay in the Mediterranean."

"Another time then," said Engelhart, rising. "Still, we will meet tomorrow morning. Your misgivings may be in vain. It is still possible that Davidson Wylie will be found in time to represent Macklin. If he is in any condition to do so, that is."

"Condition?" Livermore was startled.

"He may already be dead," Engelhart said reasonably. "Well, it is useless to speculate. We cannot know."

"No, we cannot," Simon Livermore agreed, more and more pleased that his wife had extended her stay abroad.

An hour later a phone was picked up on its third ring.

"Francesca?"

"Klaus!" she cried. "I've been waiting for your call."

4 · Energy Costs

Bruno Hauptmann taught the world that waiting is one of the peculiar cruelties of kidnapping. Since then, there have been too many racking vigils, too many anguished ordeals, too many unanswered prayers.

In the case of Davidson Wylie, there were also too many unanswered questions. During the period immediately following his disappearance, friends, associates, and even the police were preoccupied with meeting the ransom demands. But when Black Tuesday failed to honor its bargain, the queries began in earnest.

"What can they want?" Arthur Shute demanded of the men gathered in Macklin's Houston headquarters. "They must be softening us up for something. Do you have any idea what?"

But the men sitting around the table, with experience in many far-flung hot spots, had already exhausted the possibilities.

"What does Hugo think?" one of them asked in desperation.

"He says he's never seen anything like it," Shute said bitterly.

In London it was the other way around.

"I've never seen anything like it," the man at Scotland Yard reported to Hugo Cramer. "Interpol has not been able to produce any information on Black Tuesday, not one single item. It has to be a new group."

"What difference does it make whether they're old or new?" grated Cramer.

He was looking drawn and weary. Inexorably, the Noss Head negotiations had begun on schedule. By day Cramer was sitting in the chair that everybody had expected to see occupied by Davidson Wylie. By night he haunted Scotland Yard, seeking the latest information.

"On the practical level, it means we have no place to start. Black Tuesday has no known supporters or known locations. But even more important, it means we have no idea what they're interested in. They probably don't have members already in prison, so it would have to be a political issue."

"Look, they've already gotten their money, and you don't think it's prisoners. What else could it be?"

The detective looked grim. "I just hope we don't have a terrorist group with its eye on North Sea oil."

"Oh, my God!"

Klaus Engelhart, on the other hand, was growing sleeker and more content with each passing day.

"There is no doubt that Macklin's presentation is not as strong as I expected," he said, cradling a brandy snifter between his hands. "I am afraid that Mr. Cramer is far from being an adequate substitute for Dave."

"Klaus, dear, is it too much to ask you to moderate your self-congratulations and remember that my husband's life may be in danger?"

Engelhart's eyebrows rose in exaggerated surprise. "But *liebchen,* Dave has my best wishes for continued good health and spirits. I merely ask that for the next

37

few weeks he enjoy them someplace other than London."

The first public mention of Noss Head in connection with Davidson Wylie's kidnapping appeared in a London daily the next morning.

. . . still missing. Nonetheless, negotiations for the award of the contract are proceeding as planned. "It is impossible to overestimate the damage caused to Macklin by the absence of Davidson Wylie," said one of the participants in the conference. Other firms discussing Noss Head with the Department of Energy include Norddeutsche Werke GmbH of Germany and . . .

"That goddamn bastard!" exploded Hugo Cramer, before automatically reaching toward the phone and a consultation with Houston, Texas.

It took exactly three mail deliveries for Cramer's premonitions to be realized. The slit envelope had already been tossed into the wastebasket. The letter, its text crudely assembled from slivers of newsprint, lay on top of the welter of papers and charts overflowing Cramer's desk.

"Don't touch it!" he ordered.

He might just as well have told Paul Volpe not to pet a tarantula. With elaborate care Volpe leaned forward.

MACKLIN TYRANTS—
MANKIND WILL BE FREED FROM ITS CHAINS OR BLOOD WILL FLOW. IF WYLIE IS OF VALUE TO YOU MAKE YOURSELVES READY FOR FURTHER INSTRUCTIONS. LIBERTY AND JUSTICE IN EXCHANGE FOR ONE MAN. OUR DEMANDS WILL COME.

BLACK TUESDAY

"You were right," Volpe gulped. "You said something like this would happen."

"It didn't take a genius," Cramer said bleakly. "Engelhart got what he wanted, all right. You saw how that story was picked up by all the other papers. He as good as told Black Tuesday that, if they hung on to Dave, they'd have Macklin over a barrel."

"Of course they were already holding on to him," Volpe pointed out.

Cramer dismissed the past with a brusque gesture. "Hell, I don't know what that foul-up was. But I sure as hell know what's going on now."

"What do you think Black Tuesday will ask for?"

"Look at the letter. They don't even know themselves. Black Tuesday has probably sent out for an adding machine." Cramer's thick fingers tightened around a pencil. "And there's not a goddam thing we can do but sit and wait."

Turkey was one of the few places where positive action was possible. On remote highways leading east, roadblocks were still being manned. The fishing fleet had become accustomed to rigorous searches before putting out to sea. But it was in Istanbul that the latest communication from Black Tuesday caused a storm of renewed activity. The police were combing the city, from the luxury hotels overlooking the Bosporus to the noisome stews of Haydarpasar.

Captain Harbak fastidiously remained in his car, leaving subordinates to fan through every squalid warren on Begii Street.

The report, delivered by his perspiring lieutenant, was negative.

"You do not surprise me," said Harbak. "If Black Tuesday is hiding Wylie on Begii Street, they are even less comprehensible than they seem."

Pezmoglu's silence was tacit agreement. Not much could be kept secret in the teeming humanity of Begii Street. But Turkish police surveillance of secluded villas as far away as Sariyer was also proving fruitless.

Istanbul is a big city. However, it is not a city in which an American businessman can normally be kept from official attention, whether through formal or informal channels. And, contrary to what enemies of Turkey may claim, it is no simple matter to dispose of a dead body in Istanbul.

So, frustration was mounting to the boiling point.

"If we only knew something about Black Tuesday," said Pezmoglu humbly.

"If we knew anything about Black Tuesday, we would not be crawling through every alley in Istanbul," said Harbak.

Vast and intricate as the city is, the police know it as do few others. Black Tuesday, by contrast, was still a closed book. Bonn, San Juan, and Tel Aviv had been canvassed. National and international agencies had been alerted. But no link with Palestinian terrorists had come to light, no tie to Japanese anarchists, to Argentine urban guerrillas, or to Croatian nationalists.

There was only the language of the two ransom notes.

"Strange, as I say," Harbak mused. "At first they demanded all possible speed. Bankers must fly here, there and everywhere to meet their deadline. Television cameras must record for the world how their orders are obeyed. Now the tempo of their movement changes. It is a question of waiting for their next communication. They do not even send their letters to a newspaper to ensure giant headlines. They are content to work behind the scenes. What can Black Tuesday want?"

Turkish police are not notoriously overpaid.

"More money," Pezmoglu suggested.

Harbak stirred. "That is always possible," he conceded with the ingrained respect of the Near East for wealth. "But I do not think it is that simple."

"Nothing is ever simple," sighed Pezmoglu, who had just sighted his squad emerging from an alley, their leader shaking his head.

As Pezmoglu organized the intricate process of moving the police cordon to the next square on the grid, Harbak had ample leisure to pursue his thoughts. He had arrived at some fundamental conclusions by the time his driver inched the car forward to its new command post in the very heart of Istanbul's slums. When his lieutenant returned to sit out the next round of the search, Harbak was visible only as a darker shadow in the prevailing gloom, his face occasionally reddened by the glowing ember of a cigarette.

"This block will take over an hour, Captain," Pezmoglu offered.

Harbak ignored this contribution. "Of course, we have all seen these newspaper articles claiming that Davidson Wylie is necessary to his company's success in its current London activities. This Mr. Cramer who calls me so incessantly is convinced that the publicity has encouraged Black Tuesday to suppose it can raise its price. In fact, he goes further. He claims that one of his company's competitors deliberately leaked the news in order to prolong Wylie's absence."

"But Black Tuesday had already failed to release Wylie on time."

"Exactly! I am afraid that Mr. Cramer is blinded by the occupational bias of these businessmen. They ascribe all their misfortunes to their competitors. But you and I, Pezmoglu, we know better."

It was a rare moment when Harbak joined himself to his subordinate in anything. Pezmoglu tried to measure up. "They forget that the arm of Allah is over all men."

"Just so." Harbak was kind but perfunctory. "And Mr. Cramer also forgets that Black Tuesday has had an excellent source of information from the very beginning. They could have learned about these London negotiations from Davidson Wylie, himself."

Pezmoglu nodded dumbly.

"Myself, I have always doubted that Wylie was their intended victim. We know that they set up their Zurich account months ago. We know that they planned this operation meticulously. Is it not logical, then, to suppose that Paul Volpe was their original target? But when his superior appeared unexpectedly, Black Tuesday decided on a substitution. You will recall that

41

the first note did not mention Wylie by name, only the second."

As Harbak explored the possibilities of his thesis, he puffed spasmodically on his cigarette. Pezmoglu, fascinated by the pulsating red glow, began to feel he was on the receiving end of Morse code. Confused, he could only stammer, "What difference would that make?"

"Ah, you do not see the implications. Black Tuesday is a new group. Its members have not worked together, they have no tested chain of command. Then, at the outset of their first venture, they are faced with a startling development. They have much more leverage than they anticipated. Naturally they disagree as to their procedure. They have already set the wheels of the first ransom in motion. Some of them—the more unimaginative ones, I am afraid, Pezmoglu—see only the opportunity for more money. Some of them, with an eye to the future, wish to honor their commitment in order to retain credibility for their next operation. And still others wish to seize the moment and stage a spectacular coup. They go through with their original plan in Zurich. But they retain their victim while the discussion rages. That is why their pace has slowed. That is why their second note is not specific. They have still not resolved the dissension in their own ranks."

Exhausted by this speculative effort, Harbak stubbed out his cigarette and sank back on a cloud of triumph.

Pezmoglu's professional life was an uneasy balance between tendering uncritical admiration and asking the right question. Usually the traffic signals were clearer.

"What kind of spectacular coup?" he asked warily.

"Who knows? But I will tell you one thing," Harbak continued. "The answer does not lie here. Why was an employee of Macklin chosen in the first place?"

Pezmoglu did not think twice. "Black Tuesday is anti-American."

"Nonsense! All these groups are anti-American—

even the American ones. No, Macklin was chosen because it is an *oil* company. Interpol keeps saying that there is no information about Black Tuesday. But that is not true. We know that Black Tuesday ranges widely over many borders—a kidnapping in Istanbul, a ransom in Zurich, now a letter mailed in London. But there is another element in this equation that crosses national frontiers as well. North Sea oil is of importance to England, to Germany, to Scandinavia. Somehow the two are connected. That is why your men have heard no rumors, found no suspects. Turkey is an accidental location for this crime. Its center of gravity," said Harbak, soaring into theatrics, "lies on a tiny spithead in northern Scotland."

This time the green light was unmistakable.

"Extraordinary!" Pezmoglu murmured dutifully.

5 · Dry Well

In New York, two weeks later, John Thatcher's secretary was waiting too. The Sloan travel department had promised to get back to Miss Corsa by three o'clock at the latest.

It was now three-fifteen.

Miss Corsa clucked. She had many demands upon her time. John Thatcher's work continued to pile up even when John Thatcher was in Switzerland. And this absence was turning out worse than usual. Since her employer's fleeting career as a television personality, Miss Corsa had been inundated with inquiries from NBC, the *Detroit Free Press,* and the *Harvard Alumni Bulletin.*

What was Mr. Thatcher's philosophy regarding terrorism?

Was this the first time the Sloan had participated in a ransom payment?

Did Miss Corsa personally feel that Davidson Wylie was dead or alive?

Fortunately, Miss Corsa's order of priorities was deeply rooted. Crime and punishment were not her domain; the travel department was. When Mr. Thatcher's office expected a message at three o'clock, the message had better arrive at three o'clock. Miss Corsa might have to tolerate infraction of this iron law by the outer world, but within the Sloan she was a holy terror.

So, instead of typing Thatcher's latest batch of dictation tapes, she set forth for the second floor. Given a moderately just cause, as Thatcher had often remarked, Miss Corsa's strength was the strength of ten.

Her trip through the trust department to the elevators was not uneventful.

"Ah, Miss Corsa," said Everett Gabler, who was Thatcher's oldest and most dedicated subordinate. "I was just coming to see if you have copies of the Albritton report."

"I believe we do," said Miss Corsa.

"Excellent, excellent," said Gabler, a stickler for precision and order. "I would like to borrow one, if I may."

With equal punctilio, Miss Corsa assured him that the Albritton report would be on his desk later in the afternoon.

Gabler was singleminded to a fault. "Do you think you might just step back—"

"I'm afraid not," said Miss Corsa without hesitation. "I have to go down to the second floor right now."

"Oh dear, it would be such a help," he persevered.

This got him nowhere, as Miss Corsa was continuing on her way.

"Second floor?" he said, ticking over the possibilities once he saw the game was lost. "Do you mean the travel department? John is still due back the day after tomorrow, isn't he? I hope to goodness he isn't going to be tied up over there."

But Miss Corsa had passed out of earshot. If she had heard, she would not have deprecated Gabler's sentiments, or his invidious truncation of the traveling party. Charlie Trinkam ran a poor second with her, too.

Mr. Elliman, the resident mastermind of the Sloan travel department, did not seem to understand. A tall, bright-eyed man, he lived to make business travel as enjoyably broadening as possible.

"Ah, Miss Corsa," he sang out when she appeared. "I was just going to call."

"I thought I'd better come down and see you myself," she said.

This reply, which would have made the blood of any member of the trust department run cold, delighted Mr. Elliman.

"I'm so glad you did," he twinkled. "Here, do sit down. Now, it's about Mr. Trinkam—and Mr. Thatcher, too—isn't it? They're coming back Wednesday. I've ticketed them through our Swiss people, so there's absolutely nothing for you to worry about. Everything will be hunky-dory. And, if I know Mr. Trinkam, he'll really enjoy his stopover in Paris, ha ha!"

There was much in this effusion to displease Miss Corsa. But she hewed to her line.

"Mr. Elliman, Mr. Thatcher prefers not to have any stopovers."

"Zurich to New York? Oh, I strongly recommend Paris. I think they will both find—"

"Mr. Thatcher likes to travel nonstop," said Miss Corsa inexorably.

Elliman pouted. "But that will mean changing everything, including the hotel reservations."

"I'm afraid it will be necessary."

Like so many people who make wonderful plans, Mr. Elliman did not like altering them. "Well, I'll try," he said discontentedly.

"Thank you very much."

But Elliman, balked of Paris, fell prey to self-pity. "You know, it isn't easy rearranging everything at the last minute. Especially during the tourist season. You probably don't realize how many flights they've oversold."

Elliman devoutly believed that dealing with airlines and hotels required nerves of steel, the sensitivity of an artist and the heart of a lion. He glossed over the immense Sloan travel budget, which was, in fact, his weightiest weapon. "All I can say, Miss Corsa, is I'll do my very best."

Miss Corsa was not even tempted to make the obvious comment.

It was only to be expected that John Thatcher was not exhibiting comparable restraint.

For the past three weeks, he and Trinkam had quietly effected a massive reorganization of the Sloan's credits in Europe, using Switzerland as clearinghouse. Methodically working their way through currencies, they had dropped banks and added banks until the monumental task was completed.

"And not a minute too soon," he remarked, as he and Charlie Trinkam waited for their host to decide on the wine.

Herr Leopold Grimm, who was celebrating their joint achievement with the finest dinner that Zurich could provide, dismissed the sommelier and continued his review of every judgment they had made. On the whole he was pleased. Italy still bothered him, but the lira, they all agreed, was in the hands of God. Inspired by his continental survey, he ventured further afield.

"But even though your work in Europe is done, there are still problems ahead. Did I not hear that you would be financing Macklin if they obtain the Noss Head contract?" He shook his head in foreboding. "You may have more difficulty with your pound balances than you have had with everything else."

"There's time enough to worry about that. From what we hear, it appears very unlikely that Macklin will be successful. They are really feeling the loss of Davidson Wylie." Only half of Thatcher's mind was on his answer. Like a true professional, he was neatly docketing a fact. Common Market or no, Swiss bankers still thought of Europe and Great Britain as entirely distinct areas.

Herr Grimm was free of such distractions. "It cannot be easy for a last-minute replacement to join such a delicate negotiation. Quite apart from the technical details that he must master."

"The technical details aren't the problem." Charlie was fast becoming a Macklin expert. "Hugo Cramer was nerved up to sub for Wylie for a couple of days. Now that it's been two weeks, I hear tell that he's coming apart at the seams."

"And the person who tells you is Paul Volpe," Thatcher commented, amused.

Charlie conceded a hit. "Oh, I admit the kid's got an axe to grind. He thinks he should be in charge of the whole thing himself. But Cramer isn't helping by nagging at the Turkish police. Apparently he calls them twice a day."

"He even calls me." Grimm laid down his napkin with care. "I do not blame him. He feels a sense of responsibility. He is bearing the double burden, both for Mr. Wylie's welfare and for the Noss Head contract."

"Well, he has one consolation," Thatcher said. "Apparently the British government is taking Wylie's absence into consideration and not permitting it to turn into a windfall for the opposition."

Charlie snorted. "Come on, John. There's only one kind of consideration that Macklin wants—and that's a contract signed, sealed, and delivered."

This was too true to be argued. Displays of sympathy have never balanced a company's books. Only sales do that.

"All we can do is wait and see. Cramer has an outside chance of pulling it off. And," Thatcher reminded Charlie, "we've financed a lot of long shots that ended up wearing roses."

"It is still possible that Mr. Wylie may be released in time to join the negotiations," said Grimm hopefully. "Surely as long as his body has not been found, it is reasonable to think that he may be safe."

"Then why won't Black Tuesday say what it wants? Volpe tells me Macklin expected a list of demands within a couple of days of the last note. Instead, there's just silence, as if . . . Wait a minute." Trinkam's face was a study in thought. "You mean Black Tuesday wants Macklin to be really hurting before they sock them for the final installment? That the snatch was planned to coincide with the London talks?"

Leopold Grimm was obviously startled at the bird flushed by his earnest optimism. "That is not what I meant at all," he hastened to say: "The kidnapping was certainly timed, but with respect to what was happening in Zurich, not London."

Then he stopped abruptly, brought to his senses by the intense curiosity emanating from his guests.

"I believe I have said too much," he confessed.

"Or perhaps not enough?" Thatcher suggested invitingly.

The internal struggle, although severe, was brief. "I had not planned to speak of this subject." Grimm examined adjacent tables for enemy ears. Then he leaned forward and lowered his voice. "You understand that this is in the strictest confidence?"

"Oh, absolutely!" his guests chorused as one. They realized they were dealing with a man burning to talk.

"You may remember that the kidnappers required a pledge that there should be no police surveillance when the ransom money was withdrawn. Naturally this pledge was scrupulously observed. A man's life was at stake. However, nothing at all was said about bank surveillance, and I felt perfectly within my rights posting security personnel at strategic locations outside Union Suisse."

Herr Grimm glared at them defiantly as he produced this piece of casuistry.

"Splendid," said Thatcher with a thump. He had never believed in using Queensberry rules with terrorists.

Relieved on this point, his host relapsed into a conversational tone. "Of course there was nothing my men could accomplish with Mr. Wylie held hostage. All they could do was watch. But," Grimm concluded on a plaintive note rare among Swiss bankers, "I did want to know where that money was going."

"Very understandable, I'm sure," Thatcher murmured.

"And now I shall never know."

"Your boys muffed it, eh," said Charlie easily.

There was no immediate answer, but during the interval Leopold Grimm's recollections were not pleasant. "Now that I have had time to consider, I must in all fairness admit that they were not entirely at fault," he replied at length.

Vaguely intent on commiseration, Thatcher said: "If they are anything like the security people we hire at the Sloan, they are expert at preventing bank robberies, not at trailing people through Europe."

"That is very true. But I am afraid they were misdirected from the start. The directors—and I include myself—had certain preconceptions about how the ransom money would be removed."

Thatcher and Charlie glanced at each other in silent communion. It must have been the rakedown of the century if Grimm were still placating his conscience.

"But I ask you," the Swiss continued in self-justification, "how would you expect kidnappers to behave on such an occasion?"

Very few people had ever made a reasonable appeal to Charlie Trinkam in vain.

"Let's see. I'd expect them to send one man into the bank for the actual pickup," he said obligingly, "while another one waited in a fast car. The first one would leave the bank with a stream of customers, enter the car, and then the two of them would get the hell out of the country as fast as they could, with or without dropping off the money someplace."

Grimm beamed. "Exactly as we reasoned. We had cars posted at every corner, ready for pursuit. And instead . . ." He gulped. "Instead, *she* came in."

Charlie Trinkam's ears pricked up. "She?"

"This girl," said Grimm, suppressing some common epithets for undesirable young women. "She had voluminous long blond hair that was obviously a wig, she was wearing blue jeans and boots. And do you know what I had to pack the money into?" Words momentarily failed him. "A rucksack!" he finally exploded.

"A rucksack?" Thatcher stared. "But we needed four large briefcases. It wouldn't fit."

"No doubt I am using the wrong term. You must forgive me if I am not familiar with all these expressions." Grimm was heavily ironic. "It is what your American students strap onto themselves when traveling."

Thatcher thought he saw daylight. "Ah, you mean a large multi-compartmented pack mounted on a lightweight metal frame. Yes, that would just about do it."

"I do not know what you call it. But when she clumped out of my office in her mountain boots, she had money stacked on her back from her neck to her crotch."

Bankers like to see money handled with a certain respect. It was impossible for Herr Grimm to have emerged from the ransom payoff without a minimal amount of dissatisfaction. But his irritation would not have been quite so exacerbated if the dollars had left neatly packed in pigskin attaché cases.

Charlie continued his good offices as the mug who falls into every hole. "Granted, it wasn't what you expected. Though, now I come to think of it, all these Palestinian outfits seem to have a couple of girls in fatigues. But why did that make it harder to follow her to the car? She must have stuck out like a sore thumb."

"Because there was no car," Herr Grimm growled. "She did not even bother to look around. She went out the front door to the Bahnhofstrasse, turned right, and tramped three blocks to the Bahnhof, which she entered."

Grimm ended his recital on a note of high drama that left his audience in complete bafflement. He surveyed them reproachfully.

"So soon," he sighed, "and already you have forgotten Ziegelbrucke."

"I haven't forgotten," said Charlie somewhat resentfully. "It was one of those godawful rock festivals, wasn't it?"

But Thatcher was recalling the relationship of events to each other. "Good heavens, Charlie, it was Ziegelbrucke that pushed us off the front page. The hordes were already at the airport when Paul Volpe flew in."

In fact, the Ziegelbrucke Festival, featuring a galaxy of rock stars, had made headlines throughout the Western world. There were moments when it threatened to overtake and surpass Woodstock. Fortunately, Swiss prudence had prevented a debacle. The authorities had selected a site approximately forty kilometers outside Zurich. There, a large institution, unoccupied during the summer, provided space for sleeping bags, running water, and sanitary facilities. But the inevitable had occurred. Instead of the thirty thousand anticipated by the sponsors, over a hundred and twenty thousand zealots had appeared. The subsequent scene had provided a photographer's delight for three whole days.

"And just how do you get to Ziegelbrucke?" Thatcher asked in dawning suspicion.

"By train from Zurich Bahnhof," Grimm admitted sadly. "The opening concert was the evening of the day we paid over the ransom."

Thatcher was familiar enough with the terrain to visualize the situation. On one side of the station, airport buses arrive and depart continuously. On the other side, the municipal transit system deposits a steady stream of commuters and joyriders. Inside there are connections to every other European capital. And on that particular day, added to the base movement of a busy railroad junction, there would have been over a hundred thousand rock enthusiasts coming by plane, by train, and by foot to converge on the local to Ziegelbrucke.

"Beautiful!" Charlie breathed reverently. "And I suppose every damned one of them was in jeans, long hair, and a backpack?"

"Don't forget the wig," Thatcher cautioned.

"Very true," agreed Grimm. "She had only to elude my men for two seconds, whip off her blond hair, and emerge as a coal-black brunette."

"Or she may even be titian-haired," said Charlie sentimentally. "Tell me, was she pretty?"

There were realms, however, into which few bankers could follow Charlie.

"I found her singularly unattractive." Grimm was at his most repressive. "But I am told that may not have been natural. We kept the photographs from the bank cameras in case she was a known terrorist. But Interpol said the pictures were virtually useless. Not only did the wig hide her ears and forehead, but also she was wearing cheek pads. I did notice that the timbre of her voice was most unusual."

"Well, disguised or not, she must have been a worried lady during those three blocks. Of course, once she ducked through the Bahnhof she had it made," Charlie commented. "She could have gone anywhere."

Fundamentally, Herr Grimm was more interested in the money than in its custodian. "For all we know, she marched into a bank and opened another numbered account."

"Or she could have bought gold," said Charlie, entering into the spirit of things. "Or another currency, or stocks on any exchange in the world. Zurich's the perfect place."

Thatcher thought it was time to bring the other two back to earth. "Come, come," he said briskly. "We all know what the probabilities are. Why do terrorists want money in the first place? She very likely handed the cash over to an arms dealer in payment for the next shipment."

"But if they got what they wanted, why haven't they released Mr. Wylie?" demanded Grimm. "If he is alive, he must be a great embarrassment to them. The longer this situation extends itself, the more worried I become for his safety."

This same concern was voiced two hours later when the Sloan's chairman of the board put in an overseas call to Zurich. Being the humanitarian he was, George Lancer offered the latest progress report on Davidson Wylie before proceeding to his main topic.

"I've just been talking with Arthur Shute at Macklin, John. The Turkish police admit that they're at a loss. They still insist that Wylie was not smuggled out of the Istanbul area, but all their searching hasn't uncovered him."

"That doesn't sound good."

"On the other hand they also haven't found his body, which for some reason they regard as a good sign."

"I can understand that," Thatcher said thoughtfully. "The odds are that Black Tuesday would take more pains hiding a victim who was alive. A body they would just dump. And there are still no further instructions from Black Tuesday?"

"None," said Lancer.

"Odd," said Thatcher, echoing a good many people in a good many places.

"But that isn't why I called," said Lancer, modulating from man of compassion to man of business. "I do have some good news. At ten o'clock this morning Macklin got the Noss Head contract."

Thatcher produced sincere congratulations even as he began thinking of work schedules. "Then the Sloan will have to sit down with Macklin within the next couple of weeks."

"I know that you'll want to iron out the broad outlines of the financial agreement in Houston before talking to the British," Lancer continued.

"That's the way we always do it, George," Thatcher said gently.

"So I told Arthur Shute this could only be a courtesy visit. But as you said you'd be coming back in the next day or two, I thought you would not mind a stopover in London."

In other words, the hard-pressed Macklin team

wanted someone to show the flag. And, by all accounts, they had earned a little recognition.

"That's all right, George. We tied up the last details today," Thatcher admitted. "We can catch the breakfast flight tomorrow morning."

"I'm afraid it won't be pleasant for you," Lancer sounded apologetic. "They're still having that heat wave over there."

"Oh, I'm sure it won't be too bad. You can tell Shute we'll be there before lunchtime."

It is always fatally easy to underrate someone else's problems, as John Thatcher was shortly to discover.

6 · Depletion Allowance

By common consent, Everett Gabler was *primus inter pares* at the Sloan Guaranty Trust when it came to fault-finding. Everybody else there could spot a misplaced decimal at twenty paces. Everett saw the invisible defects, as well.

Charlie Trinkam's universe was totally dissimilar. At his desk, he met the Sloan's high standards of fiduciary prudence. Elsewhere, he took care to blanket life's imperfections with wine, women, and song.

Two days in London, however, had put him temporarily in Gabler's league.

"If Livermore tells me one more time how Americans must feel right at home, I'm going to punch him in the nose!" he grumbled.

"If you want to resort to violence, I believe you're going to have to wait your turn," Thatcher replied. "From the looks of him, Hugo Cramer is itching to start swinging. Ah, good morning, gentlemen . . ."

With the arrival of latecomers, the gathering trooped from the stately anteroom of the Imperial Dominion Bank to the even statelier conference room. The second day of talks was coinciding with the eighth day of the cruelest heat wave in modern English history. In the countryside, reservoirs were running dry and fields were parched. In Wales, factories were closing and water was being rationed. In London, the populace struggled on without benefit of summerweight clothing, ice cubes, or air conditioning.

The American contingent had just arrived from the Hilton, one of the few oases of comfort in the city. By native standards, they looked relatively healthy.

Across the table from them sat the Department of Energy, H. M. Treasury, and British Petroleum. To a man, they had deposited bowlers and rolled umbrellas in the foyer. To a man, they had greeted their guests with impeccable courtesy. To a man, they sank into their chairs and stared dully into space.

Chairing the meeting was Simon Livermore, who was disposing of the agenda with dogged tenacity. "We adjourned yesterday afternoon on the price-adjustment schedule, I believe. Mr. Carmichael, you wanted to discuss the appendix."

Carmichael was exhausted by the effort of finding the appendix. H. M. Treasury began doodling with desperate intensity. Livermore's thoughts were so far away that he started when it was time to call on the next speaker.

John Thatcher was old enough to remember New York before air conditioning. Even today, ice cream, swimming pools, and deodorants are not absolute necessities of life. What tried men's souls, or at least Thatcher's, was the crushing impact of weather on conversation. The standard banalities about rain, snow, heat, or cold, normally so useful in social intercourse, had been refined into a Chinese water torture.

The lunch break was a case in point.

"No thanks, Nicholas," said Simon Livermore, automatically running a finger around his wilted shirt collar. "I'd better look in at the office before we go into the import licenses this afternoon."

Nicholas, who was the Imperial Dominion Bank, was offering Imperial Dominion's renowned saddle of mutton. Yesterday it had been fine old sherry. He was not getting a second crack at Thatcher.

"Cramer and I think we should take the opportunity to consider Macklin's subcontracting commitments," Thatcher said briskly, omitting the locus of this discussion.

But Nicholas's sad smile reminded him that the temperature of the Hilton had become an obsession with most of London.

". . . used to it, no doubt," Carmichael was saying, as he and Hugo Cramer came around the table to join them.

"Heat doesn't bother me much," said Cramer, shortly. "Listen, Thatcher, I'll join you and Charlie at the Hilton. First I want to stop by the office and get them to telex Houston for those footages."

"I suppose you become accustomed to it in Texas," said Nicholas plaintively. "And you've worked throughout South America, too, haven't you?"

"Venezuela," said Cramer, his eyes crinkling. Thatcher saw that he was amused by this equation of modern Houston with the tropics. But his brevity disconcerted the others, all except Livermore.

"Odd how people differ," he said, bridging the gap. "My wife feels the cold and the damp very much. As a matter of fact, she went off to Tangiers to get away from that rainy spell we had a few weeks ago. Now, she's staying on to escape the heat. And she was born and bred in Flintshire, not Texas."

"Oh, but the heat is quite different in the Mediterranean . . ."

"Or even the desert. In Egypt . . ."

". . . Antigua . . ."

"As a matter of fact, when I called her last night, Jill told me that it was cooler at Rhamuli—that's the resort she's at—than it was in Surrey!"

They had reached Hugo Cramer's limit.

"Three o'clock?" said Cramer, making for the door. "Thatcher, I'll be with you in half an hour. I'll look for you in the bar."

"You know," said Charlie when he and Thatcher sedately followed suit, "I'm getting to like that guy."

Thatcher suspected that Cramer might be an acquired taste, and lunch proved him right. Cramer managed not to comment on the bar, which was a solid clot of relief-seeking humanity, or even on the steaming traffic along Piccadilly.

"Well, what do you think?" he asked.

"We're making good progress," Thatcher replied, interpreting correctly. "I thought the convertibility clause might hold us up longer than it did."

"It helps that British Petroleum wants to get cracking on Noss Head," said Charlie, forking his Russian egg with resignation. "Livermore's pushing things right along. Otherwise we'd still be bogged down over the tax prepayment."

They were talking a foreign language so far as Cramer was concerned. He shook his head, indicating different notions of progress.

"Livermore talks too much," he said baldly.

Nothing intimidated Charlie Trinkam, including strong silent men of the West. "That's his job. What do you think we're all sitting around that table for— to look into each other's big blue eyes? Which reminds me, did you get those specs from Houston?"

"Right here. Volpe says . . ."

In a rough-and-ready fashion, Charlie handled Hugo Cramer very well, and Thatcher left him to it. Cramer's attitude toward negotiation was not uncommon, especially among engineers pitchforked to the bargaining table. Nevertheless, he had landed Macklin the Noss Head contract. Thatcher wondered how. Almost immediately, he got some pointers.

"Cramer! I have not seen you since the award. Let me offer you my congratulations."

Two men had halted by their table. The plump young-old man accompanying Paul Volpe was correctly dressed and correctly smiling. Even before Cramer hoisted himself to his feet, Thatcher knew that Klaus Engelhart was German.

". . . Norddeutsche Werke from Hamburg," Cramer

said, yielding not an inch to pronunciation. "They were in the final round of bidding against Macklin."

"But we lost." Engelhart was determined to be pleasant. "How could we know that you are even more formidable than Davidson Wylie?"

"Sure," said Cramer, refusing the gambit. "You all know Volpe here already. Klaus, this is John Thatcher from . . ."

Upon assimilating the Sloan Guaranty Trust, Engelhart showed no disposition to depart.

"We don't want to interrupt you," said Volpe uneasily.

"Although we are more comfortable here than in my office," said Engelhart.

Paul Volpe thought this needed amplification. "We're blocking out the first subcontract proposals," he said, with a wary glance at Cramer.

"Even such a subsidiary role will help moderate NDW's . . . disappointment."

The artful pause was not lost on Thatcher. Was surprise a more apposite word than disappointment?

Hugo Cramer bristled. "Look, get it through your skull that Macklin—not Dave Wylie—was bidding for Noss Head. And Macklin's going to build it, too!"

He was truculent enough to make Engelhart stiffen. John Thatcher was moved to intervene:

"Macklin isn't going to build anything unless we get back to Imperial Dominion," he said, ostentatiously checking his watch.

As usual, this worked like a charm. Engelhart swallowed whatever he was going to say, took punctilious leave of everybody, then followed Volpe out.

"Relax! We've still got an hour," Charlie advised, as Cramer bunched his napkin. "What's the matter with Engelhart, Hugo? Does he talk too much, too?"

Thatcher's stratagem made Cramer grin. "I've got to remember that," he said appreciatively. But there was no grin when he turned to Charlie. "Engelhart? He's the bastard who—Oh, to hell with him! Let's get back to these metal estimates. Arthur Shute has rounded up some rolled steel bids—I don't know how hard they are—"

This was not a good enough answer for Charlie Trinkam.

The end of the afternoon session at Imperial Dominion did not signal release for John Thatcher. He was booked for the evening by the American ambassador, no less. The ambassador would be no trouble. Harvard, where he had preceded Thatcher by a year, and the municipal bond market, where he had spent his prime, could always keep him happy. The threat of high thinking about détente, NATO, and nuclear proliferation came from Mrs. Forbes. It was her Brahmin sense of vocation, and her lack of imagination, that had landed poor old Endicott in Grosvenor Square. A livelier woman would have taken all those trust funds and bought West Virginia.

"Well, have a good time," said Charlie, as they parted at the elevator. "I'll see you tomorrow morning."

Thatcher's practice of never intruding into the personal affairs of his associates went double for Trinkam. So he did not ask how Charlie was spending the evening. Charlie told him anyway.

"Which proves that visiting firemen can be more sinned against than sinning," Thatcher observed.

"You can say that again," groaned Trinkam. Against every inclination, he was spending an evening with the boys, trapped by the kindly intentions of Colin MacFarquar of British Petroleum.

"Now, I won't take no for an answer," MacFarquar had trumpeted with overpowering hospitality. "We can't have you come to London and miss our bright spots, can we?"

Few and far between were the bright spots Charlie had ever missed. But he had recognized and honored the friendly impulse.

Thus, that evening he found himself in a small, perfect Edwardian room, eating the most expensive oysters he had yet encountered. Gilt-framed mirrors reflected beautiful women, elegant men, obsequious waiters. *Leon's* was a bygone world of privilege and pleasure, carefully restored for the chosen few.

"They do one very well here," said MacFarquar, with the arrival of Dover sole. His enjoyment was unimpaired by the fact that theirs was the only table of men in the crowded room.

"They certainly do," said Charlie, although he had always felt that a bower of songbirds is no place for onlookers.

The third member of their party felt no such constraint. "I've been hearing about this place for years, Colin, and it's even better than they say," said Simon Livermore, leaning back to let the waiter replenish his wine. "But perhaps Charlie here is regretting his air conditioning."

"Not with food like this," said Trinkam gallantly. If everybody else could maintain standards, so could he. Furthermore, he appreciated the effort being made, including the use of first names. Colin and Simon had been on familiar terms since Oxford. But *Charlie* came easily only to MacFarquar, who was a sturdy extrovert; Livermore found it more difficult.

". . . with Angela up in Scotland," MacFarquar was explaining, as temporary bachelors always do.

Charlie had no absent family to justify his presence in *Leon's,* and the other temporary bachelor, Livermore, had let his attention wander to the staircase entrance.

"She's a looker, all right," said Charlie, following his eyes to the striking redhead who was sweeping in.

"It was her escort I happened to notice," said Livermore blandly.

For a moment, Trinkam suspected the famed understated humor. Then he, too, identified the escort. It was Klaus Engelhart, last seen at the Hilton.

The unreticent MacFarquar leaned forward with a robust whisper: "And the lady doesn't seem to be worrying overmuch about her husband, does she?"

"Is he after them with a gun?" Charlie asked, looking at Engelhart with new respect.

Livermore pursed his lips. "The lady is Mrs. Davidson Wylie," he said.

"Oh-h?" said Charlie, taking a second look.

"Exactly," said Livermore. Then, with the same precision he had shown at the conference table, he added: "I understand that she and Wylie had already agreed to divorce—before the kidnapping, that is."

"She may not have to go to the trouble," said Colin MacFarquar with gusto. Ignoring a quick frown from Livermore, he went on, "She looks like a merry widow to me. Is Engelhart next in line, Simon?"

"There's been some talk," said Livermore, unbending. "Although I myself wondered—well! Enough of that. Look here, Colin, this has been a fine meal, but I should get back and look over some papers."

MacFarquar was incensed. "Crying off now? Why the evening's young. The trouble with you, Simon, is that you spent too many years in the country. Early to bed, early to rise!"

"Surrey is scarcely the country," said Livermore, tolerantly.

"No, listen," said MacFarquar. "I have an idea. Let's push on to Crockford's!"

The magic name of a London gaming house did not produce applause.

Livermore's smile grew strained. "I'm afraid that's a little too rich for my blood. Many thanks, Colin, but I think I'd best be going along. You two go on without me. I'll see you tomorrow."

Before Colin could expostulate further, Livermore had departed. Charlie noted that he paused to pay his respects to Klaus Engelhart—or Francesca Wylie.

"Good old Simon," said MacFarquar, with one wine too many under his belt. "If you think he's dull now, you should have seen him before the divorce."

Charlie regretted having to explain that he, too, was skipping Crockford's. The Sloan Guaranty Trust allowed considerable latitude to its employees. It did not extend to roulette wheels.

"Well then," said MacFarquar largely. "The midnight show at Brown's . . ."

"You remember Klaus Engelhart?" Charlie asked when he and Thatcher strolled into Imperial Dominion the following morning.

"The young German who lost the Noss Head contract," said Thatcher.

"He may have lost a contract, only to gain a jewel," said Charlie poetically.

"The heat's gone to your head," Thatcher decided. Nevertheless, he listened with interest. Charlie's stray sidelights were sometimes valuable and always entertaining.

"Although I don't see that Wylie's marital difficulties are germane," he said, once Charlie had concluded.

"You know, the word is that Cramer suspects Engelhart of having pulled a fast one—spilling the beans about Noss Head so that Black Tuesday would hang on to Wylie," Charlie amplified.

"If he did, it hasn't done him much good. Macklin still won the award."

"True enough, but suppose Engelhart wanted Davidson Wylie out of the way for different reasons entirely."

Thatcher considered this theory a moment, then rejected it. "Not if the Wylies were already separated," he argued.

The exchange was cut short by a haggard Colin MacFarquar. Eyeing Trinkam resentfully, he said: "Don't see how you do it."

"Practice," said Charlie enthusiastically, before settling down to sterling credits as if he, too, had spent a blameless evening at the American embassy.

"We had begun our consideration of the escrow accounts," Simon Livermore announced.

Just then the door burst open. Paul Volpe, trailed by a distressed secretary, was red-faced and incoherent. Ignoring everybody else, he confronted Hugo Cramer, hunched stolidly over the end of the table.

"Hugo!" he shouted. "It's Istanbul!"

"What?" Cramer bellowed.

"They've located Dave Wylie! He's safe! He's safe, I tell you!"

Cramer fell back in his chair. "Safe," he repeated as if he could not believe it.

As an incongrous embellishment, there was a round of hand-clapping from everybody else.

Simon Livermore saw an occasion. "On behalf of my government—"

"I thought I'd take the evening flight," Paul Volpe rushed on. "Somebody should be with him, in case he needs help."

"Like hell you will," said Hugo Cramer, grinning from ear to ear. "You stay here with this nitpicking! I'm going to Istanbul!"

7 · Foreign and Domestic Fields

News that Davidson Wylie was alive and safe flashed around the world. By the time that Hugo Cramer stormed out to Heathrow, the wire services were feeding details to hundreds of subscribers. He was changing planes in Rome when Houston interrupted its regular TV programing for a special news alert. By the time that Cramer touched down at Istanbul and helicoptered to Ankara, Davidson Wylie had led the evening roundups from New York to Nairobi, then been displaced by a monorail disaster in Yokohama. Public attention marched on. Hugo Cramer was left to deal with the aftermath.

He had only one question for the official who met him.

"Is Dave in one piece?"

"Well, he seems all right physically," was the guarded reply, "but I feel I should warn you—"

"Then Dave can tell me about the rest himself," Cramer interrupted. "Let's go."

Throughout the drive to the embassy and the march

down endless corridors, Cramer brushed aside would-be informants like flies.

A budding diplomat tried tact. "You may find a certain nervous irritability," he suggested diffidently.

The local CIA man saw an opportunity to air his expertise. "Kidnap victims feel threatened for some time after release," he pontificated. "The only thing that helps is a really thorough debriefing. We could arrange . . ."

A nurse who had borne the brunt could not help complaining. "If he would only cooperate . . ."

But they were all speaking to air. Cramer's juggernaut stride had outstripped them, and he was already halfway down the hall.

He was not as oblivious as he appeared to be. Those hovering voices had conveyed a message. At the guest-room door he hesitated, not knowing what to expect.

It was some comfort to find a recognizable Davidson Wylie. To be sure, there were changes. The sunlamp tan had faded to a dirty white pallor. Instead of the trim vigor maintained by regular workouts, there was an unnatural puffiness suggesting long hours of immobility. Wylie's face was drawn, and his well-styled hair had grown into an uncontrolled bush. But far more alarming than this surface deterioration was Wylie's high, cracked voice. He was fending off a crowd of attendants so wildly that he did not notice his latest visitor.

For a moment Cramer was rooted to the spot, prey to waves of relief, anxiety, resentment, and concern. Then, without thinking, he blurted the first words that came to mind.

"My God, Dave, what happened to you?"

As a welcome, the question left something to be desired. Wylie instantly abandoned his contest with a doctor to turn a scowling face on Hugo Cramer.

"I got kidnapped, remember? I'm the one who's been out of touch. I don't even know who snatched me, Hugo. And instead of telling me something, this

67

bunch just asks a lot of questions. I can't even find out what's been going on with the Noss Head bid."

A doctor tried to stem the tide. "Now, this is no time to bother yourself with business, Mr. Wylie. What you should do is——"

The heavy omniscience that is the curse of the medical profession grated on Cramer. Effortlessly drowning the continuing prescription, he boomed: "We got the contract last week, Dave. Everything went fine, and it was all thanks to you." Then, as disapproving clucks emanated from every corner, he added a contemptuous rider. "What do you mean, this is no time for Dave to think about business? He busted a gut working on this contract for months, and it could have all gone down the drain because of those goddamned terrorists. If you're so worked up about the situation, why don't you do something to catch them instead of hounding Dave?"

Dr. Wennergren drew himself up. "I am a physician, not a policeman. And it is my professional opinion that Mr. Wylie should not be exerting himself. He should go into a hospital for a checkup."

"For Christ's sake!" Wylie exploded. "I've just been locked up by a gang of hoods for three weeks. Now you want to lock me up in a hospital. I'll be damned if I agree to that."

The soothing voice became more syrupy than ever. "But you shouldn't think of it that way. You'll have the care you need and proper diet. We could even bring your wife over so that she could stay in the clinic with you."

Gripping the arms of the chair in which he had been huddled, Wylie tried to lever himself upright. "You bring Francesca here over my dead body. Dear God, I don't want a lot of keepers. What I want is some sun and some fresh air and above all——" here Wylie glared at his tormentors "——above all, some decent privacy. Christ, Hugo, can't you get rid of any of these people?"

Back home at Macklin, Cramer was noted for the brusque efficiency with which he exercised authority.

Now was the time, he decided, for a show of force. Gesturing toward the door with a beefy thumb, he uttered one strident command: "Out!"

Then, attacking on both flanks, he turned his back on Wylie and lowered his voice to a whisper. "Leave him to me. You boys are just exciting him."

They were not as reluctant as they pretended to be. Eight hours of Davidson Wylie's hysteria had convinced them that they lacked the magic touch. If Wylie was willing to tolerate Hugo Cramer's presence, that in itself was a small miracle. After token resistance, they filed through the doorway, to congregate on the other side and justify their capitulation.

"Whew!" breathed the cultural attaché. "I suppose it's not surprising that Wylie's so edgy, but why does he act as if it's all our fault?"

It was clear as daylight to the psychologist in the group. "That's a form of transference," he lectured. "For weeks he's been furious at his own helplessness, but he didn't dare let loose in case it might be dangerous. We're simply substitute targets for his anger."

"That would make sense if he were just mad," argued the attaché. "But he's strung up tight as a drum. Anybody would think he's frightened of us."

"Not of you," said Captain Harbak, whose attempts to question Davidson Wylie had been curiously frustrating. "These terrorist animals, they must have threatened him. Even though he is safe now, he cannot comprehend it."

The psychologist nodded sagely. "A defense mechanism. He wants so much to believe the danger is over that he has to protect against a letdown if he's wrong."

"Wait a minute," objected Dr. Wennergren. "He's got more than a letdown to worry about if he's wrong."

Before the psychologist could reply, the policeman intervened. "There can be no doubt that Mr. Wylie is safe," Captain Harbak declared, drawing himself erect. "He is under the protection of the sovereign state of Turkey."

Belatedly the assembly remembered that, in one

way or another, they all represented the Diplomatic Corps, and the policeman represented the Host Country. With one accord they produced a shower of emendations that might have gone on forever if Hugo Cramer had not emerged from the guest room. Leaning his bulky shoulders against the closed door, he announced his decision.

"I'm taking Dave home with me—right away."

This simple statement evoked a chorus of protests. Cramer reserved his fire.

"All right," he said with deceptive mildness, "what do you suggest?"

There was no lack of advice. "Mr. Wylie needs the reassurance of a familiar, affectionate figure. That is why I strongly urge the presence of his wife. Then—"

"The last time Dave saw his wife she told him she was junking him in favor of a newer model." Cramer's irony had the subtlety of a kicking mule.

Without a blink the doctor shifted gears. "Then perhaps we should forget about Mrs. Wylie. But he still needs complete rest and quiet in safe surroundings. Some blood tests wouldn't be a bad idea, either. He himself has no idea how systematically he was drugged. And, above all, no excitement, no pressure, none of these business problems."

Cramer deliberately misunderstood. "I wasn't planning to have him punch into the office tomorrow morning. No, he's going to my place on the Gulf of Mexico. He can lie in the sun, snooze in a hammock, do a little fishing when he feels up to it. We can probably even manage to scare up a blood test back in the States. So my program really boils down to the same thing as yours."

He had reckoned without the psychologist.

"As far as it goes, your regimen is admirable." A persuasive smile appeared as an automatic prelude to the next sentence. "But we can't deny that Mr. Wylie is hardly in a normal state of mind, can we? It's at moments like this that a supervised environment is so important."

"I'll get to that in a minute," Cramer said ominously

before turning to the Turkish police captain. "I think I heard you making objections, too."

"Assuredly you did. It is unthinkable that Mr. Wylie should leave Turkey when he is needed as a witness."

Cramer's jaw shot forward. "A witness to what? The poor guy was blindfolded most of the time. All he ever saw was some ski masks."

"Nonetheless, Mr. Wylie might still prove invaluable. Kidnap victims in the past have often provided assistance to the police."

"Such as?"

"They have been able to identify a voice or recognize a room."

Cramer was openly challenging. "Have you got a voice for Dave to listen to?"

"At the moment, no."

"Or a room for him to look at?"

Under this catechism Captain Harbak reddened, but he held his ground stubbornly. "Not yet."

"That's what I thought." Abruptly Cramer dismissed the policeman to broaden his attack. "What gives with you people, anyway? Here's a poor guy who hasn't known for weeks whether he's going to end up dead or alive. Sure, he's jittery. I'll give you that. But your idea of the way to calm him down is to treat him as if he's crazy. Let me tell you, he'd be a whole lot crazier if he'd come out of this icy calm."

Dr. Wennergren was still trying. "Good God, you've misunderstood me. It's Mr. Wylie's physical well-being that concerns me. Of course that is partly dependent on his emotional—"

Paying no heed, Cramer continued his torpedoes. "And just because the police in this town haven't come up with a single lead in over three weeks, they can't think of anything better to do than pass the buck. Suddenly it's all Dave's fault. What in Christ's name is this crap about his not cooperating? Answer me that."

Like many speakers carried away by the sound of their own voices, Cramer had paused only to provide dramatic emphasis for his next sentence. His adversary, however, seized the opportunity.

"Mr. Wylie became completely unreasonable when I asked who had foreknowledge of his movements on the day of the kidnapping," Harbak explained severely.

"Don't tell me you're on this crazy kick, too . . ." Cramer began, before the implications of the captain's statement sank in. He was almost strangling with fury when he continued. "Dear God, now you're accusing Paul Volpe."

"I am not accusing. I am merely—"

"Then I'm not accusing either. I'm just saying that, even if Black Tuesday kidnapped Dave, somebody else is sure trying to make capital out of it. And he seems to have found himself a willing helper."

By now both men were glaring at each other with such patent hostility that alarm bells sounded for the embassy personnel. They hurled themselves into the fray.

"Captain, I assure you Mr. Cramer is not suggesting any lack of propriety by the Turkish police."

"Mr. Cramer, you must recognize the captain's duty to consider all possibilities."

Left to his own devices, the captain might have backed down, but he was never given the chance.

"I can recognize a setup when I see one," Cramer said flatly. "And that settles it. Dave's leaving right away. If anybody's got questions for him—or for Paul Volpe—they can ask them at Macklin headquarters. As soon as Dave's on his feet, he'll tell his story, but not to some kangaroo court!"

It came to pass in Houston several weeks later.

"As a matter of fact, this will be the first time I've heard Wylie's story," Arthur Shute was explaining to the delegation from the Sloan. "He's been recuperating down at Hugo's place on the Gulf."

Courteously John Thatcher hoped that Wylie was now fully recovered from his dreadful experience. "And I trust he's not coming back to the office simply to work out the revolving loan on the Noss Head contract. Trinkam and Cramer can handle it quite well."

"Don't worry about that," Hugo Cramer reassured him. "Dave's raring to get back into the saddle. I had a hard time getting him to sit still this past week."

Arthur Shute nodded approvingly. "I'm glad to hear that. I won't say it's a pleasure to be held up for a million plus dollars, but we're coming out of this better than I expected. Dave Wylie is uninjured and we've won Noss Head. Even our ambassador in Turkey has calmed down. For a couple of days there he wanted Hugo's head on a platter."

Charlie Trinkam was interested. "What have you been up to, Hugo? Misbehaving in Istanbul?"

"I never got the chance." Cramer grinned. "Let's say I had a difference of opinion with the embassy doctors about diagnosis."

"According to the ambassador," said Shute, "you got Wylie out of Ankara as if you were on a commando raid."

Cramer shrugged impenitently. "They were driving Dave up a wall. And when it comes to a choice between one of my boys and a bunch of bureaucrats, it's no contest as far as I'm concerned."

"I've been a bureaucrat myself," Shute reminded him good-naturedly. "They were probably just being over-cautious about Dave's health."

"Well you can see for yourself how my treatment worked," said Cramer as Shute's secretary opened the door to usher in the last conference member. "Hi, Dave, you look great."

He was not exaggerating, Privately John Thatcher thought that Wylie was a splendid testimonial to Cramer's methods. Macklin's European manager was not only tanned and vigorous, he was clear-eyed and alert. After acknowledging introductions, he got down to business immediately.

"I know you want my report on what happened in Istanbul, Arthur. Then I'd like to catch up on Noss Head as soon as possible."

"If you don't want to talk about the kidnapping, Dave, I don't want to press you," Shute began.

Wylie waved away his qualms. "It doesn't bother me, but I'm afraid there isn't much I can tell you. The first thing they did in the car was blindfold me. Then they must have given me a shot of some sort. When I woke up, I had no idea where I was or how long it took to get there."

"Were you still blindfolded?"

"I was blindfolded all the time I was in the first room."

This was news to Shute. "You were moved?"

"It's hard to be certain. But I'd almost swear to it." Wylie searched his memory. "After a couple of days, I blacked out again. When I came to that time, they'd taken away the blindfold and put me into different clothes. And the bed sure felt different."

His audience exchanged glances. As usual, Charlie Trinkam was the one ready to risk speculation. "That could have been about the time you were supposed to be released—after Black Tuesday got its ransom. Did you hear anything about that?"

"You don't understand," Wylie explained. "Most of the time I was alone. Every now and then two of them would show up in ski masks. One of them would hold a gun on me, and the other one would put down some food or take me to the bathroom. They never told me anything."

"And his clothes weren't any help," Shute murmured. "The Turkish police kept the clothes Dave turned up in. But they were some cheap Italian jeans and a shirt that students around the Mediterranean buy by the ton."

Wylie elaborated. "They were wearing jeans, too, if that means anything. I really don't know what else to tell you. Every day was the same until I lost all track of time. It was a shock when I got out to learn it was just three weeks. It felt like months."

"But they didn't mistreat you?"

"No, what got me down was the strain of not knowing what was going on."

For the first time there was a tremor of emotion in Davidson Wylie's voice. "You knew about Black Tuesday and the ransom notes. I didn't. To me, it was just a bunch of invisible guys holding guns on me. Anything could have been happening. A revolution in Turkey, the beginning of World War III, or a case of mistaken identity."

John Thatcher was thoughtful. "So we still don't understand why they didn't let you go on schedule. Particularly when they went ahead and released you later."

"It's a mystery to me," Wylie confessed. "All I can tell you is what I overheard the last night. They blindfolded me again, bundled me into a car, and we drove for what seemed like hours. One of them kept saying we'd gone far enough and the other one insisted we go farther. Finally he snapped something about this being the price for changing the game plan."

Cramer snorted. "Ten to one, somebody had the bright idea of hanging on to you for a second round of ransom. Then the big boys caught up with him and squashed the scheme."

"If so, I'm grateful to them. All I know is that they pushed me out of the car in the middle of nowhere. It took me hours to get to a small town and I just had one idea. I marched into the police station and demanded to be taken to the American embassy. It didn't seem safe anyplace else."

"And a fat lot of good the embassy was," Cramer growled unforgivingly.

Wylie was more detached. "You know, Hugo, I'm grateful as hell to you for coming to get me, but you handled them all wrong."

"Oh, yeah?"

"In Europe, people are very status-conscious," Wylie informed him. "When an outsider shows up giving orders, it blows their chain of command. What you should have done is gotten hold of the Turkish minister of development and the ambassador. Then they could have given the orders."

As the afternoon wore on it became clear that this was merely the first emergence of a persistent leitmotif. When Arthur Shute explained how the public relations staff in Houston planned to exploit this return from the dead, Wylie smiled gently.

"That may be all right with CBS or *People*. The American media are interested in personalities. The European press is more serious-minded. I've already called my girl in London and dictated a short statement about the economic and political implications of my kidnapping. That's what they'll be concerned about on the Continent."

Charlie Trinkam stirred restively. "Is that so?" he muttered, remembering *Paris Soir*'s helicopter above the Bahnhofstrasse and the endless columns in *Stern*.

When it came to Turkish feelers about Paul Volpe, Wylie was more charitable than Hugo Cramer. "Of course that's absurd. They know the terrorists simply trailed us to that restaurant. But the Turkish police are in an impossible situation, and they're trying to save face."

John Thatcher made a small bet with himself about the next sentence and, sure enough, it came right on schedule.

"Prestige is much more important over there than it is here. But it's unrealistic to expect the police to handle this on a national level. It's not like guerrillas in Argentina or Venezuela, who are basically local groups. These terrorists encompass the entire Mideast."

But even Arthur Shute was annoyed when Wylie zeroed in on the Noss Head award for a display of superiority.

"It was a miracle that Hugo pulled that one out of the fire," said Shute with asperity. "And I, for one, am very grateful to him."

Now it was Cramer acting the role of peacemaker. "Look, we all know it was Dave's work that set the whole thing up for the final push."

"I'm not denying that Hugo did an outstanding job," Wylie said earnestly. "And I know that getting

76

the contract was the primary goal, but was it necessary to ruffle quite so many feathers?" He tried to soften the charge by producing a rueful smile. "Your telephone bill at the beach may be quite a shock when it comes, Hugo. I decided it was politic to make a number of personal calls to Livermore and Carmichael in London. Oh, yes, and I finally tracked down Klaus Engelhart in Oslo."

"For Christ's sake, why do we have to softsoap him?"

"Because I want his outfit to bid on some of the secondary work," Wylie retorted. "And remember, Hugo, you can stay in Houston from now on, but I expect to be working with these people for years. And, in Europe, this kind of relationship has to be handled . . ."

Back at the motel, Charlie Trinkam summed up his impressions of Davidson Wylie:

"Why did they blindfold him? It would have made more sense if they'd gagged him. Given half a chance, he would have lectured them on how we experts do things in Palestine."

But Thatcher, who had made an interesting discovery when he stopped at the desk for mail, was only half-listening.

"Well, Macklin pays him to tell them how to do business in Europe. They have to get their money's worth."

"Fine!" said Charlie, rooting vigorously in a drawer. "But as soon as we start working on the fine print, I'm going to let him know who's the expert on how American bankers do business in Houston."

"I'm sure you will." Thatcher was amused. "And by that time I'm equally sure that you'll have some reliable insights into what makes Davidson Wylie tick."

Charlie emerged from the bureau with a shirt in his hand and deep suspicion on his face. "What are you talking about, John?"

"We have a new guest in this motel. Mrs. Francesca Wylie just signed in."

8 · Known Reserves

Oil and natural gas are scarce resources, hence valuable. Contrary to the opinion prevalent in Houston, there are others. Coffee beans and blue chip stocks are in short supply. So are dollars, pounds, drachmas, and yen. Big banks deal impartially with all these items. This imposed an outer limit on the amount of attention John Thatcher could spare Macklin and North Sea oil, important as they were. Sooner than he expected, he was obliged to leave them in Charlie Trinkam's capable hands. A call from Everett Gabler about a faltering department store chain in Florida summoned him back to the Sloan.

At the Sloan travel department Mr. Elliman could not believe his ears.

"Now, let me see if I understand this. Mr. Trinkam will be staying on in Houston? And Mr. Thatcher wants to fly back to New York this evening?" he asked in long-suffering tones.

"Yes," said Miss Corsa.

The London detour had been bad enough. Houston, Texas, acted on Mr. Elliman like the dark side of the moon.

"Well, I'll have the limousine there to meet the six o'clock flight," he said gamely. "I presume Mr. Thatcher will be going home."

Miss Corsa presumed so, too, which was a mistake since Elliman thought he detected fellow feeling.

"Unless he wants to take off for Quito next!"

Miss Corsa was not letting this pass. "Mr. Thatcher will let you know if he has immediate travel plans," she said, ignoring Ecuador.

But Elliman revealed a madcap side. "Oh Miss Corsa," he cried manically, "how can you!"

Miss Corsa was not kittenish. "So, if the limousine meets the six o'clock——"

"Don't worry!" Elliman said. "I'll be sure to pick up your wandering boy."

"Thank you," said Miss Corsa, swallowing hard.

Elliman was convinced they were comrades. "I suppose it's miserable for you upstairs," he said compassionately, "having Mr. Trinkam out of town for such long periods."

On the sixth floor, more correct views about the chain of command prevailed.

"If John doesn't run an eye over these new budget proposals soon, they'll be out of date. You've got to move fast to keep up with Washington, these days," said Walter Bowman, emerging from the catacombs of the research department with a sheaf of papers. A large, exuberant man, he was an optimist by nature, a cynic by necessity.

"He'll be back tomorrow," said Miss Corsa, generously.

"And high time," said Bowman, returning to his lair.

Everett Gabler, too, was happy to hear that Thatcher would be back in short order. Not only were six Bligh stores trembling on the brink, clouds were gathering over a commodity option broker in Chicago.

"John will want to keep on top of the situation," he said with somber relish.

Thus Thatcher's departure from the Tidewater Motel was of interest to several people.

But Francesca Wylie's arrival was a real blockbuster.

News that she, her husband, and Klaus Engelhart were all staying at the Tidewater roared through the ladies' rooms of the Macklin Company like a forest fire. For years Dave Wylie had been a remote employee about whom the office staff knew little and cared less. Suddenly kidnapping transformed him into an instant celebrity. Overnight everyone had become familiar with his handsome blond features. Within forty-eight hours it was household knowledge that he was forty-two, a graduate of Stanford Business School, and a married man with an Italian wife and no children.

"That poor woman," the file clerks had said, opening their brown bags in the courtyard. "How awful for her not to know if her husband's dead or alive."

When the long-awaited good news flashed from Istanbul, the first tendrils of domestic complication became apparent to the typing pool.

"You know," they said, bending over their trays in the employees' cafeteria, "it was Mr. Cramer who flew to his side, and not Mrs. Wylie!"

But all this was mere preparation for the day when Mr. Engelhart's approaching visit led to several incautious remarks by Mr. Shute. Proudly his secretary produced these nuggets at the regular weekly outing of her associates.

"Oh, it's been going on since long before the kidnapping," she reported over her shrimp salad. "Mrs. Wylie was actually in Germany when she heard what happened. She came back to England to make things look better."

Now, with the makings of a classic triangle assembled under one roof, the company gossips waited for the next development.

It was certainly no accident that Gwen Trabulsi, by day Mr. Cramer's secretary and by night most emphatically Victor Trabulsi's wife, had decided on the

Tidewater as the place to meet her husband after work. One swift glance around the poolside lounge told her that she was in luck. Two of the principals were on hand, but instead of hurling reproaches at each other, or even icily ignoring each other, they were sharing drinks at an umbrella table.

"That's Mr. Wylie," she hissed at her husband as soon as the waiter left, "and that's Mrs. Wylie. Can you believe it? They act as if there's nothing wrong."

"Maybe she isn't his wife," suggested Trabulsi. "Maybe Wylie is finding consolation the time-honored way."

This time Gwen's examination was more critical. Francesca Wylie had thrown herself into a lounge and was pulling off a wet bathing cap; her glorious mane of titian hair cascaded down her back. Beads of moisture spangled the long lovely body overflowing a minimal bikini.

"That's her all right. Paul Volpe described her and you've got to admit she's pretty unmistakable," said Gwen in an undertone. "The nerve of it! First she brings her lover here. Then she calmly goes swimming with her husband."

Vic Trabulsi had a better eye for detail than his wife. "Wylie hasn't been swimming yet," he argued. "They probably just bumped into each other."

Gwen sniffed. She had to admit that if you checked into a motel with both your men, accidental encounters were likely. But her soul thirsted for melodrama. If she could have heard the Wylies she would have despaired at their misuse of promising material.

"I don't see why you had to come here," Wylie was saying with almost judicious detachment. "We had everything figured out. You could have simply stayed in London."

"In fact, that's what you were counting on, wasn't it, David?" Francesca asked sweetly.

"I don't know what you mean. That was our arrangement."

"Our arrangement was that we were going to share fifty-fifty."

"But, honey," said Wylie, leaning forward persuasively, "that's exactly what we're doing. You know I've always wanted us to split everything equally."

"And everything includes the land in River Oaks."

For a moment Wylie stared at her. Then his features relaxed into a grin and he chuckled. "So that's what the fuss is all about. But my poor darling, that lot is peanuts compared to the rest. You could have saved yourself the trip if you'd only asked me."

Francesca's smile could have meant anything. "But then, David, your conception of peanuts has become so grandiose lately. I never know whether you mean a hundred dollars or a hundred thousand or a million."

"For heaven's sake! We're talking about one measly little lot. You know perfectly well we paid twenty-two thousand for it. I'll gladly offset it as part of my share."

"I'm sure you will. But what we paid for it and what we can get for it are two different things."

Wylie shook his head pityingly. "Now who in the world has been putting this idea into your head?"

"The realtor I went to see this morning." Her voice was creamy with satisfaction. "His figure was sixty thousand."

"Realtors always talk big when you ask for a valuation, but a bird in hand is different."

"It certainly is. And I hope you remember that, David, about all our birds in hand. But this realtor was making a firm offer to buy."

Her husband might not have heard her. He frowned, then said thoughtfully: "Since when do you know any realtors in Houston? You've only been here on short trips."

"Klaus found him for me."

"I might have known." He hesitated before continuing: "Look, this isn't the best time for you to be snuggling up to Engelhart. Can't you cool it for a while?"

"I don't see why he shouldn't make himself useful, even if he is in for a little surprise. Don't worry, I can always handle Klaus."

Wylie was half-grudging, half-admiring. "You probably can," he admitted. "But don't get carried away.

I don't need any demonstration of your expertise. And Engelhart is all right as a little playmate, but I don't want him nosing into my affairs."

"You think it might be dangerous?"

"Jesus Christ, Francesca!" he growled. "Engelhart is in the oil business. And he's damn savvy . . . at least about everything except you."

She was now openly mocking. "Really David, you act as if we have something to hide. As far as I am concerned our life is an open book, even though it is not necessarily a book that I plan to lend to Klaus."

"I'll bet you don't!"

The barb missed its mark. Head bent, Francesca was rooting inside an enormous beach bag, engaged in a search that ultimately produced a long emery board. Then, without a care in the world, she concentrated on shaping her nails to perfection. Her husband, too, seemed to have lost interest in the dispute, leaning back in his chair to watch a youthful group of swimmers leave the pool in a burst of horseplay. If it was a war of nerves, it was Davidson Wylie who broke.

"I don't see why we couldn't have settled this by phone," he complained, breaking the silence.

"We still haven't settled it. Unless you're ready to offset your share by sixty thousand."

"Like hell I am," he said promptly. "We'll sell the lot to that realtor of yours and see how much we really get—unless, of course, you'd like to offset it."

"I'm almost tempted," she confessed. "It's a perfect location."

"I don't see what's so wonderful about land in Houston."

She sighed with exasperation. "Really, David, you can be juvenile at times. You fall in love with romantic names. In case you haven't noticed, Houston is rich and exciting and expanding. If we'd had any sense we would have settled here instead of in Europe."

"You're impossible, Francesca. I've taken you to Rome and Paris and London, and you complain about not living in Houston."

The slight foreign accent became more pronounced.

"Perhaps you have forgotten, but I knew Paris and Rome long before I met you. And in Rome we lived like dreary bourgeois—we shopped in their stores, we used the beaches they chose for their children, we met them in restaurants."

Davidson Wylie was stung. "In Rome we knew a lot of artists, too."

"Artists!" Francesca scoffed. "Architects who had never built a house, actors who had once been in a crowd scene, writers interminably doing background for a book that would never be finished. Can you name one who amounted to anything?"

"And what makes the people in Houston so marvelous?"

"They're rich," said Francesca succinctly.

"Not all of them."

"The ones I would have known are. They're the kind who go to Acapulco and Barbados and Caracas," she continued dreamily.

"God, and you have the gall to claim I get carried away by names. That's just St. Tropez and Davos in a different language." He took a deep breath. "Anyway, Rome is where we started out. We did a lot better in Paris and best of all in London."

She laid down her file and regarded him with clinical interest. "We'd still be in Rome if I hadn't nagged you into leaving. But then, David, it's never been difficult to drive you into action—as long as I planned exactly what we should be doing."

"Sure!" He gave a harsh bark of laughter. "You've always loved that vision of yourself as some sort of strategy queen. Just don't underrate what the rest of us do. For starters, I'll come with you to your tame realtor tomorrow and see what we can really get for that lot."

Her eyes widened. "Don't you trust me?"

"Not your competence. I'll probably be able to jack up the price. You make the appointment, will you? I've got to be going now."

"But you never had your swim," she protested as he rose to his feet.

"That's your fault," he said. "It's already past six and I've spent the whole hour on your problem."

"Not my problem," she corrected him. "The only problems are our problems. And remember, when you're counting all those lovely dollars, that it was my idea in the first place."

He shook his head impatiently. "All right, all right. We've been through that already."

"And I won't keep you from your schedule. *A domani.*"

With a glint of malice Francesca held out her hand as she uttered the Italian leavetaking. Moved by some obscure reflex, Wylie bent to kiss her fingers.

She crowed in genuine delight. "Dear David," she murmured. "Always so continental."

Meanwhile, two tables away, Gwen Trabulsi's eyes were bulging. "Did you see that? He kissed her hand," she whispered, choking on the words. "Do you think they're having a reconciliation?"

"It sure didn't sound that way," her husband replied incautiously.

"You mean you could hear them?" Gwen had chosen the chair with an unobstructed view of the Wylies. Vic, on the other side of the table, was closer to her quarry and that much farther from the clatter of the service bar. She looked at him with silent indignation.

"I only caught a word here and there," he said, hastening to mollify her.

He was not getting off the hook that easily. "Well?" she demanded. "What were they talking about?"

"About splitting their assets, fifty-fifty."

Her face fell. "Is that all? Didn't they fight about Klaus Engelhart or anything?"

"No, they weren't very interested in him at all. I suppose they were haggling about their property settlement." His voice trailed off dubiously before he went on again. "Sure, that must have been it. After all, I didn't hear much more than half. But I'll tell you one thing, Gwen. They sure as hell were talking money."

"Then we've agreed on sixty-six point five," said the realtor the following day. "I'll have my girl start typing the papers right away."

Francesca flashed him a brilliant smile. "With payment by certified check."

"Yes, ma'am." In spite of frigid air conditioning, the realtor passed a wadded handkerchief across the nape of his neck. "You sure know how to drive a bargain, Mr. Wylie," he acknowledged.

Dave was already on his feet, restlessly collecting his belongings. "You'll do well out of the lot," he said, losing interest. "Coming, Francesca?"

"Say, folks, don't rush away like this. There's a little place downstairs where we could celebrate the deal. I like to think we're all doing pretty well out of it."

Dave did not give his wife a chance to reply. "Sorry, some other time. I'm in a hurry to get back to the office."

Francesca eyed him but said nothing until they were smoothly incorporated in the traffic flowing back to the center of town. "You were marvelous, David. I would have sworn that sixty-four was his top price."

"These real estate boys are all born actors," he said indifferently. "You don't want to pay attention to what they say."

Francesca was the world's ranking authority on the moods and caprices of Davidson Wylie. Ordinarily, he would have been basking in his triumph, lapping up her admiration. After ten years of marriage, an automatic impulse set her conning the possible reasons for his preoccupation.

"Did you mean that, about going back to the office?" she probed. "I thought we might have lunch."

"Something's come up, and I'm in a bind for time. Why don't you take the car on to the Tidewater? I'll get a cab later."

She ignored the transport problem, having reached her own conclusion.

"While I was waiting for you, I spoke with one of

the secretaries. She was quite thrilled because an Interpol man is coming to Macklin this afternoon."

"That's right. The Turkish police have thought up some more questions to ask me."

She settled her back against the car door and half-turned, examining him from beneath lowered eyelids. "That's natural enough," she decided calmly. "You were held there for three weeks. The police have to go through the motions, at least."

"They're doing a lot more than making motions. From what the embassy says, they're scouring the city to find that apartment."

"Well, why not? You're not the one who has to get nervous."

"I'm not nervous!"

He punctuated this declaration by slamming his foot on the brake as the light ahead turned red.

"There's no need to snap at me. Any more than for driving like a madman." Gingerly Francesca rubbed an elbow that had made jolting contact with the window crank. "As usual you're working yourself up for nothing. What can a man in your position tell the police? That you saw some ski masks and heard some strange foreign voices. It's that simple."

"Like hell it is," he said through clenched teeth. "They're convinced I can come up with all sorts of details if I try hard enough."

"I suppose that's possible."

The more excitable Wylie grew, the more reflective Francesca became. This progression was not having a beneficent effect on his temper.

"I don't like thinking about those three weeks, and—" he glared his fury across the front seat "—and I don't like talking about them."

Francesca shrugged. "It's your own funeral. But I know how you go to pieces under pressure. They're not going to let you pretend this never happened. Take my advice, give the police the details they want, and then you can relax."

"You act as if the police are the ones I have to

worry about. This isn't just between me and them. There are other people involved."

For a moment Francesca failed to understand. Then she burst into protest.

"Why you're afraid, that's what's wrong with you. For heaven's sake, David, this is Houston."

With a vicious twist of the wheel he swung sharply onto the approach ramp of Macklin's executive building and let the car roll to a halt with a thump.

"You make it sound like it's on the moon. You managed to get here, didn't you?"

Angrily he heaved himself out to the pavement, then had to lean back for his attaché case.

"I came to sell a lot," she stammered in confusion.

Slowly he spelled it out. "You thought you had a reason to come to Houston, so you bought a ticket in Europe and caught the first plane over. Anybody else can do the same thing, and I'm not about to forget it." Snatching up the case he turned and strode into the building.

Five minutes later the Macklin guard had to ask Francesca to clear the driveway. She was still sitting in the passenger's seat, staring at the revolving doors with a puzzled frown.

9 · Texas Towers

Wives come in a variety of guises—saints and floozies, doormats and shrews, earth mothers and prima donnas. But, one and all, they share the habit of keeping a weather eye on their husbands' emotional states.

Not so business associates. From the moment that Macklin's revolving doors accepted Davidson Wylie into their maw, he was in a world where people wanted to know what he was doing, not how he felt about it. News that a representative from Interpol would be chewing up most of his afternoon had already percolated through the upper reaches of the company. Predictably it was the chewing-up aspect that exercised Wylie's colleagues.

At first Arthur Shute saw a straightforward administration problem. "He may tie you up for hours, Dave. So be sure you got everything squared away first. He's not arriving here until two-thirty."

Charlie Trinkam introduced a more realistic note. "There isn't a hope in hell that we can be finished by then. We'll just have to let it ride over the weekend."

Thus far discussion had been amiable, because of

the nature of the participants. Arthur Shute, as a quasi-public figure, had learned that being a good citizen always costs something. A slight inconvenience, graciously accepted, was the lowest price an imperfect world could impose. Charlie Trinkam's resignation about trips away from the Sloan approached Oriental fatalism. Delays in New York, however maddening, caused him no personal inconvenience. Therefore, in New York, schedules were always met, personnel arrived on planes that landed on the dot, and appointments meshed like clockwork. In the field Charlie became a veritable Job. Strikes, epidemics, and natural catastrophes followed him in his travels as faithfully as his carry-on suitcase. If Davidson Wylie was essential, then he was sure to be *hors de combat*. What difference did it make whether fate produced a man from Interpol or a bout with Hong Kong flu?

This elevated detachment was challenged the moment Hugo Cramer learned of the shattered timetable. He came roaring up the corridor determined to get the train back on track.

"Look," he said hoarsely, "until we get that escrow account operating, we can't do a thing, and that includes signing on the local road contractor. Every week's delay on the access roads now is going to mean three weeks in the fall. If we can't wrap it up today, we'll have to do it over the weekend."

"I've already made plans for the weekend," Charlie objected. Under the best of circumstances, he was no lover of overtime. Too often, in his opinion, it did not result from the impossibility of cramming six days work into five days, but from someone's efforts to fiddle with which five days he was willing to work. "Too bad we weren't able to sit down with Wylie this morning," he added meaningfully.

Cramer took the point instantly. Interpol might be regarded as an act of God, but it was only partially responsible for the current disruption. In a very real sense, the Wylies were trying to conduct their divorce on Charlie Trinkam's time. "I'll tell you what," he urged in a more conciliatory fashion. "This stuff is all in the files. I'll dig it out, and I'll go over it with you."

Until now Wylie had been an apathetic observer of the dislocations he was causing. But some habits die hard. As if a button had been pushed, he drew himself up to lean forward, his eyes fixed hypnotically on Cramer, his voice warm with sympathetic concern.

"It's nice of you to offer, Hugo, and believe me, I appreciate it. But we don't want to take any chances on a foul-up, just as we're getting Noss Head off the ground, do we? All things considered, we were damn lucky to get the contract in the first place, but we can't count on an unlimited run of luck. Naturally all the facts are in the files, but it's the interpretation that counts. And, Hugo, you know you aren't familiar enough with customs in Britain to help Charlie out much."

Trinkam decided to rise above Macklin's internal power struggle. "Well, if someone doesn't help Charlie out today," he growled, "they're going to have to wait until Monday."

"Don't worry." Dave Wylie was already dialing another extension in the building. "I'll get Paul Volpe up here right away. He knows all about the firms on our consideration list—credit ratings, experience, principals. He'll be able to give you chapter and verse."

"Fine."

Wylie produced a wan smile. "Now I can stop worrying about what you're all going to be doing and start worrying about this guy from Interpol."

Both as a bid for sympathy and as a forecast, this remark fell flat. Those present immediately addressed themselves to the problem of financing preliminary site work in Scotland, forgetting entirely what the afternoon held in store for Wylie. On the other hand, the one man he had forgotten was on his way to lodge a protest.

Klaus Engelhart normally worked with meticulous regard for the orderings of any hierarchy in which he found himself. His system, which had proved satisfactory in Scandinavia, the Near East, and Great Britain, was soon in difficulties at Macklin. Shortly after his arrival he had been present at an extended discussion among Cramer, Wylie, and Volpe that would have defied any outsider to rank them. If there were clues, Engelhart decided, they were beyond him. The one indisputable superior whom he had encountered was Arthur Shute, and, accordingly, it was to the president's office that he brought his complaint.

"I have been here a week now, and it was Dave Wylie himself who asked me to come. Yet he is always too busy to see me," the German charged. "I cannot stay in Houston indefinitely. There are things in Hamburg that need attention, but I do not wish to leave without accomplishing anything."

"Naturally. And I'm glad you've come to me. Dave has had a lot of trouble with his schedule this week, but I didn't know you were one of the victims." As he automatically produced apologies, Shute was conscious of mounting irritation. Everyone from Hugo Cramer down had assured him that getting the Noss Head contract was the problem. Thereafter, the world-renowned Macklin efficiency would swing into action. Arthur Shute had not been with the company long enough for loyalty to displace common sense. As far as he was concerned, the award of the contract had heralded one ball-up after another. Without showing a hint of annoyance, he went on: "Let me see if I can set something up."

In spite of his previous experience with Charlie Trinkam, Shute's first attempt involved a Saturday morning session. Engelhart's short, stocky figure, his bald dome, his thick eyeglasses, all suggested a solemn dedication to business that would not begrudge an expanded work week. And, unlike Charlie, he was trying to sell something to Macklin. It soon developed that Arthur Shute was looking for objections in the wrong corner.

"I'd like to help you out, Arthur, but I don't see how I can," Wylie said with real regret. "Francesca and I are passing papers on some real estate tomorrow morning. And you know what happens to meetings the minute you let a lawyer in. There's no telling when I'll be able to pull free."

Shute was briefly thankful that Klaus Engelhart had reasons of his own for wishing to speed the Wylie divorce. Nonetheless, Macklin's European manager was not getting away with it that easily.

"Just a minute, Dave, I'm not finished. If you can't manage tomorrow, then we'll have to make it a business dinner tonight. My girl will get us a dining room at the Tidewater, and I'll ask Cramer and Trinkam if they want to sit in."

In one quarter this suggestion met with instant approval. Klaus Engelhart was beaming broadly. "That is excellent. There is a limit to what Dave and I can accomplish alone. This way Hugo and Charlie can get an overall view of NDW's participation—which will make it easier for us to work together."

Shute blinked. "There are a lot of questions still to be decided, Engelhart. We don't want to race too far ahead. At the moment NDW has simply been asked to bid on the pumping subcontracts. It's not even certain that you'll be doing that."

"Of course, nothing can go forward until the technicalities have been satisfied," Engelhart agreed. "But I expect to be interested in much more than the pumping work."

"That," said Shute with a touch of severity, "will depend on your company's capabilities."

But young men who take too much for granted are notoriously self-confident. "Do not worry about our capability. On the contrary you may find that we are indispensable."

"Perhaps. But for tonight we'd better restrict ourselves to the subcontract at hand."

Dave Wylie leaped into the breach. "And that's what you wanted to discuss anyway, Klaus. I'm glad I was able to work something out for you," he went on, taking credit for a business dinner that had been rammed down his throat. "You'll find that tonight I'll be able to settle all your problems."

But very shortly it began to seem as if tonight would never come.

"Now, Mr. Wylie," the big neutral man with the expressionless face was saying, "the room you were held in had a window so heavily shuttered you couldn't see out. Is that right?"

Dave was overeager in his response. "Yes. I never saw what was outside so there's no point in asking me about that."

"You couldn't see anything except what was in the room?"

"That's what I said."

"Then there was artificial light in the room." It was a statement, not a question. "What kind of fixture was it?"

Wylie flinched as if bitten. "I didn't say there was any light."

"But you could see what was inside in spite of the shutters. So there must have been light."

"I guess so." The agreement came slowly and reluctantly.

"And how did you turn it on and off?"

"I didn't." Wylie seemed to feel some amplification was required. "They did, from someplace outside."

There was apparently no end to the questions that could be asked about lighting.

"And what kind of light was it? Lamps? A fluorescent circle? A chandelier? If it was anything distinctive, that would be a help to the police over there."

"Well, it wasn't. There was just a bare bulb in the ceiling."

"That's odd, very odd." There was a pause for lengthy notetaking. "A bare bulb would usually have a drop cord."

"I can't help that," Wylie shot back. He had been unnerved ever since Interpol's representative turned out to be a local FBI agent. Dave had been hoping that, here in Houston, unlike Ankara, it would be the policeman who was out of place.

"You see, Mr. Wylie, we've made progress already. There can't be many places in Istanbul that have been

94

rewired to provide outside switches for a simple ceiling plug. I'd say we've narrowed things down considerably."

Dave looked anything but gratified. With a visible effort he pulled himself together and managed to speak in his usual manner. "Naturally I want to be as helpful to you people as possible, and it's great that this session has been of real use." Already he was pushing his chair back from the desk. "I'm glad I was able to fit you in but you'll understand that I'm in a real bind for—"

Agent McMurtrey simply talked right through him. "Interpol wanted me to say how grateful they are for Macklin's cooperation. And I really did appreciate it when Mr. Shute told me to take as much time as I needed, because he agreed that our investigation takes priority over any other commitments."

Davidson Wylie licked suddenly dry lips. Slowly and painfully he was beginning to realize that James McMurtrey was sitting on the other side of the blotter, not because of any expertise about Turkey, but because he knew how American corporations worked.

"Then that's fine," he said weakly. "I haven't had a chance to talk to Shute myself."

"I thought we'd better be absolutely clear about the whole thing." McMurtrey was as stolid as ever. "Now you said there were shutters over the window. Too heavy to move?"

"Yes."

"Did you try?"

"Of course I did. What do you take me for?" Wylie flared. "They weren't just heavy, they were nailed shut."

"And you couldn't loosen the nails?"

"There wasn't that much in the room to use on them. There was a tin ashtray, but it just crumpled up. And a spoon I tried wasn't any good."

"But you spent some time on the problem?"

"Until I exhausted the possibilities." Dave became sarcastic. "Those guys in ski masks weren't considerate enough to leave a lot of crowbars lying around."

"Fine! The Turkish police claim that a detailed description of those shutters will practically tell them what section of Istanbul we're dealing with."

Wylie narrowed his eyes. "I didn't take in a lot of detail."

"You just think you didn't. You'd be surprised at what you'll remember if we nudge you along a little. Were they wood or metal?"

"Wood."

The shutters became a repetition of the lights. Were they paneled or solid? Were they grilled? Did they have any decorative hardware? How many sets of hinges were there?

As Dave fiddled with some paper clips in the pencil drawer, his replies began to sound random, even to himself.

"What the hell do you think I am?" he demanded. "I was worried about my life, not taking a survey of interior decoration. I didn't notice any of this stuff."

"Come now, Mr. Wylie. You were in that room for over two weeks. If we can't get anywhere with the shutters, let's try the floor."

But Dave no longer dared admit anything. "I'm sorry, I don't remember the floor."

With no apparent chagrin, McMurtrey abandoned the floor for the walls, the ceiling, the bed, the door . . .

Grimly Wylie clung to his contention as the strange duel prolonged itself.

"I don't remember," he said over and over.

He was incapable, however, of maintaining his facade of willing helpfulness. The sullen defiance in his disclaimers accorded better with a suspected criminal than with an innocent victim. When five o'clock brought the normal bustle of departing employees to the corridor outside, he gave a sigh of relief.

"Look, I've got an appointment for dinner tonight. It was Arthur Shute who set it up."

"I know. And I've barely started on my list. Let's knock off now and get together tomorrow morning."

Dave gritted his teeth. "I've got an appointment then, too."

"I know. At eleven o'clock. Shall we make it nine?"

"I suppose you think you know everything?" Dave snapped.

"No." McMurtrey looked at him stonily. "Not yet."

When Davidson Wylie rose, he closed the drawer with a slam that echoed through the room like a pistol shot.

"He'll crack all right," McMurtrey was reporting over the phone a short time later. "All I have to do is keep squeezing him."

"You yourself have no doubts?" Captain Harbak asked.

"He's lying himself blue in the face. And he's no good at it."

"I am relieved to hear you say so. Confirmation is always welcome."

"I'll go further. You had three possibilities. You said either he was crazy, he was scared stiff of Black Tuesday, or he was in this up to his neck. Take it from me, he's as sane as you are."

"It never seemed very likely. But the psychiatrist who was present in Ankara . . ." The distant voice trailed off apologetically.

McMurtrey was a veteran of many court battles about diminished responsibility. "Aren't they something?" he remarked, before returning to the subject at hand. "What bothers me is this business of Wylie's being too scared to open up. We've never had this problem before with one of the big Che Guevara specials. Unless there's something unique about your terrorists?"

"No, even if they are novices and discordant about everything else," said Captain Harbak, who was still disseminating his theory about Black Tuesday, "they would unite in the desire for publicity."

"Then the only explanation is that Wylie can tell us a lot more than the color of a bedspread. He could tell us names. Which means Davidson Wylie wasn't casually chosen as a victim. There was some previous contact and he got snatched as a lesson."

Captain Harback was diffident. "I have been studying his dossier."

"So have I. He was just a standard American businessman based in Europe."

"Yes, but first in chemicals, then electronics. Is it too bizarre to imagine him in an arms deal? If he ever shortweighted a customer, that would explain this pattern."

When there was no audience to impress, McMurtrey stopped being impassive. Scowling in concentration, he loosened his tie and ran a hand through his hair. "No, I don't think so," he said at length. "There are plenty of reliable arms merchants, and all these groups know it. Then, you haven't seen Wylie when he wasn't being hysterical. I'd say he was the last man to decide to moonlight in munitions and go searching for customers. And he's too respectably middle-aged to fall into accidental contact with them."

Captain Harbak coughed. "Actually it was his wife I was thinking of."

There was a pause as McMurtrey riffled through his own file. What he found was not very convincing.

"She's not exactly a spring chicken herself. She's thirty-six."

"A spring chicken? Is that how you put it? It is not very gallant." Captain Harbak was mildly amused, but he persisted with his theory. "Her work takes her to all the film studios in Europe. Presumably she comes in contact with all the young actors, all the students trying to pick up some money as extras. It is a totally different environment."

"I grant you the different environment, but it still sounds farfetched to me."

Harbak clicked his tongue in exasperation. "And Wylie's manner gave you no clue?"

"When I'm there, Wylie is so scared of me that it blankets his other reactions," McMurtrey explained. "But why bother shooting down each other's theories? I guarantee you that within forty-eight hours Mr. Davidson Wylie will be telling us all about it himself."

The business dinner has become a time-hallowed institution largely because of an underlying psychological reality. A group of co-specialists laboring to meet a demanding deadline can rise above the physical discomforts of long hours, stale air, improper food, and endless cups of instant coffee. Accountants completing an exhaustive audit, lawyers composing an appellate brief, scientists summarizing research data, all are working toward a common goal. But complex business negotiations, however much camouflaged by a veneer of cordiality, are basically adversarial in nature. Different participants represent different interests. Under these circumstances, the wise executive sets a limit to physical fatigue. A dinner hour that features the relaxation resulting from one or two drinks, the warm glow of substantial caloric intake, the feeling of rich surfeit induced by a cigar after coffee, can pay for itself. Frayed tempers are miraculously restored, concessions that loomed as impossible mountains melt into manageable molehills, and more progress is made between nine and ten than was made all afternoon.

Arthur Shute had seen it happen many times, and he confidently expected similar benefits that Friday evening. Unfortunately, he had forgotten that what one or two drinks can achieve, five or six drinks can destroy. By the time shrimp cocktail yielded to steak, Davidson Wylie was a major social menace. He had arrived late, with liquor on his breath and self-pity just around the corner. When Hugo Cramer casually asked about the Interpol agent, Wylie drained his double Scotch before replying.

"The SOB claims he isn't finished with me. He wants another go-round tomorrow. And tomorrow he'll say he wants another one after that, and it'll go on and on . . ." Wylie's voice had been rising before he choked it off with an effort of will. He steadied himself with a hand on the bar. "I tell you I can't take much more of this."

Shute had not seen Davidson Wylie until he was restored to normalcy. Cramer's description had emphasized the heavy-handedness of the Ankara personnel in dealing with the malady, rather than the malady itself.

"For God's sake, Dave, I didn't realize you were still so tight about the whole thing," Macklin's president exclaimed. "Why don't I have someone from the law department stand by you tomorrow?"

"What good is a lawyer going to do me?" Wylie asked, unanswerably. "I haven't committed any crime. I just don't feel like reliving every minute of those three weeks."

Shute looked at him thoughtfully. The next specialist that came to mind was a psychiatrist, but he had no intention of washing that kind of dirty linen in front of outsiders. Instead, he resolutely steered the conversation into general channels with the able assistance of Charlie Trinkam and Engelhart. Poor Charlie was even reduced to an extended comparison of the weather in London and Houston. But, given four men vitally concerned with the acrobatics of the international oil market, it was not long before common ground was discovered to carry them through cocktails and half their dinner. Inevitably Cramer's anecdotes about Saudi Arabia and Engelhart's tales of Scandinavian intransigence led them into speculation about what awaited them in Scotland.

"From the map," said Charlie cheerfully, "it looks like the most godforsaken spot in the British Isles."

"You should see some of the places I've worked," Hugo Cramer countered. "It's not the natural site that bothers me, it's the local unions."

Rather ponderously, Arthur Shute interrupted to say that he understood labor problems had been resolved in advance.

"Don't you believe it!" Cramer snorted sardonically. "I got us an agreement with the national trade-union. But from what I hear, some of these shop stewards up north are the original wildcat strike boys."

"That is very true," Engelhart supported him. "Certainly NDW's first step on the pumping works will be to achieve accord with the local labor leaders."

There were occasions when Charlie Trinkam's genuine interest betrayed him into tactlessness. "And how much is that likely to cost you?" he asked.

Arthur Shute barely had time for one hissing intake of breath before Cramer spoke up. "That's not what Klaus meant at all. And you can spare me your famous speech about purity in business, Arthur. It's not a matter of greasing palms. You just have to be careful about stepping on toes. These shop stewards think they're God Almighty, and you've got to play along with their act."

"I still don't see why our agreement with the national union wouldn't protect us," Shute grumbled.

Cramer's hackles were beginning to rise. "Well, it doesn't. That's a fact of British life. And I got you the best deal from the labor boys that anybody's gotten in a long time."

"I'm sure you did, Hugo," said Shute, retreating. "Just as I know that you got us a damn good Noss Head contract, and we're all grateful."

This was quite enough to pacify Cramer, who cooled as quickly as he heated. Charlie and Engelhart were both pleased to see serenity restored after a gaffe for which they were responsible. But Davidson Wylie, who had long been silent, stirred restively.

"Hold it a minute!" he commanded. "Listen, Hugo, let's not forget that I'm the one who got that contract. I'm the one who did the planning, who made the contacts, and I'm the one who sweated blood for it."

"Sure, sure, Dave," said Cramer hastily. "We all know you're the expert on Europe. You put the whole package together. All I did was tie up some loose ends."

His meaningful glance at Wylie's glass was not wasted on the others. When dinner had been announced, Dave had filled a tumbler with neat whisky before following the rest of the company to the table. Since then he had been sipping steadily, toying with his food. The net result was that earlier jitters had evaporated, to be replaced by Olympian arrogance.

"And now that I'm in charge again," he said, unbuttoning his jacket and leaning back to survey his companions, "there are a few things I've got in mind. Klaus, you're going to have to watch your step in Scotland. Any trouble with the locals, I'll handle. I can do a better job."

"You think you know more about Europeans than me, too?" Engelhart asked sarcastically.

But tonight sarcasm was bouncing off Davidson Wylie's alcoholic armor. "Well, obviously, I understand the English better. It's time you faced up to the fact that I won Noss Head, not you."

If Wylie had been angry he would have been less insufferable. But his was the tolerance of an immensely wise, immensely experienced older man instructing callow youth.

In any event, Klaus Engelhart was goaded into voicing a conviction he had harbored since London. "If you had not been kidnapped, NDW would have Noss Head, not Macklin. That was your contribution, Dave—getting the English to bend over backward for Macklin. And I would not have thought they could be so stupid."

"Think you have everything figured out, don't you?" Wylie smiled loftily. "Life may be one surprise after another for you."

Arthur Shute believed in asserting dominion over subcontractors, but this was not the way he wanted it done. In a vain attempt to carry out his original plan for the evening, he said: "By the way, Dave, I thought you were going to bring Paul Volpe with you. Charlie, here, was hoping to have another crack at him."

Charlie Trinkam was anything but grateful at being sucked into conversation with the table's problem child. "That's right," he said with a grimace. "We were supposed to have a productive work session."

"Sorry about that." Wylie flapped a hand in vague apology. "Paul couldn't make it. He was going someplace else."

"What the hell do you mean by that?" Hugo Cramer demanded. "I saw the two of you pull up here together."

"He had to give me a lift because I let Francesca

have my car," Wylie explained. Then, turning to Engelhart with an unpleasant leer, he continued: "And you have to keep the little woman happy, or we know what will happen, don't we, Klaus?"

Deliberately, Engelhart ignored the shaft and aimed one of his own. "You had better get your car back so you can keep your appointment with Interpol. They might take it amiss if you do not turn up."

Wylie swept his empty glass aside so vigorously that it rolled halfway down the table. "Look, tomorrow I'm going to tell that bastard where he gets off. I've got more important things to do than fool around with him." In the last hour Wylie's speech had thickened steadily. Now his control over sentences was also slipping. ". . . got a whole field to build . . . contracts to let out . . . oil pipelines . . . property setments, no, settlements." He shook his head, stared groggily across the table, then triumphantly completed his thoughts. "But nobody's pushing me around anymore. I'm calling the shots from now on."

Not surprisingly, the party broke up shortly thereafter. Charlie decided that he was expecting a call from John Thatcher and had to be in his room for it. Engelhart and Cramer were quick to follow his lead. Arthur Shute sadly accepted the ruin of his evening's program.

"We must do this again sometime," he said automatically.

"Oh, sure," said Charlie.

By rights, the next morning should have seen Charlie Trinkam and Klaus Engelhart, long finished with a hearty breakfast, righteously watching a haggard Dave Wylie's belated entry to the coffee shop. Instead Wylie was on his way out when Charlie passed through the door.

"I see that the wonder boy managed to pull himself out of bed," Charlie grumbled to Engelhart, who was just starting his orange juice.

"He is worried about the Interpol man."

"Did he say so?"

"He did not feel like talking." Engelhart shrugged. "But I could tell."

Idly, Charlie gaped through the floor-to-ceiling glass that lined the side of the restaurant, observing Wylie's progress. "Don't let the Macklin atmosphere get to you. Wylie doesn't look as if he's hanging back from his appointment. Anyway, why should he be worried?"

"The police know he is withholding information," Engelhart said with grave certainty. "He is afraid those terrorists will kill him if he talks."

"You've forgotten what Wylie sounded like last night. He wasn't afraid of anything."

"He was drunk."

Charlie was begining to be irritated by the German's pronouncements. "He's not drunk now. And look at him. He doesn't look scared."

Engelhart turned skeptically. Davidson Wylie was tossing his case into a car. Both men watched him slide into the driver's seat. They were still watching when a flash of light was almost lost in the booming roar that followed. Instinctively they ducked as a rain of metal fragments returned to earth.

"Christ!" Charlie choked. "That was a bomb!"

10 · Boomtown!

Within minutes of the blast, firemen and an ambulance crew were struggling frantically to extricate Davidson Wylie from the smoldering wreckage of the Oldsmobile. But there was too much blood. Too many of the Tidewater's windows had been blown out. Someone had triggered a killing explosion.

"My God!" Charlie overheard the desk clerk mutter. "A single bullet will kill a man. Hell, so will a club! Why all this?"

Most onlookers remained slack-jawed, staring numbly at the scrambling emergency crew, but there was a responsive croak:

"Call it a modern improvement. Shows how far we've come from the cavemen."

"Oh, please," moaned an elderly woman. "Please."

Next to her, Klaus Engelhart swallowed convulsively, covered his mouth with his hand, then fled.

Charlie himself turned his eyes away when the firemen finally levered open the car door and waved up the stretcher bearers. With an effort, he forced himself to concentrate on the brutal, simple essentials.

Davidson Wylie had been cold-bloodedly slaughtered —and John Thatcher should be told. More slowly than Engelhart, he made his way through the growing crowd. Latecomers, he noticed inconsequentially, were excited and talkative.

"Geeze, you could feel it two blocks away . . . "

"What was it? Gas? I heard the sirens . . . "

"Have they got him out? Oh, there they go!"

In the lobby there was no sign of Engelhart or anybody else. Charlie found himself dialing New York from a vast, luxury cavern.

"No horsing around, Rose," he told Miss Corsa bluntly. "This is important . . . John? I've got the latest wrinkle from Macklin for you . . ."

"Good God," said Thatcher, once Charlie announced his news.

"And maybe doing it this way was easier than pulling a trigger," Charlie continued savagely, "but for my money, they're a bunch of maniacs. Anybody could have been walking by that car."

Trinkam was as hard-shelled as anybody John Thatcher knew. But no one is immune. Right now, what he needed was a stiff drink, not a lot of talk.

Thatcher broke in to say so, adding: "I'll be in touch later today. And Charlie, remember there is undeniable improvement in our capacity to track down killers—no matter what their methods."

"That remains to be seen," Trinkam said tersely.

But *seen* was precisely the wrong word. By the time Charlie was crossing the lobby to the bar (and he was not alone), by the time the fire department was hosing down the Tidewater's parking lot, a sophisticated apparatus was spinning into action. On a scale beyond the imagination of most Tidewater guests, and beyond the immediate vision of Charles Trinkam, the private tragedy of Davidson Wylie was being reduced to raw data.

The process began in Houston and continued throughout the day and night. But the results, in the opinion of the officer in charge, scarcely justified the elaborate information-retrieval system.

"Dead on arrival," read Lieutenant Morley Nash.

"For Christ's sake, I don't need a computer to tell me that. I was there."

Silently, the tabulating clerk handed over another sheet. The broad outlines of Davidson Wylie's life were all there—his birthdate and birthmarks, his marital status and credit rating, his education and work history. He had no police record, he had not served in the Army, he had never owned an airplane, applied for a gun permit, or been audited by the IRS.

"Who cares whether he was born in Pasadena and went to Stanford?" muttered Nash, reaching blindly for the next installment.

It was as if he were proceeding through a series of maps of the same terrain, each on a more detailed scale than its predecessor. First he learned of Wylie's arrival at Houston's airport, his stay at Hugo Cramer's beach cottage, his removal to the Tidewater. Then the Tidewater period was broken down into segments and Lieutenant Nash's eyebrows rose as he encountered Francesca Wylie's name. Finally there was a minute-by-minute chronology of the last twenty-four hours in Davidson Wylie's life, supported by interviews with secretaries at Macklin, chambermaids at the Tidewater, real estate agents and everyone present at the victim's last dinner and breakfast.

"There isn't anything here from the Fed who talked to Wylie."

Almost before the complaint was voiced, the clerk was informing Nash of an appointment set up for him at ten o'clock.

But the lieutenant was already deep in another comprehensive report, this time covering the movements of a certain Oldsmobile Delta, Texas plate MK –5892. It was owned by Southeastern Motors and leased under contract to Macklin. On September 2, after a thorough inspection in the car pool, it had been placed at the disposal of Davidson Wylie. Thereafter he had driven it himself until 1:00 PM on September 4. According to the testimony of his wife, she had driven the Oldsmobile straight from the Macklin Building to the Tidewater, where she had parked it in her husband's slot. The car had remained unmoved until 9:08 AM the next morning when it exploded. There were no witnesses to the tampering, and no suspicious loiterers had been observed by the Tidewater staff.

This stream of negatives was finally broken by experts from the bomb squad. They announced that the device had consisted of several sticks of dynamite with a blasting cap wired into the Oldsmobile's ignition. Similar contrivances, usually with the addition of a timer, had been used in 117 bombings in the United States and over 300 in Europe. Furthermore the computer, upon being told that the dynamite was that commonly used in construction work, had replied that thirty-eight cases of pilferage at construction sites in Texas during the past week were known to it. To add to the general joy, the squad had staged a simulation in which one of its men had wired dynamite into an Oldsmobile Delta, taking exactly one and a half minutes for the task.

"God!" groaned Nash. "It would have been harder to steal that car—and we all know how hard that is." Dispiritedly he shoveled together the mass of papers. "So all this junk adds up to a big fat nothing. It tells me everything about Wylie's life and death except what I want to know. What happened when he got mixed up with a bunch of terrorists? Why was Interpol on his tail? Did he know something so important he was worth blowing up?"

The tabulating clerk was not going to apologize because his equipment could not solve a problem it had never been programmed for. But, being an amiable man, he proffered the only crumbs of comfort available.

"The postmortem won't be ready for a couple of hours."

"You mean I should hope that Wylie died a natural death?"

The clerk abandoned the autopsy as a lost cause. "Maybe that Fed can tell you something."

"God, I hope so."

"Wylie was lying," McMurtrey said flatly.

"You're sure?"

"I'm sure, and so is the Turkish captain who talked to him in Ankara."

That was good enough for Nash. When two experienced policemen, with no vested interest, said a man was lying, he did not require supporting evidence.

"In a way, it's crazy, but in another way it makes more sense," he said, rubbing a hand across his weary eyes as he organized his thoughts. "If Wylie was just a random victim, there's no reason on God's earth why his kidnappers should follow him to Houston and kill him. But once you grant a tie-in between him and Black Tuesday, he could have been a danger to them in lots of ways. I suppose those are the lines you're thinking along."

"That's about it. I admit that at first I thought Wylie was putting on an act about being too scared of reprisals to open up. It seemed a lot easier to think he was behind the whole thing. But the poor guy has proved he was right to be scared."

Morley Nash had no error of judgment to haunt him. He was preoccupied with the future.

"And what the hell am I supposed to do about it? Wylie spends fifteen years in Europe, he becomes involved with some new radical group over there, gets himself snatched in Turkey so a ransom can pass in Zurich. Then by sheer accident he's murdered here, miles away from all the background. I don't know anything about all those places, I'm a Houston cop." He sketched an encompassing gesture at the window. "This is my turf."

The panorama visible through the broad sheet of plate glass emphasized his statement. Great economic power has always memorialized itself in architecture—whether it be the Great Sphinx, or the Colosseum, or Trafalgar Square. But in Texas it was not pharaohs or popes or emperors who were impressing their legends into stone and marble. The names dominating the

Houston skyline spoke for themselves. The sumptuous travertine of One Shell Plaza soared fifty stories high in the glistening sunlight. Close by, the eye-stopping trapezoid towers of Pennzoil Place symbolized the expanding prosperity that was tossing up freeways, suburbs, and modernistic shopping malls. By craning to the left it was just possible to see the delicate steel tracery of the Macklin Building.

If he could have seen that view, Nicholas of the Imperial Dominion Bank might have modified his opinion of Houston as a rugged tropical outpost. Unfortunately, Lieutenant Nash was inspired to different thoughts entirely.

"All that construction. There's probably dynamite lying around on every corner," he sighed. "Unless terrorists always carry their own brand with them."

"They would have had to come through Customs and Immigration at the airport," McMurtrey said, without much conviction.

"Ha! We've got over four million illegal Mexican immigrants. Do you think they would have noticed a couple of Arabs?"

McMurtrey nodded sympathetically. Even a four-state care-theft ring could play havoc with the jurisdictional lines of law-enforcement agencies. It was absurd to expect local police to cope with a crime spanning three continents. But before the FBI man could speak, his secretary rang through with the announcement that Lieutenant Nash's office was on the line.

"Hello, Tim. . . . Yeah, I can get back. . . . Didn't he say anything else? . . . Tell him I'll be there in fifteen minutes."

Nash grounded the receiver and turned to Mc-Murtrey, his forehead wrinkled in bewilderment. "Something's come up in the postmortem. The medical examiner is waiting to talk to me."

"But Wylie was killed by a bomb."

"I don't know what the hell is going on. But he's not hanging around my office unless he's got something up his sleeve."

110

McMurtrey, his interest piqued, was already reaching for his jacket. "Mind if I tag along?"

"Sure, but I'm not promising anything."

They were both too experienced to waste time speculating during the drive. A discussion of the Astros carried them through traffic, up the elevator, and into the Homicide Division.

The moment that Nash saw his visitor, he stopped short. Dr. Martin Zender was not a regular member of the staff. He was the high lama of consultants to the medical examiner. He was also a leading light of the Baylor Medical Center and a professor of forensic medicine. A certain degree of disenchantment might be expected in any normal man who divided his time between corpses and modern youth. But today Dr. Zender's baby-blue eyes were gleaming with excitement.

"They called me in to look at your bits and pieces," he said happily, "and I've come up with something that may upset all your ideas."

"My God," gasped Nash, sinking into a chair, "Wylie did die a natural death."

"Oh, this isn't about Wylie's death, this is about his life," said Zender, deliberately tantalizing.

Lieutenant Nash took a deep breath. "Now, wait a minute, Doc. You haven't forgotten this is a homicide case? If it turns out that Wylie was on heroin, that isn't going to help me catch a bunch of terrorists."

Serenely Dr. Zender sailed on. He might have been chatting to one of his classes. "The effects of blast are notoriously unpredictable. You can't count on your victim being blown to smithereens. In this case, for instance, there was extensive damage including . . ."

The grisly catalog that followed was intelligible to Nash.

"Okay, from the hips down he was just mincemeat. So what?"

"But the upper torso was intact. And when I spotted some interesting scar tissue, I decided to take X rays." Suddenly Dr. Zender ceased being a lecturer. "You know, I read the headlines, too. I even went back and checked the dates. I was curious about the injuries your Davidson Wylie incurred while he was supposed to be kidnapped."

The room had become completely still.

"*Supposed* to be kidnapped," McMurtrey repeated in a whisper.

"That's right. In the latter half of July, he sustained three cracked ribs, a broken collarbone, and some chipping of the ulna."

No one dreamed of questioning Dr. Zender's facts. His interpretation was a different matter.

"I suppose they could have beaten hell out of him," Nash said doggedly. "But why wouldn't he mention it?"

Zender was shaking his head gently. "The injuries were all on the left side."

Policemen may end up as specialists in homicide or fraud or vice. But very few of them get through the first years of their career without exposure to the traffic detail.

"A car accident," Nash concluded instantly. "But, Jesus Christ, the left side usually means the driver."

"He could have been on the left in the back seat. And Black Tuesday got some doctor to patch him up." But McMurtrey was speaking out of a dutiful desire to explore all possibilities. Both he and Nash could sense that Dr. Martin Zender was saving the best for last.

Zender beamed at them. "This was not a case of stealthy first aid in a hideout. The X rays show exactly how that collarbone was wired together. It was done on an operating table with surgeons and anesthetists. I can assure you that, during the period Wylie was supposed to be captive, he was receiving first-rate medical attention in a modern hospital."

Nash and McMurtrey were so excited they kept explaining the obvious.

"I was right all along," crowed the FBI man. "Wylie set the whole thing up himself. And he wasn't scared because he couldn't fake a lot of detail about lamps and shutters. He was scared because he left a record a mile wide."

"The bastard was simply ripping off his company for a million and a half. There never were any terrorists." Nash had his own reasons for being jubilant. "But then who in hell killed him?"

It was clear as daylight to Agent McMurtrey.

"Wylie couldn't have pulled this off by himself. And when he started to come apart under questioning, his buddies decided it would be safer to get rid of him," he reasoned. "They used an explosion to make it look like terrorists. But actually it could be anybody—some of his pals in Europe, or some of the people he works with at Macklin. You're going to have to start finding out about them."

Nash remembered all that apparently useless detail spewed forth by the computer about Arthur Shute, Hugo Cramer, Paul Volpe, Klaus Engelhart.

"I already know a lot. And I'll tell you one thing. They may call themselves director of operations or marketing manager, but basically they're all engineers. Any one of them could have put that bomb together blindfolded."

McMurtrey had followed the underground press in his time. "That doesn't mean a thing. If you can read English, there are plans everywhere."

"Who cares?" Nash asked grandly. "Thanks to the Doc here, I don't have to worry about a pack of politicals. That's the big thing."

McMurtrey hastened to add his own congratulations. Dr. Zender was so moved by the general approbation that he broke the rule of a lifetime and ventured beyond his own arena.

"You know," he said modestly, "I think the Turkish police might be interested in this discovery of mine."

They were more than interested. Captain Harbak seized on the new facts like a terrier shaking a rat.

"You see what this means, Pezmoglu," he declaimed to his subordinate. "All along I said the man was lying. But one thing bothered me, one thing supported his fanciful tale. You know what that was?"

Three weeks of unremitting, unsuccessful effort to verify or disprove Davidson Wylie's kidnapping had left Pezmoglu beyond speech.

"No, Captain Harbak."

"He looked the part," thundered Harbak. "He was white and puffy and unhealthy, exactly like a man who has been confined. And he had been confined! But not by kidnappers! In a hospital—surrounded by well-wishers and telephones and telegraph wires. Does he ask for the police, does he call the embassy, does he telegraph his company? Of course not! He is too busy stealing a million and a half dollars."

"He did not enjoy it for long," said Pezmoglu with mournful satisfaction.

"And that is as it should be. But now we can proceed without the distraction of these mythical terrorists. These strange, shy terrorists who made no speeches, demanded no prisoner exchanges, never mentioned Ulrike or Daoud. Pfa! Wylie must have thought we were imbeciles."

Pezmoglu continued his own strange dirge. "He created imaginary terrorists, and now he has died by one of their bombs."

"That is a matter for the Houston police. For us, there are other concerns." Harbak cleared his throat. "It is only natural that I should have been deceived by a convalescent. I make no claim to expertise in these matters. And the same is true of diplomats and businessmen. But there is one man who should have recognized Wylie's imposture."

Harbak was on his feet, pulling his tunic taut, as his assistant watched with interest.

"You and I, Pezmoglu, are going to the American embassy to have a talk with this Dr. Wennergren."

11 · Offshore Operations

The iron rules of protocol, regularly waived by affable monarchs, genial prelates, and modern major generals are scrupulously observed by diplomats, by the lower depths of bureaucracy, and by all physicians and surgeons. In our brave new world, the last surviving bastion of working feudalism is the great order of healers.

So Captain Harbak, with Pezmoglu in tow, approached the embassy medical office knowing what to expect.

Dr. Wennergren began hollering before he was hurt.

"Yes, I have been informed that Wylie has been murdered. Somewhere in Texas, I believe. I am not clear how I can help you, Captain."

"You saw Wylie three weeks ago, did you not?" Harbak said.

"What possible bearing can that have when the man has just been blown up?" said Wennergren.

Lordliness is no more endearing to a Turk than to

anyone else, which explains why sultans have gone the way of tsars and dauphins.

"The Houston police," Harbak said cunningly, "have sent us the results of their postmortem on Davidson Wylie."

He paused, but, beyond a slight pursing of the lips, Wennergren did not bite.

"The results of this postmortem are interesting to us," Harbak continued. "Perhaps they will also interest you, Doctor."

Without enthusiasm, Wennergren accepted the document that Harbak proffered. As he read, he lost altitude steadily.

A typescript from the Ministry of Interior, Republic of Turkey, left him imperially displeased with errors in the English text. But when he reached the Houston medical examiner's findings, he scented a rival power. The attached memorandum from Dr. Martin Zender of the Baylor Medical Center toppled him completely.

"A broken collarbone that was wired," he muttered. "But Wylie didn't say a thing about that."

"You do not think there is any possibility of error?" asked Harbak blowing a delicate smoke ring across the doctor's desk.

By now Wennergren the autocrat had been routed. "I think I've got an ashtray here somewhere," he said, fishing in a drawer. "Error? What kind of error? If Baylor says Wylie had a wired collarbone, that's what he had."

"I thought I remembered that it was a reputable institution," said Harbak blandly. "Not perhaps a pleasant one. It is where they transplant hearts, Pezmoglu. A gruesome thought."

Wennergren was not amused. "They're reputable, all right," he said shortly.

"With eminent specialists, no doubt," said Harbak. Although he had never left Turkey, he had a fair notion that the American colony in Ankara was not one of medicine's greener pastures. "So, you do not dispute these findings?"

"How can I?" Wennergren responded defensively.

116

"You may recall that Wylie refused hospitalization. He refused a thorough examination—"

"Aha! And if you had examined him thoroughly, you would have discovered this collarbone?"

Wennergren quivered. "Certainly."

"But without such an examination even a doctor could not tell that Wylie had been injured in this way?"

"Modern medicine," Wennergren retorted, "is not based on casual observation. My God, the man wouldn't even take off his shirt."

Harbak lost interest in Wennergren. "So now we begin to understand. Mr. McMurtrey was quite correct. Wylie conspired in his own kidnapping. But he was hurt in the wrong place at the wrong time. Nonetheless, he succeeded in concealing his injuries from you, Doctor. A very cool criminal, your Mr. Wylie."

Wennergren made an ill-advised attempt to reassert his authority. "Whatever else he was, Wylie was not cool. He was under severe nervous strain—virtually exhausted. There is no reason to doubt that he was the victim of a kidnapping. The fact that he had a broken collarbone strikes me as irrelevant."

With demoralizing indifference, Harbak rose to leave. "My choice of words may be unfortunate. But the man you saw has been murdered, and the broken collarbone will tell us why."

Outside, Pezmoglu did not have to struggle with the anarchy of English. "Wylie was not treated in any Istanbul hospital," he said. "We went to each of them."

"Go to them again," said Harbak, leaning his head against the seat cushion and closing his eyes. "Forget about Davidson Wylie. Ask about broken collarbones. But I, too, think he left Istanbul. The publicity was too intense."

Pezmoglu was gloomy. "The publicity reached everywhere—Paris, London. Even Peking!"

Irritably, Harbak straightened. "Obstructions, obstructions! First that American idiot, now you. Nothing, not even the mercy of Allah, reaches everywhere.

And remember, Wylie had three weeks, not three years. Forget China! Start with Istanbul. Then draw your circle larger and larger."

Circles radiating out from Istanbul were an old story. That was how the janissaries had carried the mercy of Allah to many lands and many peoples. Now, it was police telex messages, not scimitars, that surged across the Dardanelles.

Athens still did not like it.

"First a band of terrorists! Now an American with a broken collarbone," said the assistant minister of interior, twirling his mustache. "Do these wonderful Turks think that the Greek border is made of Swiss cheese? This is not worth our time, Matsis."

Matsis was a deep thinker. "They say the American did not have a broken collarbone when he entered Greece."

"*If* he entered Greece," said the minister.

"Exactly. They are circularizing other countries too. But they want reports from hospitals. That means—"

"I see what they want, Matsis!"

"Furthermore, this request does not come from Turkey," Matsis persisted. "In reality, it is from the Americans."

"As bad as Turks!" said the minister, martially breaking a pencil. "Very well, let it be done. Instruct the authorities in Thessaly to make inquiries. I do this only to show these barbarians that Greece is a civilized member of the world community. But myself, Matsis, I would leave these Turks and Americans to each other. They are assassins!"

Poetry was lost on Matsis. "This American, Davidson Wylie, was murdered. But all we are asked to discover is whether he broke a collarbone in Greece."

With unconcealed dislike, the minister said: "He was probably murdered by a Turk, then."

"In Texas?"

"Matsis, do not try me. Let us say that Wylie was murdered by another American. But first, his collarbone was broken by a Turk."

Little did he realize what he was suggesting. Because, if a Turk had damaged Davidson Wylie, then Cyprus was about to fade into insignificance. Within hours, routine inquiries placed Davidson Wylie on Greek soil, specifically the market town of Xanthi, not much more than one hundred miles from the Turkish border.

For three weeks, while the world thought him kidnapped, Davidson Wylie had been in Xanthi. Full reports filtered back to Matsis, to the minister, and to many others.

"No, not under this name—not Wylie, if that is the way they pronounce it. No, it was worse. Owen Gilfillan. My God, how do they keep from laughing out loud?"

"Get on with the story, Triantaphillocopoulos," said Matsis.

Triantaphillocopoulos complied. Driving a rented car alone, armed with false documents identifying him as Owen Gilfillan, of Santa Barbara, California, Davidson Wylie had passed customs with no difficulty. Eighty-five miles east, about twenty miles out of Xanthi, he had somehow lost control of the car, slued off the road, and landed in a drainage ditch.

". . . and unconscious. But he was lucky—"

"He has been murdered," said Matsis.

"Well, what do you want?" Triantaphillocopoulos asked rhetorically. "Luck does not last forever. But there, Anastasis came by with his truck. He saw, he stopped, and Wylie—or Gilfillan—was rushed to the clinic. The car was not badly damaged either."

The surgeon in Xanthi answered questions impatiently.

"Yes, I have just looked at the photograph Triantaphillocopoulos brought around. That is definitely the man who was in the clinic for ten days, under the name Gilfillan. Yes, a broken collarbone, which I attended. Some broken ribs as well. Yes, he was in pain —we naturally kept him sedated for three days. No, there was no danger to his life. But simple humanity . . . what? Oh, when he left, I told him he must rest. . . . Yes, of course, he could walk. I would not

119

release him otherwise. . . . What? Yes, he went to the hotel and came back to see me twice. He made an excellent recovery."

At Xanthi's finest hostelry, they remembered Owen Gilfillan/Davidson Wylie. But the proprietor provided more than identification. Owen Gilfillan had been expected earlier—some ten days earlier.

"I remember first, because I have an excellent memory. Also, and Triantaphillocopoulos will confirm this, I keep a complete and detailed record—especially of these crazy tourists. What uncouth things they will do, what trouble they will cause—no, I am not a philosopher. What was I saying? Oh, yes. I remember because there was a telephone call, the long-distance operator, you understand, requesting Mr. Gilfillan. And that was when he was not here, although he had made a reservation. Since I did not know he was in the clinic, there was nothing . . . what? No, for the week that he stayed here, poor sinner, he did not get any calls. . . . No, he did not make any calls. He stayed in his room, resting."

In Xanthi, publicity had been no threat to Davidson Wylie. Television sets were rare, and Greek newspaper photographs are no peril to anyone, except politicians concerned with their public image.

In neat, tidy Switzerland, this was almost unbelieveable. Captain Hummel, for one, was certainly thankful to be a policeman in Zurich. "This Xanthi is a small place. You know how they are in small places."

Leopold Grimm of Union Suisse did not reply that Switzerland is a small place too. "So at last the Turks and the Greeks have found what Wylie was doing while we were paying ransom to get him back from these phantom kidnappers."

Hummel flushed at this unkind reminder that even Zurich nods. "Yes, Wylie rented a car, drove to Xanthi and planned to stay there for three days. Instead, he landed in a hospital, first unconscious, then immobile for ten days. After that, he still bore signs of injury. So he had to delay his return to Turkey—

if he was going to claim that he had been kidnapped."

"Good," said Grimm without pleasure.

"Because he should not have been driving—alone—
in Greece under an assumed name."

"History is engrossing, Hummel, but will it retrieve
my money?" said Grimm, taking a proprietarial approach to Macklin's dollars.

"I think so," Hummel persevered. "If Wylie was a
crook, then the woman who came here to Union
Suisse to pick up the ransom was not a terrorist, but
Wylie's accomplice."

"And what difference does that make?"

Hummel reached into the briefcase at his feet. "It
may mean much, Herr Grimm. Tell me, do you see
any resemblance at all between the woman with the
knapsack—and any of these women?"

Leopold Grimm did not recognize any of the
women who had been seen in public with Davidson
Wylie during the past three months. But he was astute enough to realize what Hummel's inquiries
meant.

"The police are finished with Wylie's activities," he
reported when he called New York later that day.
"Now they are concentrating on his accomplices."

"His accomplices—and his murderers," said John
Thatcher.

12 · Pumping Stations

The truth about Davidson Wylie provoked a wide variety of response.

In London, the upper reaches of the civil service were justifiably horrified. Treasury officials who had personally extended the hand of friendship to Wylie —that is, they had accepted lavish expense-account hospitality from him—looked back on their original impressions with blank disbelief. The man whom they had regarded as a happy combination of American business acumen and European suavity stood exposed as a thief, an extortionist, a master of duplicity.

No one was more disturbed than Simon Livermore. Being a creature of painstaking habit, he wiped his feet thoroughly and hung his raincoat in the hall before entering the living room overlooking Regent's Park and bringing his wife up to date. Jill Livermore had enjoyed several nightclub evenings hosted by Wylie.

"The news from Houston today is even more appalling," he began somberly.

But Jill, a promising fashion model five years earlier, belonged to a different world and a different generation than her husband. His first ten minutes home always constituted a decompression stage for Simon as he modulated from the language and values of Whitehall to those of modern Chelsea.

"Not unless they're blowing them up in batches now," she said, her voice preceding her as she glided gracefully into the room bearing a tray of decanters and glasses.

Any subordinate who dismissed an act of primitive violence so lightheartedly would have earned a sharp reproof. But very few men, Simon least of all, felt impelled to reprove Jill Livermore. Her small, fine-boned head, its delicate modeling emphasized by close-cropped blond hair, emerged like a flower on a slender stalk from the flowing silk caftan that she was wearing. She deposited the tray and, like a ballerina, subsided into a corner of the sofa without a backward glance.

"Good God, I didn't mean there had been any more crimes," her startled husband exclaimed. "I was talking about the police discoveries. It seems they've been acquiring details at an incredible pace in the Near East. They've traced all of Wylie's movements."

With the frankness of youth, Jill rarely made any bones about her priorities. She liked wearing expensive clothes, going to famous restaurants and clubs, traveling to exotic foreign parts. She was bored by Simon's job.

"So what?" she asked, unimpressed. "You said they could tell he'd been in some kind of accident because of the postmortem. As soon as they realized that he was covering up anything, they must have been sure that he stage-managed a fake kidnapping. That's what I would have thought. But knowing where he spent the time—that wouldn't take me any farther."

Having poured precisely the correct amount of whisky, Simon carried a glass over to his wife. Then, as he had done countless times before, he mulishly tried to make her appreciate the importance his office attached to trivia.

"Now that the police have established Wylie as the author of this plot, they assume his death was due to a falling out over the money. If they can establish his actions, they may locate his accomplices."

"What a hope! Nine chances out of ten, he hired two boys who were stoned out of their minds for that masquerade in Istanbul. With all the publicity, they're probably in Afghanistan by now—if they remember anything at all, that is."

Simon hated yeilding points to Jill in this sort of argument. He was supposed to be the expert but, too often, Jill could outpace him and still arrive at the correct conclusion. Like all hard-pressed debaters, he shifted ground slightly.

"The men in the ski masks are not considered important. Wylie could have hired them anywhere," he said gravely. "The woman who went to the bank in Zurich is a different matter."

"Yes, yes," Jill interrupted, anxious to get on with it. "You'd have to be loony to think she was a casual pickup. Fancy trusting a stranger with that bank account."

"Nobody is thinking in terms of strangers," Simon retorted sharply. "Colin MacFarquar says that the police are confident of tracing a connection between Wylie and the woman."

Jill's attention was half-centered on a letter she had picked up from the end table. "Oh, the police," she shrugged. "They're always confident. That's what they say every time some IRA bomber runs loose in the West End."

"Surely there's a difference. Here they have one end of a relationship. They can pursue all sorts of inquiries."

"And they will for about ten days. Then it will all blow over. When was the last time they did anything about the man who blew up the Birmingham Crescent?" Jill asked the question and continued, all in one breath: "Simon, did I tell you we got a note from the Harrisons? They're opening their place in Corsica early this year and they've asked us to visit. Do let's run over next month."

Even as he agreed, Livermore was blinking thoughtfully. To the outsider it might seem as if he had simply stopped trying to bring his young wife to his way of thinking. Actually, these crucial ten minutes had effected their usual breach in his self-assurance.

"I suppose you may be right," he began doubtfully. "Another month and Davidson Wylie will be forgotten by everybody."

"Not by me." A puckish grin briefly ruffled her angelic fairness. "His scheme was a fantastically simple way to make money. I'm surprised no one thought of it before."

Four thousand miles away, another couple discussed the same topic. Paul and Betsy Volpe had talked of little else for the past three days. This evening, taking advantage of the lingering summer light, they had driven out from Houston to rent horses. After an hour in the saddle they descended to admire a long view.

"To think of Dave pulling something like that," said Paul for the hundredth time. "I thought he was all wrapped up in getting contracts for Macklin, and instead he was planning his own million-dollar caper."

"He wasn't planning it for two whole years. Maybe Dave was just the man you imagined when you first went to work for him," Betsy reasoned. "But you know how it is with people. You get fixated by your first notion of them, and you don't realize they're changing."

Paul was sitting in the classic posture of deep thought, his back against a fence, his chin propped against the heel of his hand. "I suppose that's possible. But Hugo Cramer says they've proved he did a lot of things in advance—hiring a car in Istanbul, renting a room in Greece. And he didn't round up that gang of helpers on the spur of the moment."

"You're talking about a couple of months, at the most. And Dave saw to it that you were pretty busy during that time."

"Of course you never liked Dave," Paul remembered, giving credit where credit was due.

It was perfectly true that Betsy had never cared for

entertaining Davidson Wylie in her own home when he visited Italy. After the first few occasions she had suggested they abandon the attempt. Even Paul admitted the evening had not been a success. Somehow Wylie's worldly anecdotes had always rung a little hollow, fallen a little flat. And Betsy, whose success as a hostess depended on hearty good will rather than polished skill, always became stiff and formal.

Nevertheless she denied any talent for prophecy. "I said Dave wasn't my kind of person. I never said he was a heist artist."

Certainly, Betsy had been understanding about the need to be on good terms with Wylie. Paul could not count the times she had stayed behind while the two men dined together or played tennis together, especially after the breakup of Wylie's marriage had caused him to spend more time on the road.

"Though now I come to think of it," Paul continued his reflections aloud, "Dave wasn't in and out of Rome all the time just because of Francesca."

"What do you mean by that?" Betsy asked.

"Well, it stands to reason. He had a lot of things to set up in Greece and Turkey, not to mention seeing this woman who was his partner. Do you know that one of the police theories is that she killed Dave after they quarreled about the loot. I don't understand that at all. They must have planned the whole thing together, and they got away with it all right. So what's to quarrel about?"

"Maybe she decided that she wanted the money and she didn't want Dave."

Betsy was lying flat on her back, with her knees lofted skyward and a stalk of grass in her mouth. In her blue jeans and plaid shirt, her curly mop of hair tousled by the ride, she looked absurdly youthful for this cynicism.

Her husband was inclined to reject it out of hand. "Come on, Betsy. Just because Dave didn't light you up doesn't mean he wasn't attractive to women."

"Oh, I can see somebody falling for him, but I'll bet it wouldn't last long. He put up a good front but it wasn't very deep. For one thing, he was always showing off. Look at the way he kept trying to play the old European hand with you."

"There was a lot he could teach me."

"Not as much as he thought. In fact there was plenty you could have told him about Europe," Betsy said loyally. "After all, he didn't know any languages and he'd never been off his little beaten track."

Here she was on solid ground. Paul Volpe was an Italo-American, thoroughly bilingual. On top of that, two years as an Army engineer in France had left him with a working command of French and an unrivaled knowledge of building suppliers on the Continent. Unfortunately, Paul could not believe that many professional expatriates envied him his immigrant parents, his second cousins in Naples, or even his ability to lay hands on a freight car of nails at distress prices. In his experience that was not what people meant by knowing your way around Europe.

"It's different if you belong to the best squash club in Rome," he said unanswerably, "or if you're on first-name terms with French banking families or you have a summer villa on the right island."

Betsy jumped to her feet in a frenzy of exasperation. "It's bad enough that Dave Wylie did a snow job on us when he was alive. Can't we forget him now that he's dead? And it was all a fake with Dave anyway. Or he wouldn't have ended up pulling a phony kidnapping."

"You can't deny it was a good way to get money." Paul sounded wistful. "And we could use some."

"There are other ways to make money. And some of it may be heading in our direction." She was brushing herself off as briskly as she did everything else. "Don't forget, Macklin is now missing one director of European operations."

In spite of himself, Paul Volpe's eyes narrowed with calculation.

In downtown Houston, another couple had not achieved the same degree of harmony.

"But it's your duty," Gwen Trabulsi insisted.

Vic Trabulsi was standing stock still in his kitchen, his stance a living embodiment of the argument now raging. On the one hand he was motionless, every frozen muscle witnessing his determination not to go anywhere. On the other hand, he was facing the door to the garage, no small tribute to his wife's persuasion, cajolery, and stamina. She had been at it now for a full hour, never losing her footing under the onslaught of Vic's varied and ingenious excuses. She knew in her bones that his recalcitrance had only one source —the ingrained reluctance of the conservative male to lend himself to anything smacking of melodrama.

"Now, honey," he rumbled, "it's not as if I could tell the cops anything that would help them."

"How do you know?" she challenged. "They've put out an appeal for everyone with information about Davidson Wylie's last week."

"I don't have any information. I keep telling you that, but you're not listening. Just the way you never do."

Strong-mindedly Gwen ignored this attempt to change the subject. Lowering her voice to a throbbing whisper, she said: "You heard him talking to his wife less than forty-eight hours before he was murdered."

Vic winced. It was precisely this sort of overcharged impressionism he was trying to avoid. "The cops already know that Wylie was staying at the Tidewater. They know Mrs. Wylie was staying there. What's so wonderful about their exchanging words? Hell, Wylie probably did as much with the waiters and the desk clerks."

"If that was all you could tell the police, it might not be important. But you heard what they were saying."

"Not all of it."

"Ah ha." Gwen was triumphant. "Then you admit you remember some of it."

"It didn't amount to anything."

"It was peculiar. You said so at the time."

Vic groaned. This was getting worse and worse.

Now he would stand convicted not only of eaves-dropping, but also of a spinsterish thirst for sensational domestic detail.

"I don't care what you say," he proclaimed roundly. "I'm not going down to headquarters."

The reason the Trabulsis could protract any dispute over an unbelievable length of time was that they had done it so often before. Every combination and permutation in their respective positions had long since been discovered, explored and filed for future reference. After the historic occasion in their first year of marriage when Gwen had forced Vic to go to the landlord about the call girl in the next apartment, there was nothing left for either of them to learn. They knew every move and countermove before it was made. And they also knew the inevitable out-come.

An hour later Gwen deposited Vic in front of a tall policeman, saying: "Lieutenant Nash? We're Mr. and Mrs. Trabulsi. I'm the one who called you."

Her manner indicated clearly that she had brought her horse to water and now it was up to Houston's Homicide Squad to make him drink. Lieutenant Nash did not do a bad job. Entering a silent pact against women, he made sympathetic noises, he nodded understanding, he admitted fellow feeling, and he waited out embarrassed pauses. His reward was greater than he anticipated.

"Now, let's see if I've got this straight, Mr. Trabulsi." Nash was as cautious as a naturalist anxious not to frighten a wild animal. "Mrs. Wylie was pressing Mr. Wylie to share everything fifty-fifty. He claimed they were, but she was suspicious and said that, while he was counting all those dollars, he should remember it was her idea in the first place."

At this bald summation, Vic Trabulsi rolled his eyes desperately. "When they started, they were talking about some lot in Houston. I missed some of it afterward, but they could have been fighting about their property settlement right along."

"That's always possible," Lieutenant Nash said without conviction. "Maybe we should ask Mrs. Wylie."

The last couple was so far from accord that they had to do their talking on the telephone. At first Klaus Engelhart did not understand the problem.

"I am sorry we cannot have dinner tomorrow. Shall we make it Thursday then?"

"No," snapped Francesca Wylie. "You misunderstood me. I won't see you at all here in Houston."

Engelhart had a rigid sense of decorum himself, but this, he felt, was carrying things to ridiculous extremes. "*Liebchen,* you were already in the process of divorcing Dave. The world will not expect a thick black veil and two years of mourning. Who are you trying to fool?"

"I'm not trying to fool anyone. That's not it at all."

"I am not asking you to put on red flounces and dance a cancan. Surely nobody could object to a quiet dinner. You have to eat."

Another woman might have started to scream. Francesca, instead, assumed a strained sweetness that was as good as a warning bell. "Klaus, dear, I do not require instruction on how widows should behave. If you have any hints on the proper etiquette for murder suspects, that would be most helpful."

"A murder suspect!" It was Klaus who was in danger of screaming. "Who gave you that idea?"

Klaus's agitation had a tonic effect on Francesca. "An unimpeachable source," she replied. "The policeman from the homicide squad who has just left."

"They must be insane. Even if they thought it was Dave who was divorcing you, when does a wronged woman wire a car with blasting dynamite?"

"Oh, they are not charging me with a crime of passion. They suspect me of cold-blooded, calculating murder for one and a half million dollars. In fact, they think I arranged that kidnapping with David."

At the opposite end of the Tidewater, Klaus Engelhart plucked his lower lip reflectively. "I can see why they think someone did. But why you?"

"Mostly because of a squabble about the property settlement. When David went to work for Macklin, I insisted that we buy land here in Houston. He was trying to cheat me out of the profit. Some cretin at the Tidewater overheard a few sentences and fabricated a theory that I helped in the kidnapping and David wouldn't give me my share of the ransom."

Klaus carefully considered what she had told him and pounced on one word. "You said 'mostly.' What else worries the police?"

For the first time Francesca was not contemptuously angry. "They know that a woman emptied out that numbered account in Zurich. If she was a casual amorous involvement, she didn't have to come to Houston, fight with David about the money, then kill him. She could simply have taken the ransom out of Switzerland and gone to the other end of the world. That is the way the police reason. But a wife, still legally tied to David, might find it easier to murder him."

"That is an absurdity, it goes without saying." Now that he was dealing with specifics, Engelhart had regained his equanimity. "Surely the police know that you and Dave had already separated. And no man in his senses would enter this sort of conspiracy with an estranged wife."

"They have managed to deal with that difficulty, too. In fact, they have alternative explanations. The separation was simply a smokescreen to deceive people. Either David and I were genuine partners at first, but I decided he was a liability when Interpol insisted on questioning him thoroughly. Or else . . ."

"Or else what?"

Francesca's voice sharpened with malice. "Or else you and I were in league and you, Klaus, with your vast engineering experience, arranged the bomb. Now do you understand why we should not be holding hands in Houston?"

His response was immediate. "We should not be in Houston at all, if that is what the police think. They cannot force us to stay, but they can make it very uncomfortable for us if we do."

"Yes, I suppose so," she said slowly. "I still have to get someone to handle probate, but I could do that in New York."

"Good God, you agree with me, don't you?"

"I do about leaving, but not about anything else. I knew David to his very marrow, and he was the last man to conceive this mad embezzlement plot."

Klaus was impatient with failure to accept reality. "If there is one thing that has been proved incontrovertibly, it is Dave's actions. Maybe he did not originate the idea. After all, he was in his forties. Men that age can go completely wild over a girl twenty years younger. A modern young student could have thought the whole thing up herself—and also made the bomb."

"That's possible," Francesca said coolly, not liking the reference to young girls. "But one thing is certain. David kept some kind of control over the money. I can assure you that he was still the same old David about cash in hand as late as last week. The girl didn't blow him up because they quarreled over a division. She did it because he was going to pieces."

"He was not himself the night before he was murdered," Klaus admitted. "But I put it down to drink."

"That's why he was drinking. I tell you, even before the Interpol man arrived, he was on the verge of hysteria. He could never have sustained several days of questioning. David never expected to explain away three weeks. He thought it was all going to be easy. As soon as it became unbearably difficult, he would have offered to deal—give the money back, turn state's evidence, name his accomplice—anything to protect himself."

Klaus Engelhart felt they should concentrate on essentials. "You may be right. What difference does it make why some imaginary girl killed him?"

"And you pretend to be a businessman, Klaus."

With crystal clarity, Francesca explained, "If David had that money when he died, there is a million and a half dollars lying around somewhere. Now I think that's interesting. Don't you?"

13 · Freezing in the Dark

The Sloan Guaranty Trust had more than a casual connection with the affairs of Davidson Wylie. There were people on the sixth floor who had stayed up half the night hand-counting crumpled bills on his behalf. But they barely glanced at the headlines screaming his murder. Unlike Houston, New York was wrestling with inflation, a whimsical bond market, and the eeriest economic forecasts since Hammurabi. Wider horizons did not afford much relief. French vineyards were being accused of mislabeling, British Leyland was being accused of international bribery, and the Japanese were being accused of almost everything.

Everett Gabler, the bank's doomsday prophet, was reveling in so many fiscal postmortems that he had no spare attention for the real thing in Texas. Walter Bowman, chief of research, was too busy preparing the Sloan for next week's debacles to have time for yesterday's bankruptcies, let alone its murders. The utilities of the nation, bludgeoned by one rate-making authority after another, had so inundated Charlie Trinkam with lamentation that he almost forgot he had ever been in Houston.

As for Rose Theresa Corsa, in sunshine or in shadow she remained untouched by vulgar curiosity. But she was always alert to the slightest strain on the delicate web of contacts she had spun throughout the Sloan. Mr. Elliman, down in travel, was fast coming apart under the onslaught of Macklin's erratic demands. First there had been Mr. Thatcher's stopover in London, involving hotel rooms and transatlantic flights unauthorized by the travel department. Then there had been the trip to Houston, first postponed out of deference to Davidson Wylie's convalescence, then hastily reinstated without reference to Mr. Elliman. Finally there had been the wholesale dislocation of yesterday's agenda due to Mr. Trinkam's arrival, fresh from the blood-boltered streets of Houston. The time had come for Miss Corsa to speak to her employer. She was ready and waiting when the elevator deposited him at nine-thirty.

She began by thanking him for the gift which had finally completed its leisurely postal route to Queens. (This time it was an embroidered luncheon set from Zurich, although Thatcher had been sorely tempted by a pair of lederhosen.) Then came the formal charges.

". . . reorganize your appointment calendar for this week, Mr. Thatcher," she was saying, as she followed him into his office. "Mr. Meager's secretary hopes that you will be able to make it *this time* at three o'clock on Friday."

"Splendid," said Thatcher, settling at his desk.

"And the letter to Associated Industries should go out tomorrow morning. Commercial credit has been waiting for your approval of the second paragraph for over two weeks."

"Send it," Thatcher directed after a cursory glance.

She persevered. "Mr. Considine sent over the minutes of the Downtown Association committee meeting that you missed. If you have any comments, I'm to

135

phone him so they can be incorporated into the printed report."

"Any comments I have," said Thatcher comfortably, "are certainly unfit for your ears, Miss Corsa—let alone, the printed word."

"Yes, Mr. Thatcher," she replied, deaf to frivolity.

"And what's this?" he demanded, making a random pass at his desk.

She was delighted to inform him that it was a list of important persons urgently wishing to talk with him. Many of them, she further informed him, had been unable to do so for over three weeks.

The duel continued with meticulous regard for the niceties. Miss Corsa brandished ample evidence that, when he departed from her script, all hell broke loose. Thatcher, an old campaigner, made no attempt to convince her that these digressions did not constitute a simple search for pleasure. Instead he methodically demonstrated that nine-tenths of all calls, letters, memoranda, and reports normally reaching him were, in fact, nonessential.

They had barely finished their preliminary warmup when they were interrupted.

"Good!" boomed Walter Bowman, gallantly letting Miss Corsa squeeze past him. "I'm glad I finally caught you. It seems as if every time I've tried to get you for the past month, you've been tied up with Macklin."

Thatcher gestured invitingly to a chair. "Well, you have me now."

But Bowman's omnivorous memory had been triggered into recalling a scene he wanted to share. "Say, did Miss Corsa tell you that maintenance put up the big TV screen in the lobby so that everybody could watch you and Charlie making the payoff?"

"She was too tactful to mention it," said Thatcher pointedly.

Walter was insulted in more ways than one. "It wasn't just the eyes of Texas that were on you. Now, I've got a dilly of a capital-spending estimate for you. Just take a look at this . . ."

At this juncture Everett Gabler arrived, bent on

analyzing every unsatisfactory twist in the Sloan's portfolio position since the election.

". . . absolutely essential that we regularize the Sloanvest situation," he concluded. "As I have stressed more than once, unless the Sloan guarantees the assets—"

"God help us!" said Walter, who had long since written off the Sloan's ill-fated real estate investment trust. "Anyway I thought Charlie was handling that mess."

"Charlie has been otherwise occupied," retorted Gabler, whose views on schedule disruptions were even stronger than those of Miss Corsa. "He has been swept up by every vagary at Macklin until a good deal of his work has landed on my desk."

For form's sake, Thatcher felt obliged to demur. "You cannot dismiss the Noss Head contract as a vagary, Everett. And Charlie was in Houston working out the preliminary financing arrangements. I will concede that his timing was unfortunate."

Gabler was a hard man to please at the best of times. Recently, the decline and fall of Sloanvest had taxed his limited reserve of patience. It was only to be expected that he would produce a burning indictment.

"First, they inveigle you and Charlie into delivering their ransom for them. Then departure dates for Houston are turned on and off for the convenience of a man who now stands revealed as a proven felon. As if that were not bad enough, this Wylie is murdered and Charlie, far from finalizing any agreements, has to spend days at the beck and call of the local police." Gabler paused in his awe-inspiring list to give his glasses a vigorous swipe. "Granted that the Macklin financing is substantial enough to warrant the Sloan's best attention. Still, we do have other serious claims on our time. Presumably Macklin should be able—"

"Mr. Thatcher," said Miss Corsa from the doorway. "Mr. Lancer's office has just called. Could you step upstairs for a few moments?"

Everett subsided into pulsating disapproval but Walter Bowman came up with the trained researcher's educated hunch. "And three guesses what it's all about!"

Somewhere in his ascent from the sixth floor to the executive tower, Thatcher left behind the trust department's parochialism.

"Sorry to call you away from your desk when you're so busy," said George Lancer, intercepting Thatcher in the hallway outside his suite. "But you're closer to the Macklin situation than the rest of us."

Thatcher raised an eyebrow. "The rest of us?"

"I've got Upton and Roberta Ore Simpson in there," Lancer explained in a lowered voice.

"They're on Macklin's Board of Directors with you, aren't they, George?" asked Thatcher easily, accompanying Lancer into quarters that could have accommodated the United Nations. "Are you hatching a palace revolution?"

"Certainly not!" said George stoutly. "But it is an appropriate time for the outside directors to take an overview of what has been happening, both in Zurich and in Houston. You must agree with that."

"Nothing to do with directors' liability?" Thatcher asked with a grin.

George did not dignify this slander with a reply.

In the good old days, notable Americans could sit on the board of directors of any Fortune 500 company, collect a handsome honorarium, and attend an infrequent meeting without a qualm. But scandal and excess ultimately led to legislation. Overnight, members of the board developed a nervous interest in what management was doing. Very often, finding out made them feel even worse. None of these generalities applied to one of Macklin's outside directors.

"Roberta, I don't think you have met our senior vice president, John Thatcher," said George Lancer. "John, this is Roberta Ore Simpson."

Some women in public life are invariably known by three names. Occasionally this designation provides continuity for a career begun under a maiden name and continued after marriage. More often it serves as a warning to the uninitiated that the lady's claim to fame rests on the grandeur of her own family rather than on her consort. But sometimes the polysyllabic mouthful signals the inadequacy of the English language. Under certain circumstances, "Mrs." and "Miss" can be grotesquely inappropriate while "Professor" and "Doctor" are irrelevant.

Certainly, in Miss Simpson's case, a mere academic title would scarcely have done justice to her wide-ranging activities. On her mother's side she was descended from an eminent Quaker family. Her father had been the founder and guiding light of one of the nation's most illustrious accounting firms. Roberta Ore Simpson had taken this mixed heritage and forged therefrom a unique approach to the American experience. Twenty-five years earlier she had been appointed president of a small college in Michigan. From this power base, she had moved onto the larger scene as a voice of morality. Corporations, innocently assuming that here was yet another innocuous do-gooder, began appointing her to their boards. Her unfailing response to any suspicion of irregularity was to throw out the company's auditors. New accountants were unleashed on the clear understanding that evidence of skull-duggery would be enthusiastically received. Nor were her interests confined to financial chicanery. Miss Simpson was concerned with the whole ethical thrust of big business, and in this cause she wielded her accountants like a virtuoso. She had discovered that conglomerates were making components that they themselves did not know about. She had bared ties with repressive regimes, stripped the mask off union kickbacks, and pursued campaign contributions to their final resting place.

By rights, her name should have been poison to any profit-making institution. But her fervor had often produced unlooked-for benefits. She had a keen eye for spotting contract overruns before they snowballed. Twice she had nagged her sponsors into the orderly termination of facilities that, a year later, would have been catastrophically closed by the FDA or the EPA.

Then, just about the time that industry was deciding her tactics might pay for themselves, they discovered they could not afford to ignore her. While they had been deliberating in closed rooms, Miss Simpson had transformed herself into a personality. That she should testify indefatigably before Congress was predictable, but she had unscrupulously seized every other forum that existed. She appeared on early-morning talk shows and late-night specials; she wrote newspaper articles, took part in panels, and addressed every conceivable convention. The blocky figure, the haphazard clothes, and the wisps of iron-gray hair were familiar to millions. By the time the great Lockheed scandal had rocked every firm that ever bribed a foreign official, there were two courses open to companies faced with embarrassing disclosures. They could make professions of repentance that nobody believed, or they could let in Roberta Ore Simpson and her kamikaze accountants.

Macklin had chosen to go the second route, and the result was Arthur Shute in the president's chair and an almost new Board of Directors. Not entirely new, however.

"And I know you haven't met Norris Upton," George Lancer continued.

"No," agreed Thatcher, thinking he would have remembered. Copper-skinned plainsmen dressed in creamy buckskin are not common in Manhattan. "How do you do."

Norris Upton was a survivor from the bad old days. A department-store tycoon from Dallas, he frankly believed that management should concentrate on earnings and let the chips fall where they might. Needless to say, he and Roberta Ore Simpson had been to the mat on almost every aspect of Macklin policy, with the luckless George Lancer acting as middle-of-the-road mediator. On the subject of repressive regimes they had nearly come to blows. Miss Simpson, her attention directed to the Middle East for the first time, had been aghast. Norris Upton did not see the problem.

"For Christ's sake!" he had said. "If your business is construction for oilfields, you have to go where the oil is and deal with whatever government you find. For all I know, Austria's got the cleanest government in the world. But it's a cinch that Macklin isn't going to do a hell of a lot of work there."

"There is a difference between dealing with a government and countenancing its domestic policies," she had replied militantly.

That time they managed to tie up Lancer for three days. But Davidson Wylie's shenanigans, Thatcher was happy to see, had generated rare unanimity among the outside directors.

"Arthur Shute has been keeping us up to date," Lancer began. "From what he says, there's no longer room for doubt. Wylie faked that kidnapping, from beginning to end."

"A guy like that, I'm not surprised someone blew him up," Upton said laconically. "They crucified those guys at Lockheed and they were just doing their best for the company. This bastard was lining his own pockets."

Roberta Ore Simpson had been hit where she lived. "It is impossible to overestimate the damage done by Davidson Wylie," she hissed. "Do you realize that he invented a form of embezzlement that is accountant-proof? The money simply passes openly through the books."

She was so overcome that she could not go on. The theme was pursued by Upton.

"You'd have to investigate every one of these goddamned kidnappings to see if it was on the up and up. And nine times out of ten, you still wouldn't know. The only reason Wylie blew it was because of that car smash."

Thatcher nodded and waited. Neither Upton nor Roberta Ore Simpson seemed self-indulgent enough to recruit an audience for their keenings. And Lancer was notorious for self-discipline. He certainly had not summoned his senior vice president to listen to empty complaints. Somebody wanted something.

Apparently it was Lancer's job to tell him what. "The thing is, John," he began slowly, "what Shute tells us is all right—so far as it goes. Wylie carried through his plan to rob Macklin with the aid of some people in Turkey and Switzerland. They got their money successfully, but then something went wrong, and Wylie was murdered."

"But you feel that leaves a good many questions still to be answered?" Thatcher suggested.

"It sure as hell does," Upton said robustly. "How come his buddies just happened to be in Houston at the right time? It's the last place they should have been. When this thing started, they were in Europe and so was the money. Why come to Texas? And if they were just strays, what difference did it make if Wylie blabbed? God knows they had plenty of cash and plenty of time. They could have been anywhere in the world, with different names and fat bank accounts." Upton paused to glare at his companions. "So maybe they weren't strays, maybe the reason they were in Texas is because they work for Macklin."

In spite of his truculence, Norris Upton had left something unsaid. In her own way Roberta Ore Simpson completed his work.

"It is extremely awkward," she said dispassionately, "that at this juncture of affairs we should be dependent on Arthur Shute for information. His interests lie in viewing this conspiracy as non-Macklin in origin, and some distortion is bound to occur, either consciously or unconsciously."

Upton folded his arms and snorted. "Just remember, it was you and Lancer who wanted Arthur in the president's chair. You were gung-ho on bringing in an outsider."

"That was two years ago," she replied calmly. "After enough time has passed, every outsider becomes an insider."

In one short sentence, Thatcher realized, she had defined the chief obstacle to the creation of independent controls—all the way from regulatory agencies to civilian review boards. By the time a man understands the problem, he has become part of it.

George Lancer was determined not to refight the battle of Shute's appointment. He pressed forward. "So you see, John, we would welcome any additional information about what's going on in Houston. And I think you may have it. Knowing Charlie Trinkam, I can't believe he let the police question him for two days without finding out what they were interested in."

"You're right, Charlie doesn't have any doubt as to what's bothering them. Wylie had only short notice before Interpol descended on him and very limited contacts thereafter. What's more, he was driving a company car that was out of his hands during most of the relevant period. The police don't seem to think there was time for someone to jet into Houston, learn that Wylie was crumbling, and identify the right car. For that reason, they are bearing down on the people who saw Wylie immediately before he was questioned and those who had dinner with him afterward."

"What did I tell you?" Norris Upton looked challengingly at his co-directors. "That means the cops are zeroing in on someone from Macklin."

"Just a minute." Thatcher raised a hand before the debate could get under way. "It is true that the group includes Shute, and Hugo Cramer, and young Volpe. But you should know that Wylie's wife and the German representing NDW are also on the list." Thatcher reviewed his statement and discovered an omission. "For that matter, so is Charlie Trinkam."

Everyone united in waving away Trinkam, but Roberta Ore Simpson wrinkled her brow over another name.

"NDW? They bid against Macklin for Noss Head, and now they're trying to pick up subcontracts," she reminded herself. "Offhand, I don't see why that should make their man suspect."

"By itself, no," Thatcher agreed, noting for his own use that Charlie's report to the sixth floor had been a good deal more comprehensive than Shute's report to the tower. "But the police have established two additional points about Klaus Engelhart. In checking the phone calls made by Wylie while he was staying at Cramer's beach cottage, they found that the first overseas call was to Engelhart. Theoretically it was an invitation to NDW to come to Houston about subcontracts, but nonetheless it represented Wylie's only contact with Europe—apart from the British government —immediately prior to his death. And second, Mrs. Wylie, who filed for divorce some months ago, has been seeing a fair amount of Engelhart."

"So Engelhart and the wife could have conspired with Wylie on the kidnapping, while planning to murder him all along? I see . . . yes, that makes sense . . . yes, that could be it!"

Roberta Ore Simpson had begun her recapitulation in a tone of consideration, proceeded to conviction, and concluded in a burst of enthusiasm. As she was the last woman in the world to favor scabrous solutions, Thatcher decided he was missing something.

"It's one of several possible explanations," he said. "I don't see that it's the most attractive."

"Oh, yes it is," she said roundly. "It means that whoever was imaginative enough to create a foolproof embezzlement scheme is now outside the company. Any other explanation, and he's still with us. There could be a systematic siphoning from Macklin at this very moment that we wouldn't find out about until too late."

Norris Upton had turned ashen. "Sweet Jesus, Roberta! Will you keep these nightmares to yourself?" he protested. "Anybody hears you and Macklin could be in big trouble."

As the interested group would include stockholders, creditors, and the SEC, Thatcher thought he had a point.

Miss Simpson, however, was above such petty fears. "There is nothing to be gained by burking the issue," she said, enunciating the policy of a lifetime. "Unless you can produce an alternative."

"I sure can. Wylie and a girlfriend dreamed this whole thing up. She collected the money, all right, but she intended to share it with some other man. So she got rid of him."

George Lancer intervened while Miss Simpson was still organizing her rebuttal. "Those are two possible theories and we can probably concoct others. But what we're interested in, John, is keeping abreast of this situation as it develops. And that's not easy when we all have full-time commitments elsewhere." Gently he glided over their distrust of progress reports relayed from Houston. "In that respect it's fortunate that you'll be going to London for the Noss Head loan. You're bound to see a fair amount of the Macklin team."

Thatcher was resigned. "If it's like most negotiations, Charlie and I will be living in their pocket."

"Good," said Lancer, sacrificing his vice president's comfort without a twinge. "I don't have to tell you how much we'll appreciate any information we can get. When are you leaving?"

"Too soon," said Thatcher, as he consulted his pocket diary. "There appears to be some wretched social function to launch the Noss Head project— sponsored by the Arabs for unknown reasons. Charlie and I will have to take the plane tomorrow."

As might have been expected, Lancer's stratagem had succeeded in distracting only Norris Upton. Women do not accede to corporate power by being fibbertigibbets. Roberta Ore Simpson was still riding her hobbyhorse.

"It is almost impossible to evaluate these police discoveries without knowing something about Davidson Wylie's wife." She looked keenly at Thatcher. "What kind of woman would you say she is?"

"I have never met the lady," Thatcher was happy to reply. "And now that her ties with Macklin have been severed, I don't suppose I ever shall."

He did not know what was waiting for him in his office.

14 · Secondary Recovery

John Thatcher hoped to spend the rest of the day on his own work, but Destiny had other plans for him. He came downstairs to find Miss Corsa's desk impassable.

"Mr. Thatcher?" she said, as he headed toward his own quarters.

This stopped him in his tracks. Miss Corsa was consulting her calendar, as was right and proper. But the other feminine presence, registered by his peripheral vision, was not Mrs. Penn from the typing pool, or Miss Friar.

Thatcher did not possess Charlie Trinkam's built-in tuning fork when it came to women and their manifold vibrations. But he knew Miss Corsa, and her many voices. Volume and timbre were, as usual, immaculately impersonal. But somehow or other, in four short syllables, she outdid most Toscas.

Despite appearances to the contrary, Miss Corsa was seething.

"Mr. Thatcher," she vocalized, "Mrs. Wylie says she has an appointment with you. This morning."

All Thatcher's appointments, including those with his dentist, were artistically choreographed by Miss Corsa. Nevertheless, he was incautious enough to say: "Mrs. Davidson Wylie?"

Francesca Wylie approached him with a rueful smile. "Yes, I have just flown up from Houston. Arthur Shute said that he was sure you would be able to find time for me."

Naturally, the musical hint of an Italian accent was not going to charm Rose Theresa Corsa. But, judging by the speed with which a totally fictitious appointment had become a pretty plea by a pretty woman, Thatcher guessed that Francesca Wylie did not waste her charms on secretaries. At the moment, for instance, she was pretending that Miss Corsa did not exist.

Thatcher was not going to join her.

"How booked am I this morning, Miss Corsa?" he inquired, simultaneously transmitting information and rallying team spirit.

Miss Corsa loyally searched her records, then announced that he had a little free time.

Throughout, Francesca Wylie kept her attention trained on Thatcher. She was a man's woman, and she looked it.

Graceful, self-assured, she accepted Thatcher's escort as her due. This, together with an emerald green silk raincoat, settled one small point for him. Mrs. Wylie was not here as a grief-stricken widow.

Even so, Thatcher was old-fashioned enough to feel the need for solemnity. "How can I be of assistance to you, Mrs. Wylie?"

"I wish to put my affairs in the hands of the Sloan," she replied with a fluency that suggested rehearsal. "I myself must return to London, but my late husband's property is here in the United States—real estate and securities. Therefore, I think it would be wise to have the Sloan represent me here."

Thatcher listened with his usual courteous gravity. Mrs. Wylie's statement was remarkable for its assumptions and omissions.

"Do you anticipate residing in Europe permanently?" he asked.

Even the most routine question set off ambiguous resonances, given the police activities in Zurich and Houston.

With skilled evasiveness, Francesca Wylie said, "I cannot be sure I shall remain in England. Most probably, I shall stay in Europe, where my work is."

"I see," said Thatcher, assuming the lady was taking refuge in the long view.

He was disabused when she leaned forward and confided: "Despite what many people seem to believe, I do not have plans to remarry immediately. So I cannot tell you where I shall be living."

Tilting her head, she appraised the impact of this candor on him. Apparently satisfied, she went on: "That is why I am so anxious to have the Sloan care for my business here in America. I am sure you can sympathize, Mr. Thatcher."

This blatant appeal to his chivalry, Thatcher appreciated, was not as disingenuous as it sounded. Francesca Wylie was telling him something. But was it about Davidson Wylie, Klaus Engelhart—or herself?

This raised the specter of the possible permutations and combinations underlying a pseudo-kidnapping. And a murder. It also raised another phantom that irresistibly appealed to Thatcher's sense of the ludicrous.

Could this estate, which Mrs. Wylie wished the Sloan Guaranty Trust to administer, include the ransom that the Sloan Guaranty Trust had been gulled into delivering for Macklin?

Thatcher chose his words with care: "Mrs. Wylie, I think you would be wise to have professional assistance with your American assets, particularly if you envisage remaining abroad. And the Sloan does offer such a service to its clients. Normally, however, this service is limited to estates in excess of a million dollars. Anything less—"

"A million?" she said with a trill of derisive laughter. "If only it were! No, Mr. Thatcher, I am talking about something far less than that—unhappily!"

"Then I am afraid that the Sloan is not the place for you. I would be happy to give you some recommendations—"

She did not let him finish. "I know you are wondering if I have the ransom money. That is why you talk of a million dollars. There is really no necessity for all this tact. The police do not hesitate to brand my husband a thief. And when I tell them this is not so, they become kind and look at each other, convinced the wife is always the last to know. These imbeciles act as if we are discussing infidelity."

From what Charlie Trinkam had told him, Thatcher realized the police were also thinking that, in this case, the wife might have been the first to know. Sternly he confined himself to Francesca's specific allegation. "Surely that truism has a general application," he suggested.

"Nonsense! All men have a capacity for infidelity," she said flatly.

Thatcher was not going to argue that one. "The police may simply feel that an intimate does not always know what a man is capable of."

"But the cases are not the same. There are different kinds of crime." She was relaxing her vehemence to introduce a note of cajolery. "Come now. I am sure you agree with me. In this bank of yours, which is so great it does not deal in petty sums under a million dollars, do you not attempt to distinguish the employee likely to rob you?"

Bull's eye! Given sufficient motivation, some men might rob at gunpoint, some might concoct ingenious paper frauds, and others might quietly melt away with a bag of cash entrusted to them. The Sloan had an elaborate system for channeling certain personality types away from certain temptations. But nobody, either at the bonding company or in personnel, claimed he could spot a potential adulterer at thirty paces. Thatcher had to admit that Mrs. Wylie knew where to aim her arrows.

149

"You may be right," he conceded. "There are different way to steal money."

She seized on her victory. "David had not the temperament to plan such a public crime. I, who was his wife for many years, can assure you of that. So you see, it is ridiculous to speak in terms of a million dollars. I doubt very much whether David ever had that ransom. I know that I do not."

"Mrs. Wylie," Thatcher replied, "you misunderstood me. I was simply explaining that the Sloan has certain minimum standards in the accounts that it handles."

She clasped her hands together in her lap. Then, quietly, she said: "There has been so much talk about this ransom. So much—and so wrong! I am tired to death of it. I leaped to a conclusion—but I see that I misjudged you. Please forgive me."

Point, game, and match, he thought. Mrs. Wylie had succeeded in putting him at a disadvantage. She was a woman who would try to exploit the situation to its utmost. But her attempt was foiled by an earlier tactical misstep. Before she could mobilize, the door opened to admit Everett Gabler and Walter Bowman.

"I have the Sloanvest tax liabilities here, John— Good heavens! I beg your pardon. I didn't realize you were occupied."

Everett Gabler was genuinely dismayed. Walter Bowman, as soon as he assimilated the circumstances, was not, although he concealed his curiosity admirably as he too apologized for the intrusion.

"No, don't go," said Thatcher, wondering if his secretary had abandoned the fort or was simply encouraging interlopers. When she was trying, Miss Corsa could bar the Golden Horde. "You may be able to help us. Mrs. Wylie, may I introduce my associates?"

Mrs. Wylie responded as if she already knew them, Thatcher's subordinates as if they had never heard of her. It was an artful performance by everybody concerned.

"Mrs. Wylie and I have been discussing the possibility of having the Sloan take charge of her husband's estate," said Thatcher, proceeding to outline the situation.

"But," she interjected, "Mr. Thatcher tells me that it is too small for the Sloan. Unless . . . tell me, do you think that perhaps this once you could make an exception?"

Both Walter and Everett were still pretending that the Macklin Company did not exist. Hoping that their self-control would continue, Thatcher, who had come to a decision, frowned.

"It would mean very much to my peace of mind." Francesca Wylie was almost tremulous.

"Perhaps we could arrange something," said Thatcher, avoiding eye contact with his unruly subordinates.

"Oh, Mr. Thatcher!" she breathed.

A better man would have managed a fatuous smile, Thatcher knew. "If you will instruct your attorney in Texas to communicate with us . . ."

When Francesca Wylie departed, trailing gratitude and expensive perfume, audience reaction was swift and merciless.

"Just a pushover for feminine wiles, eh, John?" Walter smirked. "What are you up to?"

Everett never let disapproval prejudice his analytic powers. "I assume you are undertaking this paltry account in order to maintain surveillance on this woman, or at least on this woman's financial situation. Not that I believe we can recover the ransom money that way."

Thatcher was willing to accept this gloss on his motives.

But Walter was the devil's advocate. "Oh, come on, Ev. Maybe John here just wants the Sloan to take good care of that lovely lady."

"Preposterous!" said Gabler.

"Thank you, Everett," said Thatcher humbly.

Gabler looked suspicious but Walter was still sorting the data.

"The real question is what was Mrs. Wylie doing here? And why does she want the Sloan to hold her hand?"

Thatcher did not know, and he said as much, adding: "She may simply be disseminating her theories about Davidson Wylie to all and sundry. Or possibly trying to create a presumption of her own innocence, wherever she can."

"Distasteful," snorted Everett. "Really, this Macklin situation goes from bad to worse."

Walter wanted facts, not value judgments. "Speaking of lovely ladies," he said, "what brought Roberta Ore Simpson and the original Marlboro man here today?"

In a flash, Gabler forgot Sloanvest and sermonizing. "The outside directors?" he asked sharply. "Are they taking action?"

"They don't know exactly what action to take," said Thatcher, condensing drastically. "They're scared to death that somebody at Macklin may be implicated in Davidson Wylie's murder."

Gabler brooded darkly, then said: "John, in view of these circumstances, perhaps it is a good thing you are flying to London tomorrow. The Sloan should keep abreast of Macklin—no matter what happens."

Bowman had other ideas and Miss Corsa entered in time to hear them.

"Macklin, huh? Well, for my money, I'd keep an eye on the widow. Your Mrs. Wylie looks capable of anything to me."

"A very impressive woman," Thatcher agreed.

Being a perfect lady, Rose Theresa Corsa said absolutely nothing.

15 · Petrodollars

But her trials for the day did not end with Francesca Wylie.

"Going back to London again, are we? Well, here are the tickets for you. I only wish I were going along," Mr. Elliman prattled. "It sounds absolutely fabulous!"

The vision of Elliman, safari suit and all, accompanying Mr. Thatcher anywhere in the world staggered Miss Corsa, but she rallied. "There is a possibility that the hotel accommodations may be needed for a second week."

Elliman took notes, but his head was in the clouds.

"Do you read the *Washington Post?*" he suddenly asked.

Miss Corsa received it, logged it, renewed it. She did not read it.

"They say this party's going to be a bigger bash than the one the Shah of Iran threw," said Elliman reverently. "Here, have you seen *Women's Wear Daily?* Even the *Times* wrote it up."

He pawed through a stack of clippings.

"I read the *Times,*" said Miss Corsa.

"Listen to this," Elliman burbled. " 'Invitations to the best Arabian Night of them all are in demand from London to Singapore!' My!"

The *Times,* although Miss Corsa did not care to say so, had called it "The Do That's Got Society Quivering."

" ' . . . calling embassies to beg for invitations!' " Elliman read, as if from scripture. "And to think our Mr. Trinkam and Mr. Thatcher are going!"

Between Mr. Elliman and the tittle-tattle of modern journalism, Miss Corsa was hard-pressed. "Do you think there will be any difficulty about hotel arrangements?" she asked.

"For this?" Elliman cried. "If I had to, I'd rent Westminster Abbey."

Miss Corsa could reconcile herself to another business trip. But reading about beautiful people converging on London was a heavy cross to bear.

"They're just another byproduct of petroleum," Thatcher had commented when he caught her at it.

"Yes, Mr. Thatcher."

Familiar with her uncompromising views on work, play, and travel, he added: "Don't be misled by all this froth, Miss Corsa. Properly speaking, this party should be covered by financial reporters."

Thatcher knew that his forthcoming trek to London was going to involve him in festivities that could be described as social only by the preternaturally innocent.

The Organization of Petroleum Exporting Countries was hosting a party. Besides the tinsel reported in the press, the guest list included half the British cabinet, the senior advisers of the Department of Energy, oil companies from Exxon and Texaco to Royal Dutch Shell and British Petroleum, tanker owners from Athens, construction firms from Stockholm, shipbuilders from Tokyo, and bankers from Zurich.

OPEC, Thatcher suspected, wanted to illustrate the distinction between promise and achievement. Just as every oil well, before it is drilled, is going to be the biggest gusher ever seen, so North Sea oil might become the bonanza of bonanzas. Yields might outstrip those of the Persian Gulf, Europe might dispense with the Emirates, and world energy prices might plummet.

But, in the meantime, OPEC was doing very well, and they had decided to prove it. Their soiree was going to show what money and power can do. In a rare moment of accord, Libya and Iraq, Saudi Arabia and Iran decided that neither the pedestrian pleasures of a London hotel nor the dubious delights of the West End sufficed for the occasion. An Arab chieftain does not extend hospitality in a commercial establishment. For that matter, neither does an English gentleman. Fortunately for the two cultures, the ideal site had already passed into Arab hands. This particular jewel consisted of a manor house in Twickenham, set in manicured grounds running down to a substantial frontage on the Thames.

The best that most guests could do to meet this challenge was a chauffeur-driven Rolls-Royce. But, for once, Elliman had surpassed himself.

John Putnam Thatcher had been routed from the Sloan to the Concorde, from the Concorde to the Hilton as if he were a mere mortal. But then, on the night of the party, the Elliman touch came through loud and clear.

The Sloan Guaranty Trust did better than hold its own. Its senior vice president was wafted to Twickenham under the fluttering banners of a magnificent river launch.

"Mind the step, Mr. Thatcher," cautioned an attentive steward upon debarkation.

"God, it makes me feel like Henry VIII," remarked Charlie Trinkam when his turn came.

Thatcher examined his companion as they made their way up a gravel path lined with flaming torches. Charlie was looking his dapper best in an impeccable dinner jacket. Nonetheless Thatcher shook his head.

"You're not dressed for the part," he said kindly.

Their arrival at the main entrance hall provided Charlie with his answer. "Then I'm almost the only one who isn't," he said, eyeing the splendid throng eddying up the broad divided staircase.

John Thatcher had been exposed to the domestic architecture of Regency England before and had admired its many excellences. Now he realized that there had always been a sense of incongruity, of gentle friction between dissonant elements. Those Adam ceilings, those swagged draperies, those crystal chandeliers had never been meant for men in business suits and women in tweed skirts. They had been designed as backgrounds for peacocks, and tonight the Arabs did them justice. As they ascended to the drawing room, their flowing robes and brilliant headdresses improvised unexpected harmonies with the cool celadon green of the paneled walls.

"Yes," Thatcher agreed, as he and Charlie attached themselves to the tail of the procession, "Beau Brummel would have been right at home tonight."

He was not the only one to sense the lingering presence of neck ruffles and snuffboxes. Almost the first group he recognized after leaving the reception line consisted of Paul Volpe, Klaus Engelhart, and a young woman soon identified as Betsy Volpe. Predictably, the men were slightly uncomfortable at these intimations of a more elegant past; the lady was glorying in them.

"Have you ever seen anything like this?" Volpe asked, unconsciously fingering his starched collar and dress tie as if expecting to encounter a jabot. "I think the champagne coolers may be solid gold."

Klaus Engelhart was more direct. "Surely there can be no reason for such display at what is, after all, business hospitality."

"You may have put your finger on it," Thatcher said dryly. He failed to see any distinction between NDW's lavishness in Hamburg and what was happening tonight. The Arabs simply did a better job.

"I think it's wonderful." Betsy Volpe's tanned face was aglow with enthusiasm. "Have you met Sheikh Yemeri? The one in the robes?"

Charlie Trinkam was always ready to encourage

the ladies. "And which one is he?" he asked. "The whole gang is in robes."

"His are royal purple," Betsy said impressively before breaking off to laugh at herself. "Only this afternoon I was worrying about what dress I should wear to such a fancy party. It never occurred to me that the competition was going to be men. The women aren't in it at all."

"Some of them are." Charlie, after one glance at Mrs. Volpe's dinner skirt and blouse, dropped the subject of dress. "That one over there is fighting the real battle. Did you notice her diamonds?"

The object of Charlie's attention was a middle-aged woman who had already turned aside to cross the room. Like most trust officers, John Thatcher had a workmanlike knowledge of jewelry. Even so, he had noticed only a multiplicity of brooches and necklaces, all radiating the glitter of the genuine article. Betsy Volpe, on the other hand, proved herself to be in Charlie's near-expert class.

"The stones are wonderful, but she ought to have them reset. That's what I'd do. I wonder who she is?"

Klaus Engelhart, who had spent most of the last six months in London, was ready with the answer. "She's the wife of a junior minister."

"Well, those diamonds didn't come from a junior minister's salary," Betsy said with calm certainty. "She probably inherited them and doesn't have the cash to get rid of those old-fashioned settings. You'd think she'd sell a bracelet and upgrade the rest."

This cavalier disposition of somebody else's assets roused Engelhart.

"I don't see how you can be so sure of that, Mrs. Volpe. She may think it worthwhile to show she is not nouveau riche," he began, thus swatting the entire delegation from Texas. With his usual studious precision, he commenced a list of alternatives. "For all we know, those are famous heirlooms. Or maybe they came through her husband's family and traditionally go to her son's wife. Or it could be that . . ."

Both Thatcher and Charlie could see that he wasn't

making a dent. Betsy Volpe was courteously waiting for Engelhart to finish speaking before she reasserted her position, as confident as ever. With one accord the two men scanned the horizon, searching for diversion. Thatcher's cast was the lucky one.

"Ah, Shute," he said with real cordiality, as he spotted Macklin's president. "And Cramer, too. I think we all know each other."

Both Arthur Shute and Hugo Cramer were beaming broadly.

"A wonderful evening," said Shute, inclining his white head with majestic approval.

"Couldn't be going better," echoed Hugo Cramer.

Thatcher did not have to search far for the source of all this satisfaction. For others, tonight might be the civilized expression of a fierce rivalry. Oil companies had to worry about the costs of exploration before a strike and the possibility of expropriation afterward. Tanker fleets had to worry about shortened ocean routes. But Macklin was in the happy position of making money from oil, no matter whether it involved port facilities in Kuwait or pipelines to Valdez, Alaska. For Shute and Cramer tonight was an anthem to the profitability of black gold, and God bless it, wherever it was.

Klaus Engelhart answered the spirit, rather than the content, of their remarks. "Not just for the Arabs, but for Macklin, too." He went on generously. "I was talking to the people from Shell and they agreed that you will be a force in Europe from now on."

Shute was mellowed enough to become philosophic. "Strange how things turn out. This should have been a great night for Dave Wylie. The whole oil world is here, and they would have been showering congratulations on him. Instead we all know he was a criminal, murdered by his accomplice. And if he had only known there was this coup in store for him, he probably never would have bothered."

"Oh, come off it, Arthur." Cramer might be happy, but his feet were still on the ground. "It turns out that

158

Dave wasn't interested in congratulations, he was interested in money."

But Shute had fabricated an explanation for Macklin's notorious defector that was too convenient to be abandoned. "Only yesterday I said to Mrs. Wylie that we should regard her husband as a kind of mental casualty. He was working so hard that the strain became too much and he simply broke down."

Thatcher had no difficulty rejecting this vision of Davidson Wylie as a gallant foot soldier whose shell-shock had taken the form of feeding a Swiss numbered account. But instead of fighting, he let a moment of silence intervene before asking: "Then Mrs. Wylie has arrived in London?"

"Yes, and I felt it was only right to have a few words with her. I would have done so in Houston, but what with one thing and another," said Shute, delicately skipping over postmortems, police suspicions, and hasty decampments, "she had left before I could make an opportunity."

Engelhart stirred restively. If Shute had bothered to ask, then he knew that Klaus and Francesca had left on the same Houston-to-New York flight. "I understand Mrs. Wylie had to get back to work. You know she is dubbing the Italian on a new British film."

"So I understand." Arthur Shute directed his bushy white eyebrows toward Thatcher. "She told me that was why she handed over the probate proceedings to the Sloan. Our personnel people will have to thrash out his pension rights."

"Yes," said Thatcher, wondering if Francesca Wylie was using his name in the same free-and-easy manner she had used Shute's. "I'll be putting one of our young men onto it."

"Well, if you find a million dollars in Dave's estate," said Cramer with heavy jocularity, "just remember that it belongs to Macklin and not the Wylies."

Before Thatcher could reply, Klaus Engelhart rushed to Francesca's defense. "Mrs. Wylie is as interested as anyone else in correcting the situation."

159

He spoke stiffly and his back was ramrod straight. "She had no advance knowledge of her husband's plans and has no intention of profiting from them."

Too late, Cramer realized that he had stirred up a hornet's nest. "Hell, I'm not accusing Francesca," he blurted. "I wouldn't have the nerve to accuse anybody after the way Dave made a patsy out of me."

"He tricked the rest of us, too, Hugo," Shute reminded him.

"It's not the same. He tricked you long distance. Me, he did eyeball-to-eyeball," Cramer said stubbornly. "When he had me there in Ankara, I was sorry for the poor SOB. I could kick myself now, but I thought he'd been through three weeks of hell. So I let him play me like a violin. When he said the doctors were driving him up a wall, it never occurred to me he was hiding a bunch of scars. I just thought his nerves were shot to pieces. Even in Houston, when a couple of questions from Interpol sent him diving into a bottle, I still figured he couldn't face up to it."

"You even began to believe he was seriously afraid of terrorists following him to Texas," Charlie suddenly remembered.

"Sure I did. And what else was I to think when he got blown sky high?" Cramer spread his hands helplessly as he turned to Engelhart. "The point I'm making is that I'm in no position to blame Francesca for not figuring out what was going on. Hell, I saw more of Dave than she did."

Engelhart was softened enough by this appeal to drop the "Mrs. Wylie" nonsense. "Francesca, too, is puzzled by her lack of insight. She claims that this crime was totally out of character for Dave. It may be that she is technically correct. But I doubt if Francesca is attaching enough weight to that girl in Zurich. She was probably the master-mind. It would not be the first time that an older man acted out of character to the point of folly for the sake of a young girl."

"What's that you're saying?" Arthur Shute demanded. "Who's this older man you're talking about?"

When Klaus patiently explained he was still referring to Davidson Wylie, Shute's confusion merely deepened. The difficulty was self-evident to everyone except the two principals. Wylie had been ten years older than Engelhart but fifteen years younger than Macklin's president. He would have had to have lived a good deal longer before qualifying as an older man in Arthur Shute's lexicon.

There was general relief when Betsey Volpe broke the impasse. "Francesca can't be as smart as I thought," she declared. "I wouldn't be silly enough to let Paul fool me that way."

Shute, still trying to work off his exasperation on somebody, frowned at her. "You're not in the middle of divorcing your husband, young woman."

She grinned at him cheerfully. "No, I'm not silly enough for that, either."

Paul Volpe half-choked on a spurt of laughter and Shute, his good humor restored by this model corporate wife, tucked Betsy's hand into his arm and insisted on taking her to the dining room.

"Come on," he invited the rest of them. "I've been hearing about this spread for hours."

Obediently they trooped forward to another breathtaking room, where the buffet was more than worthy of its rave notices. Needless to say, every luxury known to the Western world—caviar, smoked salmon, paté—was present. But the wonders of modern transportation and refrigeration had enabled the commissariat to plunder the East as well. There were pyramids of fruits and confections never before seen this side of Suez.

Shamelessly Thatcher broke ranks and headed for a silver bowl heaped high with apricots, each rosy with ripeness, each still bearing its bloom. Lost in gluttony, he was oblivious to his neighbors until he finished plying a napkin over his juice-drenched chin. At first the surrounding waves of Spanish convinced him he was lost among the Venezuelans. Then he spied a familiar face emerging from another napkin.

"Good evening, Livermore. I see you're a fancier of apricots, too."

For once, Simon Livermore was wholeheartedly enthusiastic.

"They have ripe dates at the other end. Really ripe," he said, delightedly. "And something called sweet lemons. You shouldn't miss them."

"So this is where you've gotten to, Thatcher," boomed the voice of Hugo Cramer. "And Livermore. That's great. I want you to meet our president, Arthur Shute."

In an instant Livermore reverted to form. Caught fast in the bone-crushing exuberance of Cramer's business handshake, he murmured a distant greeting. Arthur Shute, with more perception, satisfied himself with the regulation two-finger salute.

"I'm glad we've run into each other," Shute said sedately enough to reassure an army of civil servants. "You'll have heard about Dave Wylie's death. Paul Volpe will be taking over for him. I'm sure you've been wondering about that."

"I knew you'd find somebody," Livermore said with gentle irony. Corporations do not generally abandon multi-million dollar contracts because one employee bites the dust. "But Volpe and I have already done some work together and that will certainly make it easier to continue doing so."

"Well, none of us are going to be strangers by the time we get back from Noss Head." Cramer seemed to welcome the prospect. "On that kind of site, everybody gets to know each other."

"Splendid," Livermore forced himself to say.

"Now, I don't want to break this up," Shute lamented, as if they were having a roaring good time, "but there are some pumping people that I want Cramer and Volpe to have a word with. And I'm sure that you'd be interested too, Livermore."

But Livermore was already signaling over the intervening shoulders. With a ghost of a smile he said: "I'm afraid we'll have to make it some other time. My wife is coming this way, and nothing will persuade her to take pumping stations seriously."

The Macklin contingent withdrew, shadowed as persistently as ever by Klaus Engelhart.

"Why does he want to tag along?" Charlie asked the world at large.

"Engelhart seems unable to tear himself away from any aspect of Noss Head." With calculated indiscretion, Thatcher continued to Livermore: "In Houston he wasn't making any secret of the fact that he expected your department to award the contract to NDW, instead of Macklin."

Either Livermore did not care to match indiscretions or he was only half attending. "That's not uncommon after a major award, Thatcher. I've known . . . ah, there you are, dear. Having a good time?"

When Charlie Trinkam saw Mrs. Simon Livermore and friend, pumping stations were a lost cause with him, too.

"A smashing time!" Jill cooed. "Tell me who everybody is, darling, so that I can introduce them to Sheikh Yemeri."

Thatcher had already guessed it. There could not be two sets of robes like that in one building. The Sheikh was obviously the catch of the evening and, God knew, Jill Livermore had earned the right to snare him. Either divine Providence or native cunning had inspired her toilette. In a room where the overwhelming impression was that of billowing fabrics—draperies falling from eighteen-foot ceilings, silk rugs fluttering on the walls, women enveloped in clouds of chiffon, Arabs in their burnooses—she had eschewed the bouffant effect. Jill was showing not only her shoulders, but her legs as well. Her little slip of gold lamé ended above her knees and was supported by two string-like straps. With her smooth, gliding walk she wore the minimal garment as if she had train bearers behind her. The result was spectacular. Other people were showing off textiles. Jill was showing off herself. An observer might have been excused for thinking

163

that it was Sheikh Yemeri who had carried off the prize.

"And you were wrong, Simon," she continued, after the introductions. "There is dancing. They've hidden it off in a corner, but the sheikh showed me."

Simon, with a flourish of marital authority that fooled no one, said he hoped she hadn't pestered the sheikh into partnering her.

Her first response was a peal of laughter. "Oh, Simon," she sputtered, "don't you ever look at the society rags? The sheikh is more at home on a dance floor than I am. He does the hustle like an expert."

The sheikh's white teeth gleamed beneath his mustache. "We try not to be too backward," he said in fluent English honed by three years at Harvard Law School and many seasons on the Riviera. "But when I saw your wife's dress, I was afraid we might have missed the latest craze. I thought maybe it was the Charleston."

Trinkam immediately protested that Jill was far too young to know about the Charleston.

"Oh, I can do it," she corrected him, fluttering her eyelashes outrageously. "I bet I could teach you."

Grinning, Charlie said it would be a pleasure. He knew he was in no immediate danger. At the moment, Jill was training her guns on the sheikh.

And John Thatcher's guns were trained even farther afield. "By all that's holy, they've even got Leopold Grimm here," he exclaimed.

"Looking like a fish out of water." Charlie, who could see what was coming, was unsympathetic.

"It's only decent to say hello," his superior said inflexibly.

"Business tonight?" Jill wrinkled her nose in a parody of distaste. "Well, not for me. I'm going to force my husband, willing or not, to dance with me."

Laughing over her shoulder, she swung away, an escort on either arm.

"You're a hard man, John," Charlie said reproachfully, "when you ask me to trade Jill Livermore for Leopold Grimm."

Certainly Grimm was not contributing to the gaiety of the evening.

"Foolishness and more foolishness," he replied to questioning. "I have business with NDW that could best be accomplished either in Zurich or Hamburg. Instead we must both come to this extravaganza. Then Interpol says, as long as I am in London, will I please secretly observe Mrs. Wylie."

Charlie was less bored than he expected. "You mean, to see if she was the pickup girl?"

Grimm flapped a disgusted hand. "Already, last week I have looked at hundreds of pictures of Mrs. Wylie. I have seen her walking, sitting, reclining. I tell them it is out of the question. Nonetheless, I must lurk in a doorway at Harrod's for twenty minutes before they are content."

"I thought you said you probably wouldn't be able to say one way or the other," Thatcher objected. "What with all the changes in hair and voice."

"The hair, the face, the voice, they are all beyond me," Grimm proclaimed. "But a Valkyrie, I would have noticed."

Charlie, the connoisseur, was inflamed. "Come now, Leopold, Francesca Wylie is not exactly a battle maiden."

"Visualize her in blue jeans and mountaineering boots," Grimm commanded.

Charlie blinked. "I don't think I can," he said finally.

"I think we see what you mean," Thatcher agreed. "There's no denying the effect would be memorable. So Harrod's was a waste of time for you. You'll have to fall back on your business with NDW."

"Which we will accomplish in an uncomfortable hotel room, with briefcases in our laps," said Grimm clinging to his grievance.

"Then why in the world did you come?" Thatcher pressed.

"For the same reason you did," Grimm replied starkly. "Everyone is here tonight because of money. We have it, or we share it, or we want it, or we merely wish to be near it. But it comes to the same thing. We have been brought together by its power."

It might have been the voice of Mammon, so elemental was his analysis. But two hours later Charlie Trinkam, as wise in the ways of the world as any man, was quibbling with Grimm's verdict. He and Thatcher had joined a knot of onlookers in time to see Sheikh Yemeri speak to the band conductor. Then, as the music began, the sheikh led Jill Livermore onto the dance floor, and the purple robes began flicking to the beat of the Charleston.

"Somebody should tell Leopold that there's more than one kind of power," Charlie whispered.

16 · Blowout

John Thatcher could take desert hawks or leave them. Bedouin splendor in Twickenham, ceremonial robes, and jeweled daggers left him essentially unmoved. OPEC was undeniably fierce and predatory. But when it came to the wellhead price of oil, the Venezuelans in their pinstripes were as wild and untrammeled as any nomad.

So, when the Arabs struck their stately-home tent and silently faded back to the Savoy, Thatcher expected to revert to the pedestrian and colorless real world.

Instead, he plunged directly into the Western world's equivalent of a pilgrimage to Mecca. This did not entail donning a burnoose. A space-silver jumpsuit was protecting him from the relentless icy spray of the North Sea. His daffodil-yellow hard hat may have guarded him from falling objects. It undeniably stamped him as a visiting bigwig.

Thatcher was trudging down a bleak stone-shingled shore along Noss Head. Through a rainy mist he could see a greasy gray sea stretching out past barren rocks to a greasy gray sky. Sound effects were provided by disconsolate seagulls wheeling overhead and scummy water slapping against a decaying rock.

It was scant comfort that he was not alone.

The official party inspecting the site of Macklin's projected installations was large. Since all of them were outfitted like Thatcher, a fanciful spectator might have been reminded of a garland of buttercups carelessly dropped into an overflowing gutter.

Not Charlie Trinkam. "I suppose you're going to tell me that when it's not raining, this is a beautiful spot," he said to Simon Livermore, with a gesture encompassing the austere landscape, the muddy scars of construction, the derelict village.

Livermore was becoming hardened to American idiom.

"Exactly," he said, without the awkwardness of three weeks ago. "Unfortunately, it always is raining."

"The weather's just one of the reasons this is going to be such a tough job for Macklin," said Arthur Shute proudly.

"I thought that was Exxon's line," said Charlie, squinting into the gloom. "Say, there's a boat out there, isn't there?"

Thatcher had no desire to figure as the bearer of bad tidings. But the only way to survive an endurance test is to take its measure in advance.

"After we have seen the site of the onshore pumping facilities—which is here where we are standing, I take it—we are going to ride that launch, Charlie, out to where the tanker berths will be. Do I have that right, Shute?"

Shute, wincing against a frozen rivulet that had tipped down his neck, nodded.

"Great," said Charlie.

"That will give you a better idea of the magnitudes involved, together with the conditions the crews will have to face," Shute explained.

Site inspections are sacred rituals of modern capitalism. Underwriters, bankers, lawyers, and stray investors are regularly and religiously subjected to intricate technologies they do not comprehend, wastelands rich in some invisible resource, and experiments revolutionizing the unknown. In theory, these outings bridge the gap between the world of money and the world of goods. In actuality, as Thatcher had ample reason to know, they were a penance for all concerned. Chemists, metallurgists, or, as today, construction engineers like Hugo Cramer labored inarticulately to convey abstruse complexities in terms that even a vice president could understand. Some vice presidents made fools of themselves admiring big pipes, small computer banks, or deep holes. Those who kept their wits about them tagged along, too polite to remind the experts that the ultimate titanic achievement is the ring of the cash register.

Arthur Shute, president of Macklin, and Simon Livermore, representing among other things the hard-pressed pound sterling, felt obliged to evince respect for the prodigies of drilling, blasting, and excavating that would transform this desolation into a cornucopia of energy for Western Europe. It was noticeable, however, that they were not up ahead with Hugo Cramer who was knee deep in engineers, blueprints, and survey results.

Charlie Trinkam was always game to go through the motions, but awe was alien to his nature.

"Well, Hugo," he said, plodding damply onto the dock, "this all looks like a piece of cake to me. You don't have any caribou like those poor fish on the Alaska pipeline."

Cramer, the only visiting fireman who looked as if he had worn a hard hat before, stuck his clipboard under an arm and detached himself from storage capacities, depth soundings, and pipeline welding.

"Don't you believe it, Charlie," he said, standing aside to let Klaus Engelhart and Paul Volpe precede him through a string of puddles. "There's some kind of rare bird that nests over there." He indicated a rocky hillock that rose on the easternmost arm of the harbor.

"Paul says people are writing letters to *The Times* about it."

His words were wind-borne beyond Trinkam.

"Macklin has made extensive provision to respect the environment," said Shute, puffing from his exertions.

Simon Livermore was hauling himself up the heaving gangplank. "Yes, every attempt is going to be made to preserve the local flora and fauna," he echoed.

There was a dank silence, during which the party trailed aboard ship. Then Klaus Engelhart spoke up.

"That is easier said than done," he said dispassionately.

This harmless remark produced a disproportionate reaction, attributable in part to the extreme discomfort of their new surroundings. Ordinarily, shipboard is the only comfortable portion of any amphibious undertaking. But the *Macklin Star,* now chugging steadily out to sea, was not much of an improvement over the receding shore. Thatcher suspected that "launch" was a misnomer. The *Macklin Star* was a maritime utility vehicle, part tug, part tender. Thus, six visitors, four resident Macklin surveyors, and three crewmen—most of them large and bulky—were jammed into an inadequate space. The resultant clammy body heat generated a steamy bouquet of bilge, long-dead fish, and some unknown but malodorous chemical.

Even so, the response to Engelhart was not all atmospherics. He had been odd man out all day—asking too many questions, airing too many opinions, taking too much for granted.

Paul Volpe was still testing his new authority. "Don't worry, Klaus," he said, bracing himself against the *Macklin Star*'s bucking. "We'll meet our contract terms, and that includes all the ecological safeguards."

Engelhart's almost colorless eyebrows sketched surprise, as he glanced quickly at Hugo Cramer and Arthur Shute.

Cramer was hunched over, peering through the rain-spattered window, ostensibly indifferent to this interchange. But he heard all right.

"Especially the birds' nests," he said, bringing a flush to Volpe's thin cheeks.

Arthur Shute tried to make things better, and blundered.

"Paul's absolutely right," he said, clutching at the nearest prop, which was John Thatcher's arm. "Our agreement with the British government worked out in detail our obligations, such as resodding the hills when we've finished construction. And the careful disposition of waste materials. Dave . . . that is, our European office, spent a lot of time on that part of our specifications during the bidding. Isn't that correct, Livermore?"

Livermore was embarrassed by this reference to what everyone had agreed to forget. "Yes, that's right," he said, literally turning his back on the subject by staring out at the featureless sea.

The entire cramped cabin could hear Klaus Engelhart's next contribution.

"You forget, Mr. Shute, that my firm—NDW—also submitted a bid to the British government, to Mr. Livermore. So I know all about the performance standards and penalties."

This amounted to gratuitous discourtesy. Under better circumstances, Thatcher thought, it would have been met with cool silence, blank faces, then a new, innocuous subject—like drilling platforms. With all the engineers at hand, this treatment should have been easy.

Unfortunately, the engineers had retreated into solid silence. So, as the *Macklin Star* shuddered into another swoop, Paul Volpe did the best he could. "Look, Klaus, we all have to live with the fact that Macklin got the contract," he began.

Looking briefly over his shoulder, Cramer intervened: "Knock it off, Paul. Look, up ahead at that red buoy is where the first tanker berth is going to be. We're running a line . . ."

171

The tanker berths were followed by the offshore islands, where Macklin was going to build storage tanks. By nightfall, a scarcely noticeable darkening of the western sky, when release should have been in sight, Arthur Shute made an announcement that could not have been welcome to anyone.

"Busby's just radioed," he said, as the *Macklin Star* nosed back into harbor. "There's some kind of snag with the plane. I'm afraid we're not going to be able to fly back to London until tomorrow morning."

Charlie Trinkam groaned aloud. This morning, the Macklin plane that shuttled to Noss Head had been part of the daily grind. Now, after pumping stations and tanker berths, it was a flying carpet.

"Don't worry," said Shute with a false cheer. "We can make you comfortable for the night up at the inn."

Ignoring a broad grin from Cramer, Charlie spoke from the heart. "You may be able to turn this place into Houston East, Arthur, but until then that's beyond you."

He was correct. There are limits to what technology can do; there are even limits to what money can do. The inn at Noss Head illustrated both. Macklin had taken it over, introduced deep freezes and steaks flown in from Kansas City, and stocked a bar that made the natives blink.

But the essential inn remained, a huddled, ancient structure of haphazard, low-ceilinged rooms, redolent of the smoke and damp of centuries.

"When we get a full crew working here, we're going to throw up dormitories and commissaries," Cramer explained, accompanying Thatcher inside. "This is just a stopgap."

"I see," said Thatcher temperately.

"Anybody can see," said Charlie with robust bitterness.

"Oh, come on, Charlie, it isn't so bad," said Cramer, unzipping his sodden jumpsuit.

And it was not. Macklin provided unexpected guests with emergency kits containing everything from toothbrushes to malt whisky. Food and drink were more than adequate. The public rooms were stuffy with warmth and the bedrooms were clean, if not inviting. As Thatcher pointed out, they were roughing it in reasonable comfort.

Trinkam preferred bright lights, but he was adaptable. "It's not the plumbing I mind, John," he said, joining his superior in a corner of the minute taproom. "It's all these smiling faces. I didn't expect this jaunt to be a laugh riot, but who wants to be locked in a closet with the cast for World War III?"

Allowing for hyperbole, Thatcher had to agree. The fine drizzle that had marked the daylight hours was now a steady downpour. Given the weather and the village, no one was tempted by an after-dinner stroll. In effect, the inn was simply an extension of the *Macklin Star*.

Neither of them was a happy ship.

"And it's more than the clash of uncongenial personalities," Thatcher mused aloud. If North Sea oil—or modern banking, for that matter—demanded real affinity from its followers, they could all go back to barter and rubbing sticks for fire.

"Adversaries are one thing," Trinkam said. "Sure, everybody's out to protect his own interest, whether it's Macklin, or the ministry, or NDW—"

"Or even the Sloan," Thatcher, no mean adversary himself, interjected. "But are these interests what they seem to be? As you once pointed out, business isn't the only jungle, Charlie."

"What do you . . . uh-oh! Here comes one of the wild animals now. . . . Sure, Klaus, pull up a chair."

Engelhart was not a mountain lion, thought Thatcher watching the young man's stiff self-control. It was just possible, however, that he was a beaver.

"Thank you," Engelhart said. "A brandy will be very welcome after such a long, cold day. Although it was most interesting to see what Macklin plans. Of course, I had been here before with NDW engineers, when we were preparing our bid."

Dull and deliberate, Thatcher decided, watching Charlie suppress a yawn.

"NDW also made special provisions with regard to the environment. Even now, when we can hope only to do the superstructure work, we have careful procedures outlined in our contract."

"Back to the birds' nests," Charlie murmured.

Across the tiny room, Paul Volpe was huddled over a small table making notes while Hugo Cramer talked.

"The birds' nests," Engelhart agreed with a mechanical smile. "I did not realize that Macklin was so sensitive about these ecological issues."

"Today, everybody has to be," said Thatcher carefully.

But Engelhart had something to say, and he intended to say it. Clearing his throat, he continued: "For example, I did not get the impression that Davidson Wylie was deeply concerned—with birds' nests, as you say."

The name brought Charlie's nodding head up. It also froze Paul Volpe and Hugo Cramer. Only Shute and Simon Livermore, discussing the OPEC fete in Richmond, seemed untouched.

"But of course, now it is not Davidson Wylie, but Paul, who has taken charge of Macklin's European operations," Engelhart went on mischievously.

"Volpe is running the London office," said Thatcher, lowering his voice. "But I do not think Macklin has decided whether he is in charge of all European operations."

With what appeared to be real amusement, Engelhart replied: "He would not be pleased to hear you say so. He thinks he has already stepped into Davidson Wylie's shoes."

Some sixth sense told Paul Volpe they were talking about him. Self-consciously, he concentrated on Cramer's instructions.

Cramer spoiled the effect. Rising, he rubbed the small of his back to get the stiffness out, then lumbered across the room to loom over Engelhart.

"Still talking business?" he asked genially. "I've got a better idea. How about unwinding with a small friendly poker game?"

Thatcher could not tell whether or not he had overheard Klaus Engelhart.

Engelhart himself hastily jumped to his feet. "I'm afraid you will have to count me out," he said, abruptly. "I have an important telephone call to make."

With a bob of the head, he scurried out into the hall.

"Queer duck," said Cramer, looking after him.

"Is Macklin going to find it easy to work with him?" Thatcher asked bluntly.

"I don't know," said Cramer. "Hell, NDW doesn't even have a contract yet. Engelhart rubs a lot of people the wrong way. If he and Paul can't meet without tangling, I'm not so sure there's going to be a contract."

Paul Volpe swung around to face them. "Klaus sounds worse than he is, Hugo. If you'd just leave him to me, I can handle him."

"Like we saw this afternoon," Cramer replied.

"That was no sweat," Volpe insisted. "Anyway, we've got to have NDW. They're the best in the business."

"Macklin's the best in the business," Cramer reminded him.

"All right, all right," Volpe said. "But we really need NDW. Everyone will tell you that."

Cramer's patience was running out. "We don't need anybody," he said gruffly. "We sure don't need a trouble-making little bastard like Engelhart. What's the matter with you, Paul? Didn't you see what he was doing? He was trying to needle you about your promotion."

Volpe did not back down. "He really wants to know how much authority I've got. And for that matter, I wouldn't mind knowing myself."

Cramer had become so angry that Arthur Shute was forced to take a hand. "This is neither the time

175

nor the place to discuss company reorganization," he said with impartial displeasure. "You both should know better."

This effectively terminated the bickering, but it did not end the quarrel. Volpe and Cramer relapsed into a sullen silence that threatened to engulf the whole room.

It was Simon Livermore who rescued them all. Imperturbably, he resumed the conversation he had been having with Arthur Shute. "As I was saying, I expect both my boys will insist on visiting Noss Head during their next vacation. When I stopped by to visit them in Surrey, they were thrilled to hear where I was going. The younger one is at the age where he cannot imagine anything more adventurous than drilling for oil."

Arthur Shute wanted to keep the ball rolling. "And you did say your older son is going to Oxford next year, didn't you?"

"Yes, I hope he'll be at my old college," said Livermore.

Paul Volpe was too young to appreciate the lubricating effect of small talk. He shoved back his chair as noisily as possible. "I'm turning in," he announced curtly, before stalking out of the room.

His duty done, Simon Livermore was ready to call it a day. "I think I'll follow his example," he said decorously. "Good evening, gentlemen."

This left four men, each with his own thoughts. Charlie Trinkam spoke his aloud.

"I like Livermore's officer-and-gentleman style, don't you?"

Nobody replied.

Because, as John Thatcher recognized, nobody was thinking about Simon Livermore.

17 · The Independents

In Scotland Macklin was tackling the Noss Head project with platoons of technicians, the latest computing equipment and a budget large enough to satisfy many small nations. Back in London, Betsy Volpe, with one notebook and a ballpoint pen, was mounting a campaign that was almost as complex. She was proposing to move an American household, complete with appliances, furniture, potted plants, recreational gear, pets, and Lenox china, from Rome to London. She dismissed as trivial changes in language, currency, and national habits. Here, as in every other city in the world, the chief obstacle to relocation was going to be the real estate agents.

"I wouldn't call it large," one of them was saying to her with an ingratiating smile. "Rather, I would call it ample. Ample accommodation for entertaining, for house parties, for—"

"There are six rooms more than I want," Betsy interrupted.

"With spacious grounds," he continued.

"That would need two gardeners full-time."

"And a splendid view of the park!" he concluded triumphantly.

"From the attic." Betsy was collecting her belongings and rising. "I'm afraid it won't do."

So far the day had produced houses rich in Old World charm (an antediluvian heating system and one bathroom as far from the bedrooms as possible), strong on compact efficiency (built-in fixtures demanding zany domestic routines), mellow with the memory of departed servants (endless stairs, basement kitchens), and lacking in every detail required by the Volpes.

"In other words," thought Betsy, crossing off yet another name on her list, "just about normal for the start of house hunting."

Undismayed she examined the Kensington street sign to orient herself and debated alternatives. It was too late in the afternoon to open dealings with the next agency. It was too early to return to her hotel for dinner and her nightly task of dividing the Volpe belongings into movables, salables, and discards. It was too far to . . .

In the midst of these reflections, the teasing doubt that had kept her stationary clarified itself. She checked the sign again. Two years was a long time. But surely the first or second turn on the right led to the Wylie apartment. If so, Betsy Volpe had no intention of wasting a golden opportunity.

Within fifteen minutes she was tripping into the building, a small parcel in her hand and a self-congratulatory smile on her face. Really, it couldn't have worked out better if she had planned the whole thing. What was more natural than that the wife of Davidson Wylie's assistant should pay a courtesy call on Mrs. Wylie? She could offer Francesca condolences and good wishes. She could stay for tea. And, in order to make sure that tea was offered, she was bringing the cakes with her.

From the moment the doorbell was answered, this simple script had to be revised. Tea was a lost cause. Francesca was already carrying a tinkling glass. Almost without asking, she supplied Betsy with a good three fingers of Scotch as soon as they were seated. And before Betsy could establish her brand of cozy, all-girls-together intimacy, Francesca was well along the road to the much franker woman-to-woman variety.

Their first exchange set the ground rules.

"Oh, Francesca," Betsy murmured softly, "I was so upset you left Houston before I could see you. I wanted to tell you how sorry Paul and I are about Dave."

"That is very kind of you," Francesca replied promptly. "And, of course, I too am sorry that David should have been killed. But I know I do not have to hide from you that everything had been over between David and me for some time."

"Well, Paul did mention that you were having trouble," Betsy faltered. It is never easy to have one's condolences dismissed, however politely.

Francesca refused to play on this level of half-truths. "Come now," she reproached her guest. "You must have known that David moved out of here months ago."

"Naturally Paul had to know where he could get in touch with Dave."

"And that I filed for divorce," Francesca continued remorselessly.

The conversation was not proceeding as planned. Betsy had become the defendant while Francesca flourished her skills as cross-examiner. In an attempt to break the pattern, Betsy Volpe moved into generalities.

"That was all common knowledge at Macklin," she agreed with a rush, "but, after all, couples often run into a bad patch and manage to get together again. I've known quite a few wives who decided to divorce and then changed their minds. Sometimes just the threat of a breakup is enough to start people doing something serious to save their marriages. We always hoped that you and Dave would work things out."

"Ah," Francesca sighed, infusing her words with

immense world-weariness, "but David and I were long past that stage. There is a point of no return, you understand, and it is not difficult to recognize. When all anger is gone, there is nothing left to save. I can truthfully say that it has been over a year since David was able to inspire any interest in me whatsoever. All the little hurts, the foolish jealousies, the unreasonable grievances"—Francesca's hand fluttered in illustration—"they had evaporated in the sunshine of my indifference."

Wisely, Betsy did not attempt to pursue Francesca into the ether. "One of the other ways of recognizing that turning point is when your interest shifts to another man," she said, bringing them back to earth with a thump.

"Yes, yes, what you say is true." Francesca's agreement was slow and judicious, as if she were examining a novel hypothesis. "As a matter of fact, I have become interested in other men."

"Hugo Cramer says you're going to marry that German," said Betsy flatly.

"These men!" The rich laugh was a masterpiece of lazy, good-natured tolerance. "They are all the same, so confident about everything. Hugo Cramer knows what I am going to do, Klaus Engelhart is equally positive, probably your Paul is too. In the meantime I am all confusion and self-doubts. Is is they who are the little children, or are we?"

This philosophic query was destined to retain unanswered. Betsy's jaw tightened, but then she stopped short. She was allowing herself to be hypnotized by Francesca's Madame Récamier act, in spite of the fact that Francesca was sitting upright wearing a tawny brown pant-suit with a crisp shirt. Another two minutes and they would be lost in the underbrush of an interminable discussion about the sexes. She choked on a genuinely appreciative giggle.

"Don't try to fool me, Francesca," she said, on surfacing. "You haven't been uncertain what to do about a man since you stopped wearing pigtails. Maybe you're not going to tell me, maybe you're not going to tell him, but you know all right."

Far from being offended, Francesca seemed to regard this speech as a compliment.

"That's better," she said approvingly. "Next time, don't try to ask me questions by telling me what Hugo Cramer says. And to spare you unnecessary trouble, my intentions about Klaus Engelhart are not ready for publication."

"I'll bet your timetable has been disrupted," Betsy speculated shrewdly. "Your divorce wouldn't have gone through for months, always assuming you and Dave really did split. Has it occurred to you that that may be what sent him round the bend?"

Francesca frowned. "On the few occasions we met, David gave no evidence of going round any bend. I suppose that it's possible I overlooked something. I find quarreling about property settlements tends to absorb my attention." Her eyes slid to her guest in silent appraisal. "But why am I telling you what I thought? After all, you have seen more of David than I, recently."

"Actually," Betsy said with precision, "it is Paul who has been seeing him."

Francesca's lips curved. "And men can be so blind," she lamented. "So Paul noticed nothing?"

"Paul thought Dave was all wrapped up in trying to deliver Noss Head." Betsy struggled against disloyalty for a moment before surrendering. "For heaven's sake, Francesca, you know perfectly well that Paul admired Dave so much he would have been easy to fool. He wasn't suspicious, he wasn't even normally critical."

"Perhaps not. But David was not surrounded exclusively by admiring fans, you know."

"Don't you believe it! Dave was more of a salesman than you're willing to admit. He sold Hugo Cramer a song and dance about Europe requiring a special touch. He did such a job on Simon Livermore that there's been trouble ever since. First, Livermore didn't want to deal with Hugo, and now he's edgy with Paul.

Good God, Dave even sold the whole British government on Macklin!"

"And me?" Francesca asked with a half-smile.

"You married him, didn't you?" Betsy said crossly.

"That was quite some time ago. I meant during the past few months."

"You said it yourself. You've been concentrating on real estate in Houston." Betsy made it sound like a dereliction from duty.

Francesca shook her head, mildly reproachful. "There is something in that. But still, you must admit that it's odd David seems to have hoodwinked so many people so completely."

"What's odd about it?" A demon of perversity gripped Betsy. "People were seeing him in offices, talking to him about business. In that atmosphere they weren't likely to ask themselves if he was planning to stage a fake kidnapping. Once David moved into his own place, nobody was seeing him with his hair down. It was probably at midnight, after he put his feet up and had a few drinks, that you could tell he was planning to slip the leash." The relevance of these words to her own situation suddenly struck Betsy. "And while I'm on the subject, would you mind if I threw the rest of this stuff out and had a glass of water instead?"

"Oh, I think I can do better than that." But Francesca did not permit the production of a glass of orange juice to deflect her. As if there had been no interval she went straight on: "If that was the case with David, he certainly covered his tracks. I went through his apartment yesterday—with the kind permission of the police—and you would think he only had two subjects on his mind. Noss Head and divorce."

Betsy's eyes were alert. "The police? You mean here, in London?"

"My poor child, did you think we had left them behind in Houston? We may have had a kidnapping in Istanbul, a ransom in Switzerland, and a murder in Texas, but the one man Interpol knows about lived in London. And the officer I spoke with was very interested in the fact that, at the moment, all David's associates are here—his wife, his superior, his subordinate, his customers, and his rivals."

"Those are just the ones they know about," Betsy protested. "Why don't they look for those men in Istanbul, or the girl who picked up the money?"

Francesca was staring into the depths of her whiskey as if pondering a crystal ball.

"I imagine they are," she said dreamily. "I can see some very persistent men asking questions all over Istanbul and Zurich, Athens and Rome. I hear that they even brought over that Swiss banker who paid the ransom, to see if he could recognize me."

"You!" Betsy heard the incredulity in her own voice and tried to justify it by blurting: "But that was supposed to be a girl!" Then she blushed fiery red to the roots of her hair.

This social maladroitness failed to fluster her hostess. "Real girlhood may end quite early," Francesca said drily, "but attempts to reproduce it artificially have been known."

Betsy was beyond the stage of offering apologies. In her opinion, Francesca was already getting the lion's share of satisfaction from the encounter. "So the police let you search Dave's apartment?" she asked pointedly.

"It would be more accurate to say that they let me stand there while they searched. They couldn't very well keep me out of the place, because I am executrix of David's will." She shrugged lightly. "But they were damned if they were letting me run loose there, not until they put everything through a sieve. And much good it did them. All they got for their pains was David's elaborate calculation of the current worth of our Houston land and a pack of canceled checks proving no unusual payments in the last year."

Only an expert would have realized that, as Francesca delivered this information, she was waiting for some reaction. Certainly Betsy, her forehead wrinkled, her thumb compulsively rubbing a roughened fingernail, had no attention to spare for these fine details.

"But that's nonsense," she said at last. "Dave had lots of expenses. He was hiring accomplices and cars, he was buying submachine guns and false identity papers. It must have cost him thousands. You can't tell me he did it all on credit."

"That thought had occurred to me," Francesca admitted.

"Well, it's really quite simple. Dave was keeping all his records at his girlfriend's place. That's why his apartment was so clean."

Very gently, Francesca stopped holding her breath. "That is certainly one explanation," she said politely.

Unfortunately, Betsy's appetite for information was far from sated. With unflagging energy she proposed one avenue of exploration after another. Even if the girlfriend had flown, surely it was not impossible to discover where she had been. Maybe Dave had been paying the rent for her. Had the police tried that route?

"Maybe she was a married lady living with her husband," Francesca retorted. "So many mistresses are."

Undeterred, Betsy continued her theorizing. There was no reason to suppose the girlfriend lived in England. If Dave had traveled regularly to meet her, there must be airline records.

"Unless she lived in Hong Kong, David could see her on legitimate business trips."

So intent was Betsy that it took her some time to realize that Francesca was deliberately stonewalling. Then, without rancor, she demoted Francesca to the same category as unsatisfactory real estate agents.

"I'm afraid I have to be going," she said, collecting her belongings and rising.

She left behind her an arena in which the honors had been just about evenly divided. Neither lady had obtained all that she wanted; neither had emerged empty-handed. And they were together in considering that afternoon as a mere preliminary.

Betsy, the less patient of the two, was able to hurl herself at the phone the moment she returned to her hotel room.

"This is Mrs. Paul Volpe," she announced. "I would like to come by tomorrow morning . . ."

Francesca, constitutionally better fitted to endure delay, waited for the Noss Head expedition to return to London before making her call.

"This is Francesca Wylie. I think it essential that we should speak together. . . ."

But, however disparate their characters, both women knew how to set aside their personal preoccupations when it came to gratifying their menfolk.

Francesca was practically purring when she agreed to Klaus Engelhart's plans for the evening. Of course she did not object to making a foursome of it. And seeing that young Volpe couple again would be charming, simply charming.

As for Betsy, she agreed absolutely with Paul that if they could do a little social favor for Klaus Engelhart it might pay handsome dividends. Besides, it would be fun to see Francesca again. She was feeling quite guilty at not having thought of it herself.

In the end, their histronic talents were not put to the test.

Betsy had finished dressing and was putting on earrings when Paul burst into their suite.

"You'd better hurry. We're going to be—" she began, before she saw his face in the mirror. "Paul! Has something happened?"

He was standing in the doorway, one hand clutching the jamb. "The switchboard operator caught me in the hall. It was Klaus on the line." He paused and swallowed painfully.

"Yes?" Betsy was white, almost afraid to ask more.

"Francesca's dead. She put her head in the oven and gassed herself."

18 · Oil Slick

Until he heard his own words, Volpe was obsessed by the personal horror of Francesca Wylie's tragedy. Suddenly his thoughts began to scurry in wider and wider circles. This was not an isolated death. This was the latest in a terrible sequence—first robbery, then murder, now suicide.

"My God, isn't this ever going to end?"

Betsy Volpe, watching him pace back and forth, bit her lip.

"Well?" he demanded roughly, wheeling toward her.

"Of course it's terrible," she said.

"Of course it's terrible," he repeated dully. "Betsy, you don't have a clue about how bad this is. We're not sitting around being polite at a funeral home, you know. Three guesses what people are going to say when they hear Macklin's got another corpse on its hands. Just how many deaths is this deal going to take?"

His outburst shook Betsy. "But Paul," she said, trying to think it through, "if Francesca committed suicide—"

Electrified, he pounced. "What do you mean *if?*"

By now, Betsy was rattled. "I don't know—it's just that when I saw her, she didn't sound suicidal to me."

Paul stared at her.

"Don't look at me like that, Paul," she cried.

He shook his head helplessly. "You went to see Francesca?"

"Yesterday afternoon," said Betsy, with a lift of her chin. "I just wanted to tell her how sorry I was—about everything."

When Paul rolled his eyes, she added: "She was perfectly normal when I left. Oh, she'd been drinking. But she wasn't thinking about putting her head in an oven—"

The phrase made her gag. But with the volatility she had come to know and dread, Paul had switched from reality to a dark world of his own imagining.

"They'll say you had something to do with it. They'll say you went back. Or—" he flung out his arm with uncontrolled abandon "—or me! I've been chasing all over London since I got back last night. They'll say I went to see Francesca. Or even that I hit her over the head. God, Betsy, what are we going to do?"

Betsy fought with her own nightmare. "But Paul, Klaus is the one who was there."

"Klaus!" Paul reacted violently. "Klaus suggested this dinner. Maybe Hugo was right. Maybe Klaus has been setting me up all along."

Desperately, Betsy struggled to keep her footing. Right now, the most important thing in the world was to stop Paul from whipping himself into a nerve-ridden frenzy.

Sounding years older, she said, "Paul, what you should do is tell the company. Hugo, or Mr. Shute. They should know about this as soon as possible."

As she hoped, this arrested him. "The company?" he said dazedly. "You're right. That's absolutely right."

When he made no move, she took the next step too. "Do we know where Mr. Shute is staying—or Hugo?"

The Hilton said that Hugo Cramer was out but

Arthur Shute was with some other guests in the dining room.

"Excuse me, John," he said, touching napkin to lip in a gesture reminiscent of prewar movies. "This is probably Houston. I've had a call in for a couple of hours."

Self-importantly, he bustled off to the telephone.

His bankers took advantage of his absence.

"John, I thought Shute was supposed to be one of those hard-nosed businessmen before he went to Washington," said Charlie.

"To the best of my knowledge he was," Thatcher replied. "But that was fifteen years ago."

"Well, he's sure softened up."

"He has certainly forgotten everything he ever knew about banks," Thatcher agreed. "Shute seems to feel that our primary allegiance is to Macklin, not the Sloan."

All things considered, this was a very temperate comment. Somewhere along the line—and Thatcher suspected that the *Macklin Star* was responsible—Arthur Shute had led himself astray. From business associate, he had progressed to colleague, with co-conspirator looming ahead. With boring simplicity he shared Macklin—past, present, and future—with them. Today, over drinks, they had relived the bad old payoff days. Soup had brought the Roberta Ore Simpson shakeup, complete with Arthur Shute's soul-searching before accepting the presidency. The roast beef, which was excellent, had been salted with Noss Head and estimated earnings per share.

"And when he gets back, he'll take up where he left off," Charlie predicted.

In essence, this meant dessert and new worlds to conquer.

But the Arthur Shute who rejoined them had lost his self-indulgent desire to wander down memory lane.

"What? No, I do not want a trifle, whatever that

may be," he snapped at the hovering waiter. "Will you get us the bill? We're in a hurry!"

Scenting another Macklin crisis, Charlie was inclined to demonstrate the Sloan's independence even if it took treacle tart.

Thatcher was more direct.

"What's *your* hurry, Arthur?" he asked, emphasizing his own detachment.

Shute's officiousness melted away. "That was Paul Volpe," he said limply.

With a triumphant glance at Thatcher, Charlie reached for the dessert menu.

"Volpe thought I should know," Shute amplified, with visible effort. "Apparently Francesca Wylie has just committed suicide."

"Francesca Wylie?" said Trinkam, disregarding the menu. "I don't believe it."

"That's what Volpe said," Shute mumbled distractedly. "My God, I don't know. Maybe this means the whole damned Wylie mess is cleared up at last. Unless, of course, it means something else. . . ."

Charlie cut in ruthlessly. "Did she leave a note?"

All Shute knew was what Paul Volpe had told him. ". . . and that was damned little," he said bitterly.

During this exchange, Thatcher had been lost in his own reflections. Francesca Wylie's death by her own hand inescapably resurrected the living woman who had been such an enigmatic presence in his New York office hardly a week ago. But her tragic end could be a climax in the Macklin saga. Either they were finally out of the woods, or they were compromised beyond retrieval. It was a matter of moment to the Sloan to discover which. Resolutely, Thatcher concentrated on business, not human interest.

Unlike Charlie, he did not waste time trying to elicit nonexistent information.

"Where were you proposing to hurry, Arthur?" he asked.

Shute's mouth worked. Then he said: "I want to talk to Hugo. After all, he's working mose closely with the British. He'll be the one to know if this will make

189

any significant difference—to Noss Head, I mean. Hugo's sharper about this sort of thing than he looks."

When catastrophe struck, Betsy Volpe's instinct had been to spread the burden, conscript aid and support, blur the stark outlines. Arthur Shute's initial reaction was identical. John Thatcher naturally could not know about the Volpes, but he recognized action for action's sake, movement masquerading as decision.

"Do you know where Cramer happens to be?" he inquired with a fair notion of the answer.

"Well, no," said Shute resentfully, as if Thatcher were splitting hairs.

"That's going to make it tough to find him," Charlie pointed out unkindly.

Shute was in turmoil. Obviously somebody else had to take charge.

"I agree it would be wise to contact Cramer," said Thatcher, without explaining why.

"Yes of course. Macklin has to consult—"

"But," said Thatcher, firmly overriding him, "very little will be gained by pooling ignorance. It would be an excellent idea if we could equip ourselves with some information before descending on Cramer."

This went past Arthur Shute directly to Charlie Trinkam, as intended.

"I'm with you so far," he said. "What exactly do you have in mind?"

"Well," said Thatcher, working it out as he went along, "the police are not likely to release any details to us. Indeed, I have no desire to present myself to them. I do not wish the Sloan—or Macklin—to figure as a voyeur of crime. However, Simon Livermore—"

"Livermore?" Shute was adamant. "Absolutely not! Good Lord, that's what I've been trying to explain. I have to talk to Hugo before Livermore hears about this. We have to decide how to handle it."

Thatcher spelled it out. "In view of the circumstances, Arthur, I think it is safe to assume that one of the first things the London police did was communicate with the Department of Energy. As well as Interpol. Mrs. Wylie has been the object of a good deal of official attention recently. And that attention has been intimately connected with Macklin and Noss Head. I am sure that Livermore already knows—and probably has more information than Paul Volpe."

"I want to talk to Hugo first," said Shute mulishly.

It took hard persuading and an affronted waiter with the bill to budge Arthur Shute. Even then, Thatcher suspected it was the restless itch to be doing something that prevailed.

But for once good advice was more productive than anybody could have expected.

A tight-lipped Livermore opened the door of his apartment. Behind him, watching the procession file in, stood his wife, Jill, and Hugo Cramer.

"Yeah, Simon and I were going over the revised figures on that back-up platform. We wanted to have them finished by tomorrow," Cramer explained as they trooped in. His face was hard.

"We were getting ready to go out to dinner," Livermore said somberly.

But news of Francesca Wylie's death had been dispatched to the Department of Energy, just as John Thatcher predicted.

". . . so, instead of having that marvelous paella, I had to make sandwiches," said Jill Livermore with an uncertain smile. "I call that bloody unfair."

Nobody, including her husband, paid the slightest heed.

"Do sit down, won't you all?" she continued into the silence. "I think we can offer you brandy, can't we, Simon?"

"What? Oh, yes, yes."

Brandy was offered and declined with funereal solemnity. Somebody, and Thatcher guessed an interior decorator, had made the living room a gay, insouciant blend of timeless elegance and bravura color. There was some gleaming silver, masses of bright flowers, and a lustrous ikon over the mantel.

Little Mrs. Livermore, vivid in batik print, curled up dejectedly in the corner of a long white sofa.

Thatcher thought he could understand why. This was her room and usurpers had invaded it.

Charlie knew better. Jill Livermore thrived on gaiety and flirtation. She could not handle the black pall introduced by Francesca Wylie's death.

"Once I heard the news, I wanted to stay by the phone," Livermore explained.

This remark galvanized Arthur Shute.

"Have you heard anything more?" he asked. "What really happened?"

Cramer, more rumpled than usual, was brutal. "Francesca shoved her head into a gas oven about two hours ago. That's what happened, Arthur."

This sent a shiver through the room, diminishing Arthur Shute but, surprisingly, reviving Livermore.

"The police called to inform my minister," he said with a semblance of his customary competence. "Apparently Klaus Engelhart was taking Mrs. Wylie out to dine this evening. He found her when he arrived."

Hugo Cramer stirred restively.

"When Engelhart got there, he smelled gas. He rushed inside, broke the kitchen window, pulled Mrs. Wylie out. But it was too late."

Studying the impeccable crease of his trousers, he added: "According to Engelhart's statement to the police—and I gather he was somewhat shaken—they were going to join Mr. and Mrs. Volpe for dinner."

Charlie felt something had been carefully omitted. "Did she leave a note?" he asked for the second time.

"No," said Livermore. Then, meticulously, he continued: "I should say that there was no note when the police arrived."

"Funny," said Charlie, "usually they leave something, don't they?"

Thatcher watched his henchman expressionlessly.

All innocence, Charlie looked around. "Francesca Wylie didn't strike me as the kind who would want to kill herself. She looked like a gal who had a lot to live for."

Cramer, who had been holding himself in check, seized on this. "Christ, that's what everybody is going to think. They're going to say that Francesca must've been in this up to her neck." He slammed the arm of his chair. "Then they're going to want to know why Paul was buddying up to her. Hell, why won't that kid listen to me? I told him Engelhart was out to make a patsy of him."

Stiff with disapproval, Livermore retorted: "I can assure you that our police are not easily misled. Especially in cases of foul play."

"Foul play!" Shute exclaimed. "But that means murder. Good God, if she and her husband were together in this plot, who's left to kill her now?"

Thatcher did not think it was quite so simple and neither, apparently, did Cramer. "Plenty of people," he said savagely. "For God's sake, Arthur, didn't she tell you anything? She sounded as if she wanted to."

Shute gaped at him. "What are you talking about, Hugo?"

"When she called you this morning," Cramer said impatiently. Suddenly aware that everyone was staring, he expanded: "The switchboard at the office put her through to me."

Thatcher could see that Arthur Shute was about to explode. "Perhaps you had better start from the beginning, Cramer," he suggested.

"There isn't that much to tell," said Cramer. "Francesca said she had to get hold of you, Arthur. I told her to try the Hilton."

"Well, she didn't reach me," said Shute.

"More to the point, do you have any idea what she wanted?" Thatcher asked Cramer.

"Not a clue," he said indifferently.

Charlie was stung into expostulating: "Use your head, Hugo. Don't you see that you may have put your finger on it? If Francesca wanted to talk, maybe somebody was afraid of what she was going to say."

Simon Livermore could not silence speculation about Francesca Wylie's death. He did not have to countenance it in his own home. "There is very little to be gained by theorizing. At the moment, the only thing we know for a fact, is that Mrs. Wylie's death is compatible with suicide."

Arthur Shute was too grateful to be perceptive.

"And, if she was Wylie's accomplice she must have been terrified. When the police started closing in, she decided to end it all."

His transparent hope that Francesca Wylie's suicide had ended Macklin's troubles was contemptible. Jull Livermore was not the only one to look disgusted.

"There are other possibilities," sad Thatcher frostily.

But Shute could not leave it alone. "All right. But they are all outsiders. Nothing has happened to imperil our contract, has it? Even if Engelhart was—"

Simon Livermore was not making any commitments. "I am in no position to comment," he said distantly.

For once Hugo Cramer had to remedy Shute's clumsiness. "It's a helluva thing," he said rising like an old man. "But I guess this isn't the place to chew it out. I think we'd better move on."

Neither of the Livermores pressed their guests to stay.

"I'll be in touch with you tomorrow, Livermore. Possibly by then, the situation will be clarified," said Arthur Shute.

"Yes, indeed," said Livermore tonelessly.

Cramer was apologizing to Mrs. Livermore: ". . . make a real night of it at the best restaurant in London," Thatcher overheard him saying, as they eddied into the corridor.

Jill Livermore rebuffed him. "Perhaps we can get together sometime. Good night, Mr. Cramer."

"You sure made a hit with her," Charlie remarked, as they rode down in the elevator.

"Nothing that an expensive dinner won't take care of," said Cramer offhandedly. "She's a party girl. She didn't understand what was going on."

"And neither do I," complained Shute. "Hugo, do you think—?"

Still casual, Cramer said, "Right now I don't know what to think, except I didn't like that crack about Volpe. I think we'd better get over and make sure Paul doesn't get himself—or Macklin—into deeper trouble."

Here was where the Sloan cut off. "Then," said Thatcher firmly, "we'll be leaving you."

"What are you thinking about, John?" Trinkam asked, when they hailed a cab.

Thatcher was thinking about money.

"The ransom?" Charlie asked. "The ransom that Francesca Wylie claimed she didn't have?"

"That," agreed Thatcher, "and money in other forms as well."

19 · Wildcatting

Journalistic reaction the following morning was violent. Davidson Wylie's kidnapping had made the headlines. His wife's death filled the front pages. Without compunction, newsmen focused on the Wylies as archconspirators. Thereafter, the medium shaped the message.

For tabloids, the story was a natural. They knew the classic recipe for concocting a tragic figure—start with unpromising beginnings, rise to astronomic heights, then plunge to a fated doom. With a little ingenuity, Francesca could be fitted into this mold. They saw her as struggling through a war-torn childhood (she had been three when the war ended), to become a familiar of the great (the publicity stills showed her with notable Italian directors and actresses), only fall prey to the inexorable demands of the third act, encompassing divorce, crime, and death. There was a strong suggestion that Davidson Wylie had been her Svengali, and that her desperate attempts to free herself had merely hastened their predestined ends. This broad treatment, avoiding all problems of consistency and probability, satisfied the tabloids and also many of their readers.

One group particularly spellbound by this version of the Wylies was the staff of a small hospital in northern Greece. They had plucked Davidson Wylie out of a car smash and made him whole, only to have him die in yet another car a few weeks later. It had seemed as if they were the victims of some playful deity. But no longer. Now they saw themselves as part of a deep, sinister, and incomprehensible plot.

"Can you believe it? He involved his own wife in his misdeeds," said a pharmacist disapprovingly. "That is not right."

"And she was so beautiful," breathed a young nurse, mooning over a large photograph.

The ambulance driver was shocked. "That's not her, that's Sophia Loren." He pointed to the second woman. "This one is Francesca Wylie."

"She's still beautiful," the nurse said stubbornly.

Television commentators had neither the time nor the desire to be fanciful. For them, it was yet another sordid example of the unscrupulous materialism they regularly espied in elected officials, business executives, blue-collar workers, suburbanites, and everyone leading a life unsanctified by a major network. Davidson and Francesca Wylie were dismissed as criminals who had chosen to live by the sword and die by the sword. Unlike tabloid readers, television viewers were expected to provide their own romance.

Gwen Trabulsi had no trouble at all.

"Just think, Vic," she said, her eyes like stars, "we were sitting right next to them while they were arguing what to do with a million and a half dollars."

For once, Vic had not a single deflating sentence at the ready. He might accuse his wife of overdramatizing, but Walter Cronkite?

"He was trying to cheat her," Vic remembered. "That was plain enough."

"Yes." Eagerly Gwen began to embroider the theme. "That must be why she killed him."

The course of twentieth-century history was teaching Vic to beware the sweeping generalization. Instead of a crisp negative, he hazarded only a personal impression.

"She sure didn't look like the kind of lady that makes her own bombs."

Only the elevated portions of the press—those expecting their public to keep abreast of disarmament negotiations, the ballet, and African geography—regarded the Wylie deaths as constituting something less than a closed circle. Of course it was possible, they conceded, that Francesca had killed her husband and then committed suicide, but this explanation left a good many questions unanswered. Had the separation and divorce been a sham? Why had the couple then disagreed so violently? What had happened to a million and a half dollars?

"None of it makes sense," Charlie Trinkam decided.

"Certainly the police don't think so. Have you noticed that every statement they've released avoids any mention of suicide?" Thatcher agreed, following Charlie out of the cab and into the Hilton.

There the low-ceilinged lobby was packed with chattering groups, barring access to the elevators. "I wonder if this hotel will ever return to normal," Thatcher remarked, detouring around a mountain of luggage.

"Not until we all forget that heat wave. It's not just Americans flocking in. They're getting the Japanese and the South Americans and—"

Thatcher took Charlie's elbow and turned him in the direction from which they were being hailed.

"And the Germans as well," he said, as a threesome approached. "Good evening, Grimm. Good evening, Engelhart. So this is the uncomfortable site of your deliberations."

"Just so." Leopold Grimm was still hankering for the delights of Zurich. "Engelhart you know, but I do not think you have met Herr Pleuger, the managing director of Norddeutsche Werke."

Herr Pleuger was the first to suggest that they repair to the bar. Grimm seemed to welcome enlargement of his party. Only Klaus Engelhart remained wrapped in gloom.

As soon as they were settled, Charlie faced the problem of condolences. "Must have been hell for you, Engelhart, finding Francesca Wylie's body that way," he said with unforced sympathy.

"It was extremely unpleasant." After gazing into his glass for a moment, Klaus expanded on his constrained response. "What makes it harder is that I might have saved her if I had been earlier. The police are not sure how soon she died before I arrived."

Tact came naturally to Charlie Trinkam. It was not part of Herr Pleuger's armory. He shook a finger at his subordinate and said: "You must learn to face disagreeable facts, Engelhart. What the police are really saying, is that they are not sure she was dead *before* you arrived."

"I am well aware of that. It is not particularly surprising to me," Engelhart said woodenly. "After all, if the police do not accept suicide—and I myself told them that was out of the question—they must suspect someone of her murder."

"I fail to see why it is out of the question. Surely it explains everything, if she killed her husband and then became remorseful."

Engelhart's fingers tightened on his glass. "Francesca did not commit suicide," he repeated stubbornly. "You forget that I spoke with her on the phone the day she died. She was eager to see me. She was even looking forward to going out with the Volpes. Women do not gas themselves immediately before a dinner engagement."

Pleuger, a pontifical man, did not enjoy having his theories punctured by his juniors. "Much may have happened after you spoke with her. Perhaps evidence of her crime was coming to light."

"As for Francesca killing anybody, that is absurd. She could not even bring herself to believe that her husband planned his own kidnapping."

As Herr Pleuger was looking alarmingly apoplectic,

Thatcher interceded. "It's not as if the police were devoting themselves exclusively to Engelhart. Naturally they link both Wylie deaths together, which makes them suspicious of everybody who was first in Houston, then in London. They're asking quite a lot of people for alibis, including Trinkam here."

"They sure are," Charlie said feelingly. "I'll bet that Engelhart and I didn't get much of a workout compared to the Macklin boys. Hell, Paul Volpe tells me that they took him through his trip back to the hotel with a stopwatch. And they still don't like the fact that he was twenty-five minutes late."

"I am sure that what you say is true and that Macklin is enduring much annoyance. But—" and Pleuger came at last to his real grievance "—they can console themselves with the knowledge that they profited from their association with Davidson Wylie."

Leopold Grimm could not let this pass. The memory of his travail in Zurich was still an open wound. The proverbial salt was supplied by the knowledge that he and Thatcher had played their puppet roles in response to a chimera.

"Mr. Wylie embezzled a million and a half dollars from them," he said in unforgiving tones.

"What is a paltry million and a half dollars?" Pleuger asked magnificently. "He got them the Noss Head contract, didn't he? No matter what your calculations, Macklin remains a gainer."

As his resentful gaze rested on his subordinate, his thoughts were obvious. Should Scotland Yard sweep Klaus Engelhart far from the haunts of man, he would leave no such golden legacy for NDW.

Goaded, Engelhart retreated to his time-hallowed contention. "If Wylie had not been kidnapped, NDW would have gotten that contract."

"What the hell," said Charlie cheerfully. "You win some, you lose some. There are a lot of big outfits playing the oil game."

"I am not so unreasonable as to expect to win all major construction bids," said Pleuger, lying in his teeth. "I merely expect intelligence from the field that is accurate enough to permit NDW some advance planning on a rational basis."

So that was Engelhart's crime, thought Thatcher. He had failed to forecast the outcome.

"Am I expected to anticipate mock-terrorist outrages?" Engelhart was addressing the heavens, rather than Pleuger. "Who would have expected the British to bend over backward merely because of some obscure fellow feeling? So they have had their IRA experiences. We have had Munich."

Pleuger was icy. "It was not necessary to predict, only to recognize!"

Thatcher was beginning to understand why Grimm had been so eager to leaven his little band with newcomers. Fortunately, Pleuger waved aside the suggestion of a second round, announcing that he and Engelhart were due to study a Norwegian invitation for bids.

"Now, more imperative than ever. Perhaps in Oslo there will be no inducement to foolish optimism," he declaimed, sweeping his employee along in his wake.

As Grimm, too, decided that it was time to retire, he paused for a last aside. "You must not judge Herr Pleuger by this evening," he said to Thatcher. "NDW had been hoping to arrange certain financial accommodations with Union Suisse—which we would have been happy to provide to the prime contractor for Noss Head. However, it has been my unhappy duty to inform Pleuger that NDW would be well-advised to defer its plans for the present. Under the circumstances, a certain amount of nervous irritability is only to be expected. I am sure you meet with this situation at the Sloan."

"We understand," Thatcher assured him gravely.

There had, indeed, been many unfortunate experiences with this kind of nervous irritability at the Sloan. Now the room reserved for breaking the bad news was stripped of throwable objects and furnished with a powerful pneumatic door-closer.

Charlie waited only long enough for their recent

companions to move out of earshot. "Well, Engelhart sure isn't NDW's boy wonder anymore, is he?"

"Fair's fair," Thatcher countered. "Engelhart himself seems baffled by his failure to sell the British."

Charlie was unimpressed. "He's got to say something with Pleuger chipping away at him. After all, he's getting it on all sides. Pleuger isn't crazy about his choice of girlfriends, either."

"I think it's a little more than that."

"I know, I know. The police probably wonder if Francesca and Klaus didn't team up to do a job on Wylie, and then Klaus decided to go it alone. Pleuger doesn't care for that kind of image in his marketing manager. I don't know that I blame him."

But Thatcher was not thinking about NDW's personnel policies. "Has it occurred to you that all the theories we've heard about these crimes involve some falling out among co-conspirators? First there was talk of some unknown paramour turning on Wylie, then it was his wife, and now Engelhart and Mrs. Wylie are supposed to have united in killing Wylie, only to divide thereafter very rapidly."

"As a matter of fact, I've been thinking about it ever since I ran into the Volpes. They're still on the unknown-girlfriend kick. Paul doesn't understand why the girl should split off once they'd salted away their million and a half. Betsy doesn't go along. She's really got her knife into the late departed Dave Wylie and thinks it's natural anyone would want to get away from him. But, let's face it, Betsy's a nice healthy girl who hasn't had much experience with million-dollar deals."

"Exactly."

In the banking business it is axiomatic that elaborate contracts are superfluous except when the venture in question sours. Successful partners can always iron out their difficulties.

"So we look for a scheme that was so unsuccessful it left the partners ready to lynch each other," Charlie postulated. "And the most unsuccessful operation lying around is NDW's bid on Noss Head."

Thatcher could feel his own imagination taking

flight. "Suppose, just suppose, that Engelhart approached Wylie with a proposition. First, he said, you make yourself indispensable to Macklin's presentation. Then I will arrange a fake kidnapping and all you have to do is remain passive. At the end of this charade, my company will have the business and you will have a million and a half dollars."

"And the beauty of it is the source of the money. Macklin gets its throat cut and foots the bill for the surgery."

"It would explain why Engelhart was so confident his bid would prevail."

Charlie decided to be counsel for the defense. "Engelhart could just be built that way."

"Even more, it would explain his bewildered resentment when the British went ahead and gave the contract to Macklin, anyway," Thatcher continued serenely. "You could say the kidnapping backfired by producing sympathy."

"You can think up other reasons for all that." Charlie waved away Klaus Engelhart's emotional responses. "What I like is that it ends up with two partners who really have something to fight about. Regardless of who was sitting on the money, there was bound to be trouble. Engelhart didn't get what he bargained for, and all those secondary contracts Wylie was trying to throw his way didn't satisfy him. And nine chances out of ten, Wylie didn't have his money, even though he'd done what he promised."

By now the two of them were no longer listening to each other. "Then there's Mrs. Wylie's conviction that this was not the sort of crime her husband would have conceived," Thatcher mused. "Perhaps Engelhart did all the thinking for him."

Charlie was remembering more details relayed through Betsy Volpe. "None of the expenses to set up the kidnapping went through Wylie's checkbook. Could be that good old Klaus was taking care of all that from Germany."

As befitted his seniority, Thatcher came out of the clouds first. "Wait a minute. There are a few unresolved questions still. Wylie reserved a room at that hotel in Greece for only two days. He didn't plan to be away for the Noss Head negotiations. That delay was introduced by his car accident."

"Maybe he was supposed to go on someplace else."

"No." Thatcher shook his head. "If he had planned to be away for three weeks, he would have had a story ready for Interpol. He wouldn't have had to improvise. Quite apart from the unknown woman in Zurich."

"A girl from Engelhart's office?" Charlie hazarded.

"Would you trust anyone on Pleuger's payroll to keep a secret from him? I wouldn't. And we haven't tackled the biggest problem of all—the money. Davidson Wylie didn't look like the kind of man to trust Engelhart. How could he have enforced payment after the kidnapping? The girl must have been *his* accomplice." Thatcher was regretful. "It's a shame. At first sight, the Engelhart theory seemed to explain so many inconsistencies."

Charlie never wasted time on vain regrets. Suddenly he laughed outright.

"Boy, the British must he wishing they'd never seen either Macklin or NDW. They were trying to run a nice, clean construction job, and look what they end up associating with. I can tell you one thing, we're not going to be overburdened with official hospitality on this trip. First, all those immaculate civil servants start running around with Dave Wylie, and they find out he's an embezzler. Then they've got to be having doubts about Engelhart. To top it off, a stuffed shirt like Simon Livermore asks Cramer into his home and, before he knows it, he's part of the guy's murder alibi. It looks like we're going to be eating a lot of hotel food, John."

Pleasant memories of ripe apricots and the Charleston came floating to the surface. "He's not all stuffed shirt," Thatcher corrected.

"You mean the lucious Jill?" Charlie accused with a grin. As usual, he had not let business interfere with a lively interest in passing female acquaintances. "You're going to have to get along without her, John.

She's giving the rainy season here a miss. And guess where she's gone."

"The South of France?" The minute he spoke Thatcher realized he was missing something.

"Baghdad! It seems Sheikh Yemeri's invitation was irresistible. Ah well," said Charlie tolerantly, "I'm glad somebody's getting some benefit out of this Noss Head deal."

Thatcher took a larger view. "Come, come," he objected. "Let's not forget a substantial supply of oil for Europe."

20 · Twin Gushers

Charlie Trinkam's pawky attitude to life and its concomitants was an after-hours affair. From nine to five he abided by the old-fashioned precept that the simplest way to undertake a task is to get right down to it.

When he arrived at Macklin's office the next morning, prepared to draft the final loan agreement, he had metaphorically rolled up his sleeves and sharpened his pencil. At first, the omens were propitious. Arthur Shute presented him with a private office, a private secretary, and the latest dictating equipment. He then rendered all these aids to productivity completely nugatory by refusing to leave.

"You're sure you've got everything you need?" he asked for the fifth time.

"Absolutely. I can lock myself in and start plugging away," Charlie said hopefully.

But Shute settled further into his chair and lit a pipe. "As soon as we finalize the paperwork, I propose moving forward with Noss Head and putting the Wylie deaths behind us."

"Then I'd better hop to it. I certainly don't want to hold up Noss Head."

Charlie had intended his words as a crowbar to pry Macklin's president from his resting place. Instead they transfixed him.

"I am glad to hear you agree with me," said Shute as if a great weight had been lifted from him. "After all, there can scarcely be any doubt that the important thing is the oil. From a social point of view, even from a humanitarian point of view, the sooner Europe gets it, the better."

"I'm all for more oil." Charlie had been victimized before by businessmen experiencing sudden moral qualms about the profit motive. To forestall turgid elaboration by Shute, he added: "Even if someone makes a buck out of it."

"Exactly," Shute beamed. "Understand, if corrective action were possible, I would be the first to insist on it. I am very mindful of the fact that Roberta Ore Simpson expected me to put a stop to these practices. But with Wylie dead, there is no alternative—except a futile washing of our dirty linen in public."

Charlie realized he had misjudged his man. Shute was merely following in John Thatcher's footsteps by theorizing that Engelhart had bribed Wylie to disappear for the Noss Head negotiations. And reminding Shute that Miss Simpson had intended to stop Macklin's employees from giving, rather than taking, bribes would be mere carping.

"You may find a couple of flaws in your idea if you look further," he remarked. "Have you talked this over with Cramer?"

"I tried to," answered Shute plaintively, making it all too clear why he was reduced to seeking solace from an outsider. "Of course, Hugo agrees with me, but nothing will get him to admit it. He simply blows up when I ask him to consider the facts. Naturally, he feels he's under the gun because he's the one who hired Wylie. But nobody could possibly blame him for failing to foresee what happened."

So much for shoving Arthur Shute out of this office

and into Cramer's. Ostentatiously Charlie began feeding a new reel of tape into his recorder. "Maybe that's not what he's worried about. Maybe Hugo simply doesn't go along with you."

"Nonsense!" Blind to all evidence of activity, Shute leaned forward earnestly. "Just listen to what he proposes. Instead of giving Paul Volpe full authority in Europe, Hugo thinks we should both stay over here to keep an eye on Noss Head. That is simply absurd. I have to get back to Houston, and very soon Hugo will, too. On top of that, he insists we get rid of Engelhart. I admit that I'd be happy to see the last of NDW under the circumstances. But it's foolish to rock the boat. Particularly when everything has turned out so well."

This blatant display of egocentricity penetrated Charlie's glaze of boredom. Macklin had its contract. Macklin's black sheep, together with his ill-gotten gains, had disappeared from the stage. So everything was fine.

"Not from Engelhart's point of view," he felt obliged to remonstrate.

Shute stared. "I don't see why not. He got what he wanted."

"How's that again?"

But Shute was talking to clarify his own doubts, not to dispel the confusion of others. "And while I may concede Engelhart's mercenary guilt, I refuse to go further. I can tell that Hugo is playing with some wild fancies for which there is no foundation whatsoever. Why does he insist on looking for trouble? It's not as if we didn't have a perfectly good explanation at hand. Mrs. Wylie was part of the plot from the beginning. She killed her husband, thinking that would clear the way to over a million dollars. When it didn't, she became depressed and killed herself."

At the beginning of his speech, Arthur Shute had been feeling his way from word to word. By the end, his voice was ringing with conviction.

"I remember your trying to sell that one the other night to Livermore. It didn't go over with a bang."

"That was different. I didn't understand what was

going on, then." Shute was undismayed. "It's been a real help, thrashing this out with you, Charlie. And it's a relief to know that you see it my way. When I came in here, I wasn't really certain in my own mind. After all, you can be ninety percent convinced of something, and still welcome another person's opinion. Especially when it's someone whose judgment you respect. I can truthfully say that I value give-and-take before coming to a decision. But now that I know you agree with my policy, I can regard the whole thing as settled." At last he was rising from his chair and heading for the door.

"Any time, Arthur," Charlie growled, turning on his recorder and beginning to dictate at top volume in order to discourage any postscripts.

Charlie should have finished his draft by noon. Thanks to Macklin's president, he was late. Fortunately a patch of unusually free-flowing thought compensated for most of the damage. As a result, by one o'clock, he had not only corrected the typescript, he had even had time to diagnose why he and Arthur Shute had been at cross-purposes. Mellowed by these twin victories, he accepted Paul Volpe's luncheon invitation. He was halfway through his tankard of ale before he noticed that his companion did not share his sense of well-being.

"Nobody lets me alone," Volpe answered, upon being challenged.

"It doesn't seem to be their strong point."

"Macklin's bad enough, but now Betsy's gone crazy. You remember all that business about going to have tea with Francesca and trying to pump her?"

Charlie nodded. "Sure, you were there when she was telling me."

"Well, that wasn't enough for Betsy. When she found out the police hadn't uncovered a clue to the money in Dave's apartment, she decided to have a stab at his office. So she called the switchboard and told them she was coming in to see if the office needed any redecorating for me. While she was there, she went through the drawers and the file cabinet and everything else she could find. Of course, she didn't come up with a thing."

"So what's the big deal?" Charlie asked. "Does Betsy want a million dollars to become one of the beautiful people?"

Paul Volpe refused to be flippant. "No, that's not it. But she's got this bee in her bonnet about how I ought to have Dave's job. When Hugo only came through with a watered-down version, she was burned up. All right, so I was burned up, too. But Betsy has to have a brainstorm. She figures that if I can help Macklin recover its money, they'll promote me out of gratitude. Why the hell can't she leave it to me? I can manage a promotion without digging up any buried treasure. On top of that, I finally got it out of her why she's always poormouthing Dave. You'll never guess why!"

"I won't?" asked Charlie, confident he already knew.

"It seems Dave made a pass at her the first time he visited us in Rome. And Betsy's still steamed up about it."

Paul thought he was retailing wildly improbable behavior, but in the face of Charlie's lack of response, he became defensive. "I thought women were supposed to be flattered by that sort of thing. I know damn well that when one of those Italian counts propositioned Betsy, she giggled about it for days."

Charlie Trinkam knew that women untouched by a suitor may regard him kindly. A wife whose loyalty to her husband is threatened—however momentarily—is likely to blame her tempter. And the stronger her marital affection, the more unforgiving her reaction. But he had no intention of exposing Paul Volpe to these depths.

"I'll bet her count was a passing acquaintance," he said carefully. "But Dave Wylie was supposed to be your friend. Betsy didn't like his trying to seduce her behind your back."

"That's what Betsy said," Volpe confessed, proving that great minds think alike. "Anyway, I wish she'd stop telling me how much better I'll be at the job than Dave was. Particularly when Hugo Cramer has got different ideas."

"What makes you think that?"

Volpe frowned. "He's another one who won't let me alone. You've seen how it is with Klaus Engelhart. Every time I'm getting somewhere with Klaus, Hugo comes busting in and makes things ten times worse. There's nothing wrong with Klaus. He may be a little stiff and formal, but there are thousands of guys like that in France and Italy. But for some reason, Hugo thinks I'm so wet behind the ears I'm going to let Klaus steal the pants off me."

Charlie was beginning to feel sorry for Paul Volpe. Unless the brass at Macklin broke down and opened some internal lines of communication, the misconceptions flying around were going to be compounded.

"Poor old Hugo probably has something altogether different in mind," he said.

"Oh yeah? He may be poor old Hugo to you, but he's my boss. And he's not going to like this latest end-run by Shute. Nine chances out of ten, he'll think I engineered the whole thing." Given these sentiments, Paul Volpe did not sound half as downcast as he should have.

"What end-run?" Charlie asked curiously. "Arthur Shute has been a busy little man this morning."

"There's no reason I shouldn't tell you. It's going to be public tomorrow." The grin that had been controlled so long finally surfaced. "An hour ago Shute gave me Dave's job—the whole shebang. But don't think it was a normal operation. Honest to God, you would have thought he was trying to hire me away from another company, he was so nervous about it. He's breaking the news to Hugo over a steak. And he was full of hot air about how I'd stood by Macklin in the past and he knew I'd do it in the future."

"Son of a gun!" said Charlie to himself.

"On top of that, he's giving me a bigger salary than he gave Dave. Do you have any idea what's going on?"

"He's paying you to keep your mouth shut."

The grin died a rapid death. "What's that supposed to mean?" Volpe demanded with a face of stone.

"Nothing to get uptight about," Charlie reassured him. "Shute is scared that you spotted something or you will, and he wants to be sure it gets swept under the rug."

"I don't know what the hell you're talking about."

"Just that your esteemed president has convinced himself that Davidson Wylie bribed Engelhart to throw the Noss Head contest. And Shute is perfectly willing to kiss his million and a half good-bye, to keep it under wraps."

Volpe shook his head like a swimmer battling heavy seas. "But that's plain crazy. You've heard Klaus. He expected to get Noss Head, and he still doesn't understand why he didn't. You can't shut him up on the subject."

"Sure. But that's exactly what he would say, if Shute's little pipedream is true."

Volpe waved aside the objection. "Look, you weren't here. Klaus busted his ass for NDW. You've gotten the wrong idea from seeing him and Hugo strike sparks off each other. Klaus made it a race right down to the wire."

Charlie Trinkam examined the younger man curiously. "You've got plenty to say about Engelhart's probity. I don't notice you rushing to Davidson Wylie's defense."

"Dave?" Paul Volpe rasped a hand along his chin ruminatively. At last he said: "If you want to know, I can see Dave pulling a stunt like this easier than I can see him stealing the dough for himself. In fact, it would be right up his alley. Dave was a real schemer. And this way he'd be forcing Macklin to pay a whopping bribe, without the controller's office knowing what he was up to."

"He'd be doing more than that," reasoned Charlie, yielding to technical enthusiasm. "By staging a big public kidnapping he'd be forestalling any questions from the IRS or the SEC about the payment. They'd think it was a legitimate ransom. Hell, Macklin would get its tax writeoff without a quibble."

Paul Volpe was an engineer. He was necessarily familiar with tax deductions, but he was not overcome by their beauty.

"I still say it's a lot of horse water. Klaus made the most of Dave's disappearance, and plenty of people were surprised that Hugo managed to pull Noss Head out of the bag. Besides, I suppose Shute doesn't stop with bribery. He must think Klaus killed Dave when it looked as if he might talk."

"Not on your life!" Charlie chuckled. "That is most emphatically what Shute does *not* want people believing. How could he justify his inaction? Shute's got Francesca figured for the bloodstained villain. She's supposed to have murdered Wylie, thinking she could latch onto Klaus and all his shekels. When Klaus didn't see it that way, she had nothing to look forward to but the police closing in."

For once, Volpe did not reject his president's theorizing out of hand. "That's the only part of this rigmarole that makes sense. If Dave was cooking up something with Klaus, he'd need a middleman. Dave could spend all the time in the world with the Department of Energy people, because he was selling them something. But he didn't have any excuse to hobnob with the competition. He could've pretended to split from Francesca so she could set up the details. I suppose if she saw enough of Klaus, she could have persuaded herself she had him hooked."

Charlie remembered the titian hair, the ripe charms, the assured manner. "She didn't look to me as if she was still making elementary mistakes. I wish I'd gotten to know the late Mrs. Wylie a little better," he said regretfully. "There is just so much to be learned from bumping into a lady at a motel."

"Well, there's no point in asking me. I don't even understand Betsy." Volpe spread his hands wide. "I've

213

got to admit it. I don't know the first thing about women."

Charlie could not keep a certain measure of self-satisfaction from his voice.

"It's a subject that repays study," he recommended.

21 · Capping the Well

John Thatcher, meanwhile, was touching home base.

"Mr. Thatcher, you don't shop at a store called Free Wheeling, do you? It's on Eighth Avenue," Miss Corsa asked during a pause.

Eighth Avenue had very little meaning for Thatcher in New York, and none at all in London. "No," he said absently. "Now, once you've told Kendrick to revise the option clauses—"

"I didn't think so," Miss Corsa congratulated herself.

"I beg your pardon?" said Thatcher. A Miss Corsa who interrupted was a Miss Corsa gripped by strong emotion.

"Nine hundred and seventy-two dollars," she said, giving the full dimensions of some enormity.

"A tidy sum," he agreed, fleshing out these bare bones. "Who is charging me nine hundred and seventy-two dollars—and for what?"

This was no leap in the dark. Miss Corsa not only double-checked his bills, she double-checked his monthly statements from the Sloan Guaranty Trust.

"Wait a minute," he corrected himself as his numerate faculty stirred. "My grandson's birthday! That's it. Somehow, one bicycle led to another."

"And all of them ten-speed," said Miss Corsa dispassionately.

Whether this was a criticism of grandparents or bicycles, Thatcher did not care to inquire. "At any rate, nobody has run amok with one of my credit cards," he said lightly.

Miss Corsa, who believed that eternal vigilance is the price of everything, preferred to treat the subject seriously or not at all.

"After Mr. Kendrick revises the option clauses?"

Thatcher finished Kendrick, approved several letters going out over his signature, and dictated a memorandum for the Investment Committee.

"And that should take care of it," he said, ticking off the last item on his list. "I'll be calling tomorrow morning."

But the Sloan also had a list. "Mr. Lancer wants to talk to you," said Miss Corsa. "He says that it is urgent. And Mr. Bowman, too."

Thatcher had relaxed prematurely. He continued doing so until it became evident that Miss Corsa herself wanted a word.

"Do you know when you will be returning to the Sloan?"

"I'm still not altogether sure," said Thatcher. "With luck I may be able to finish here by the end of the week. If so, I'll fly to New York and leave Trinkam to do the signing. I can take care of the tickets at this end."

There was a slight hesitation, the significance of which eluded him. But Miss Corsa did not let Mr. Elliman color her response.

"Fine, Mr. Thatcher."

"I assume Lancer wants to talk about Macklin?" Thatcher asked, as if it were not inevitable.

"He did say it was urgent," she repeated, before unbending. "I do know that he has been in conference with Miss Simpson."

"Tell him I'll call back later, and put me through to Bowman," said Thatcher decisively.

Postponing the Macklin Board of Directors did not postpone Macklin for any appreciable time.

"John," Bowman came on the line. "How's the weather over there?"

"Raining," said Thatcher briefly, reflecting on the rich variety of atavism lurking at the Sloan. Miss Corsa feared evil spirits inhabiting computers. Walter Bowman, who spent nine-tenths of his time on the phone, insisted on horse-and-buggy niceties.

Thatcher was not paying transatlantic rates to find out if it was raining in New York. "What's on your mind, Walter?" he prodded.

"Macklin," said Bowman succinctly. "John, the papers here are having a field day with these murders of yours."

Thatcher ignored the attribution. Bowman had not flagged him down for ponderous whimsies or idle curiosity.

"It set me thinking," Bowman proceeded. "Macklin closed off a fraction yesterday. But on the whole, it's been holding up pretty well, considering what's happening to the averages. But if they fumble Noss Head, I have a hunch that there could be a slide. Not that we have a helluva lot. But if you've heard anything, we'd better take steps."

Thatcher contemplated this shorthand.

"As yet, there are no solid indications that Macklin has been compromised here," he said. "True, there is enough uncertainty to cut with a knife, but it is being kept out of official channels. Or, at least, out of some official channels. The Department of Energy is pushing ahead with our financing discussions as if the police were not out in full force. The British are eager to get Noss Head into production and so is Macklin." Finishing his own analysis, he went on: "Is the market saying something else?"

Right or wrong, market opinion was always worth a hearing. Management weighed everything it could see; the market examined management, too.

"I'm not sure," said Bowman. "Right now, my guess is that everybody's been shaken up by the headlines. But if Noss Head proceeds according to schedule, the worry will die down. Of course, any more bombshells—"

"In the context of recent happenings," said Thatcher, "that is an unfortunate metaphor."

"What's that? Oh, you mean down in Houston?" Bowman jogged his memory. "Hell, Wylie was good riddance to everybody. I don't know about the wife, though. Well, if you hear anything, pass it along."

This specialist attitude was not heartlessness, Thatcher reflected. Bowman simply had another way to look at Macklin.

Thatcher himself was going to improve on it—by not looking at Macklin at all. He consulted his watch. Thanks to ducking George, he had finished with the Sloan earlier than expected. His next appointment was not until late in the afternoon.

Between Miss Corsa and equipment leasebacks, a stretch of free time beckoned.

Thatcher decided to fill it profitably at the National Gallery.

But before he got to the portrait of Oliver Cromwell, Charlie Trinkam—warts and all—caught him.

"John, are you sitting in at British Petroleum this afternoon?" he asked, overtaking Thatcher at the curb.

"I have another engagement," said Thatcher, shamelessly.

Charlie was preoccupied. "Hell!" he said, as a cab pulled up. "I wanted to get you before I forget the gory details. But I'm late for MacFarquar already."

Hardened by his recent exposure to the Sloan, Thatcher would have gone his way if Charlie had not added: "Either Shute's crazier than a coot, or there's something rotten in Denmark."

"Something New York will hear about?" Thatcher asked, mindful that rumors do not stop at the water's edge.

"If they do, we're in for some real fun."

Thatcher's conscience got the better of him. "Come on. I'll drop you off. You've got until we reach BP."

London taxis are notoriously comfortable and ample, but London traffic is notorious, too. Charlie had time to spare for a report of his morning's haul.

"You may not believe it, but you're attracted by Shute's theory," Thatcher accused as they crawled along.

"Well, you've got to admit it's a beautiful wrinkle," Charlie countered. "Oh, Volpe must be right that Engelhart didn't take a dive. But what a sweet way to make a payoff. I'll tell you one thing, I'm revising my opinion of our pal Shute."

"Upward or downward?" Thatcher asked dryly.

Charlie replied with cheerful amorality. "It's too early to say. I have to wait until I know if Shute is just pretending to overlook the practical difficulties."

"There certainly are plenty of them," said Thatcher. "Klaus Engelhart could not deliver Noss Head to Macklin. In the first place, the NDW performance was so good that everybody was surprised when Macklin edged them out. Engelhart may be clever, but I refuse to believe he would risk such fine tuning. Furthermore, I think he is on a tight rein. Pleuger was not giving him much room to maneuver."

"And there was no way to buy off NDW," Charlie said, just as they pulled up to British Petroleum. He was too busy struggling with his umbrella to notice that Thatcher was reaching quite another conclusion.

Thatcher was barely conscious of his departure.

"Where to?"

"Trafalgar Square," said Thatcher, rousing himself, although second thoughts convinced him that the National Gallery was receding steadily. Right now, words were worth a thousand pictures. Cavemen may have painted walls, but they told stories around the campfire first.

Thatcher lacked the campfire. But he was beginning to think he had the ingredients of a story.

Start with some definitions by that grizzled hunter, Walter Bowman. Throw in Arthur Shute, trying to appease the forces of darkness. And for chorus, you could add Roberta Ore Simpson.

If it was not an epic, it was a damned good cautionary tale, Thatcher thought, debarking at his destination. Heedless of the rain, of clouds of pigeons, of bustling shoppers, students and tourists, he began to stroll around the fountain. The moral of this particular fable was too simple to miss. But, as he turned his back on the National Gallery, it occurred to him that his source materials had to be similarly obvious. His bards, after all, were twentieth-century Americans. Their omens and portents came from tax returns, not solar eclipses. Expense accounts and ledgers had replaced the entrails of a cockerel long ago.

If you interpreted Macklin's drama in terms of standard operating procedure rather than poetic license, what did you have?

An accounting record for the costs of a crime . . .

A passport revealing two trips to Zurich . . .

A long-distance call originating from the wrong telephone . . .

"Good Lord," he said, stopping short to the peril of two sari-clad women behind him. Barring the car crash, which was an act of God, and the murders, which were acts of desperation, this was the one perfect crime for an otherwise honest man. The rewards were great and the risks were minimal.

Abruptly, Miss Corsa rose to haunt him. To her, there was no such thing as a minimal risk or an unnecessary precaution. If she had arranged that kidnapping in Istanbul . . .

One unnecessary precaution would be enough. Thatcher was in the mood to gamble on a long shot. Narrowly escaping injury, he plunged across traffic, forgetting to look to the right as he headed for a taxi.

"Yes," he agreed with the driver, "it does take an American a while to get used to looking in the opposite direction. But I think I've got the hang of it now."

It was a curiously apposite remark.

His subsequent exertions touched off three fruitful conversations.

In Istanbul, Captain Harbak was bemused.

". . . no, while we looked at everything else, we did not look at that. If you are correct, it will be small consolation that Houston also erred. But it will take a moment. . . . Pezmoglu, bring me the copy of the ransom note. . . ."

In London, an hour later, Herr Leopold Grimm examined his surroundings with dismay.

". . . naturally, every effort to apprehend these criminals. However, I must tell you that such a place as this, with pictures of naked women wherever one looks, does not fill me with confidence."

In Grosvenor Square, good old Endicott Forbes was himself.

". . . anything the embassy can do to help. Interpol? Oh, I'm sure somebody here knows how to get in touch with them."

By the time John Thatcher reached Imperial Dominion the next morning he had labored long and hard. Entering the conference room late, he discovered that he was not the only delinquent.

Charlie, already sitting next to Paul Volpe, looked up to greet him. Then, in an undertone, he said: "What have you been up to, John?"

"Quite a lot," said Thatcher with truth.

"You look like the cat who swallowed the canary."

"I hope not," said Thatcher. But he had no regrets, either. The mechanics of problem solving were always exhilarating. Murder did not make them any less so.

Unfortunately the future was going to be filled with painful debris. Intensive salvage efforts would take care of the corporate damage. But there was no such remedy for the personal tragedy of a man who had stumbled blindly from one crime to another, until he found himself a double murderer.

To be forewarned is not always to be forearmed. Thatcher had made one miscalculation by underestimating the speed of the forces he had set in motion.

"Boy," said Hugo Cramer heavily, "will I be glad when you experts hammer out all your numbers. I'm fed up with all this talk. I want to get back to work."

With an oblique look at MacFarquar and Nicholas, across the table, Arthur Shute bantered clumsily. "You're more at home in the field, aren't you, Hugo?"

"It depends on the field," said Cramer unhelpfully. "Look, what are we waiting for? I've been here for half an hour."

"We're waiting for Livermore," said Volpe wearily. "You know that, Hugo."

"Well, why the hell don't we start without him?" Cramer rumbled, flushing a confused babble of explanation from the English and advice from Charlie.

"Relax, Hugo," he said. "A few minutes one way or another—"

"Yes," Shute broke in: "Where is Livermore? Paul, why don't you go call his office and make sure he hasn't forgotten."

"Oh, I don't think—" Nicholas began.

"Yeah, Paul, go on," said Cramer crudely.

Volpe got up and smiled unhappily at Nicholas. "All right if I use your phone?"

"Yes, of course."

When Volpe left, complete silence descended. No one ventured any small talk. Since Francesca Wylie's death, any attempt to simulate normalcy foundered on what was said, and what was not said.

"Perhaps we should start considering these investment credits," Thatcher said, to dispel the general embarrassment.

"Yes," said MacFarquar eagerly. "We can sketch it in. Then, when he gets here, Simon can give us the department estimates."

"Great," said Hugo sarcastically. "We sit here and work our butts off, then we do it all over again when Livermore gets here."

"For God's sake, Hugo," protested Shute.

Just then, Paul Volpe returned, his face drawn.

"Did you get Simon?" MarFarquar asked, happy to abandon Cramer.

Paul Volpe might have been reciting a schoolboy poem. "They've arrested him at Heathrow. He was on his way out of the country—and they arrested him."

This time it was shock that stilled the room.

Then, like a storm bursting, their voices began battering against each other with questions that had no answer.

And quietly, two large men pushed Paul Volpe to one side and advanced on the table.

"Hugo Cramer? I have here a warrant for your arrest . . ."

22 · Refining the Crude

"So Hugo Cramer was the SOB behind everything," Norris Upton marveled. "To think I've known that guy for years and I never figured him to run around Houston bombing cars."

"And some British civil servant was involved, too, wasn't he?" George Lancer mumbled without lifting his eyes from the ornate menu.

"Surely it would be preferable to allow John to tell his tale in an orderly manner." The words were those of Roberta Ore Simpson, but the tone—mellow, benign, non-censorious—was not.

If Thatcher had been surprised that his report to Macklin's outside directors was taking place in an uptown New York restaurant, he was even more surprised at the extent of the report they required. To all appearances, even the newspaper accounts had passed them by.

It took him some time to realize that vintage wines, out-of-season asparagus, and rack of lamb represented a song of triumph that had nothing to do with Macklin. While he had been gallivanting around the British

Isles, his companions had been fighting on other fronts. For example, Miss Simpson, on a flying trip back to campus in Michigan, had uncovered an audacious coup in the making. Faculty, students, deans, and alumni were conniving to replace her with a twenty-two-year-old husband-and-wife team. Defeating this unnatural alliance and its appalling standard bearers had been an invigorating but time-consuming interlude. The foes of Norris Upton sprang from an older tradition. By the skin of his teeth, he had retained control of Upton Enterprises against the combined attack of his two sons. It had been a ferocious proxy battle—even by department-store standards. True to form, George C. Lancer had not been a combatant, only a mediator. He had been sucked into New York City's latest fiscal crisis, to emerge a sadder but wiser man.

Naturally the absence of juvenile intellectuals, voracious offspring, and His Honor, the Mayor, encouraged an atmosphere of euphoria. No man could have asked for a better audience.

"Thatcher can do it any way he wants," Upton said, holding a wine bottle to the light. "Here, son! Another one of these."

The speed with which the order was filled gave Thatcher pause for thought. It was axiomatic that every busboy in New York could distinguish Savile Row tailoring from Brooks Brothers. But were the personnel of La Garonne also connoisseurs of Stetsons, boots, and silver trappings? Could they tell at a glance if they were dealing with off-the-rack buckskins? Thatcher decided they probably could. After all, everyone at the Sloan knew that the real money these days was in the Sunbelt states. The headwaiters of this world are never far behind its bankers.

George Lancer had finally decided that hothouse strawberries were worthy of the occasion. Setting aside his menu, he said mildly, "Yes, but first John has to tell me what was really going on. You mean Dave Wylie wasn't stealing for himself?"

"Precisely. What's more, we had Klaus Engelhart

constantly telling us that if there had been no kidnapping, Macklin would not have won the Noss Head bidding. He said the right words, but gave them the wrong interpretation."

"I fail to see how Mr. Engelhart's statement clarifies anything." For once, Roberta Ore Simpson did not sound like a college president. She was simply offering a neutral fact.

"Come now, Roberta," said Thatcher, taking the plunge into intimacy as he let the axe fall. "What if I rephrased his sentence and said that Macklin would not have gotten Noss Head if a million and a half dollars had not changed hands?"

It was a godsend for all of them that she had her recent victory to sustain her as the implications of his words sank home. She was almost bereft of speech. "A Lockheed payoff," she whispered hoarsely.

Thatcher bowed his head in silent assent.

Norris Upton's views on bribery were, to say the least, a good deal more flexible. But he liked to see the thing done right—no publicity, no bombings, no Scotland Yard arrests.

"For God's sake!" he demanded. "Why do it in front of television cameras?"

"Because that was an integral element of the plan. Let me start at the beginning," Thatcher suggested. "When the Noss Head job was first announced, Wylie realized that it was his big chance. He immediately went to work. He became familiar with the customers, he fed information back to Houston, he nagged Cramer into producing a Macklin bid that was a virtual replica of British needs. Inevitably he came to know Klaus Engelhart and the NDW bid. Engelhart was not ingratiating himself with anyone. He took the position that his offering was superior and the Department would be fools not to choose it. Wylie was a salesman pure and simple. Instead of realizing that Engelhart was suffering from youthful arrogance, he accepted this evaluation. Wylie could see his golden opportunity going up in smoke, unless he managed to fix the race. It was at this point that he redoubled his hospitality to the Department of Energy. He was no longer making friends; now he was looking for someone corruptible—and in Simon Livermore he found his man. But almost immediately, he ran into problems."

"I should hope so!" Miss Simpson grated.

"Mainly thanks to you," Thatcher said generously. "Hugo Cramer said the plan was impossible. There was no slush fund in existence. Arthur Shute would never authorize its creation, and the new accountants made it impossible to establish one on the sly. Nor were Wylie's difficulties confined to the payment end of the bribe. Simon Livermore was petrified with fear at the action he contemplated. Bribery is not a way of life in England—far from it. So Livermore's conditions were almost impossibly exigent. Nobody at Macklin except Wylie and Cramer was to know that there had been a bribe, let alone the identity of the recipient. There must be absolutely no paper record leading to him. The money had to be laundered and relaundered. Given all these obstacles, Wylie's grand plan seemed doomed to abortion. And then one day—no doubt after reading of a terrorist outrage in South America—he was visited by an inspiration. He could not only meet Hugo Cramer's objections, he could achieve a small miracle on the receiving end."

Norris Upton only saw half. "So he could fool Arthur Shute. But what did this do for Livermore?"

"Livermore insisted that there be absolutely no paper record, and that is not easy when you're talking about a million and a half dollars. Even the Watergate burglars were paid by check. Both Charlie Trinkam and I have spent our lives transferring funds from one place to another. But, as we lugged those briefcases in front of television cameras, neither one of us could remember ever doing it with cash before. For that matter, I doubt if there are any other circumstances in which Arthur Shute could have persuaded George to count out over a million dollars in small denominations—not without a lot of questions."

Lancer had not forgotten a single detail of that emotion-packed night. "I still asked a lot of questions," he recalled grimly. "Like why we couldn't use a bank credit. But every time I said anything, Cramer waved that ransom note at me."

"Well, believe me, by now he regrets he ever showed that note to the Sloan," said Thatcher, with a surge of satisfaction.

Lancer caught his meaning immediately. "Did the note help trip him up? Good, I'm glad."

"Yes, but I'll come to that in a minute. Right now I am emphasizing how well the fake kidnapping served Wylie's purpose. Until the money entered that numbered account, its movements were open to public inspection. But when it left on Jill Livermore's back and disappeared in the Zurich railroad station, there was a complete discontinuity in its paper record. Nobody could incriminate Simon Livermore by tracing the money. And after the Watergate and Lockheed investigations, that is the peril that preoccupies corrupt officials around the world."

Miss Simpson was nothing if not resilient. "I had not realized it was the man's wife who made the pickup," she said thoughtfully. "But surely that made them just as vulnerable as a laundered check would have. She would always be subject to identification."

"Livermore was afraid of evidence that might lead an investigator to him. It never occurred to him that someone would first suspect him and then go looking for proof," Thatcher argued. "As for the danger inherent in Jill's role, Davidson Wylie managed to factor that into his game plan. You see, Livermore insisted that he be paid before throwing the contract to Macklin. Quite naturally, as he would have had no recourse if payment had not been forthcoming thereafter. But Wylie, in his turn, wanted some hold over the Livermores to ensure compliance after the money was out of reach—and Jill's involvement gave him exactly what he needed."

George Lancer was shaking his head as if he could scarcely believe what he was hearing. "It all sounds so simple the way you put it," he complained. "Wylie stages his charade in Istanbul, Cramer sees to it that the ransom is paid into the numbered account, the Livermores pick up the money and there you are."

"Yes, with the addition of a few details. Jill Livermore set up the numbered account months in advance. Wylie arranged his hideaway in Greece and then hired two drifters with criminal records for the scene in the Turkish restaurant. Even when these drifters realized they'd been part of a major embezzlement, they wouldn't risk a kidnapping sentence by pitting their word against Wylie's. And then all this carefully contrived simplicity fell apart because of a car crash."

Thus far Norris Upton had been content to let his co-directors do most of the talking. Clearly his famous tolerance of bribery was going to need a little rethinking. In the past he had stymied more than one opponent by asking: What harm does it really do? Now, instead of reaching for murky ethical precepts, they would merely say: Two murders.

With a wary eye on Miss Simpson, Upton cautiously asked his question. "Why did everything fall apart after Wylie's accident? Even if their schedule was fouled up, the scheme had worked. So what difference did it make?"

Thatcher might have been reading his mind. "Quite a lot. The seeds for two murders were planted when Wylie skidded on that Greek road. The plan called for Jill Livermore to pick up the money and jet out of Zurich to Algeria. She reasoned that, if the Swiss police had followed her, they would never let her fly off to such a well-known terrorist haven. Once she was safely in North Africa, she rejoined her friends in Tangiers and called Wylie to give him the signal to reappear. He would produce his well-rehearsed tale of being blindfolded for thirty-six hours and proceed to London for the final round of the Noss Head negotiations. The whole operation would have been so swift and so slick that the principals could have forgotten it ever happened. Above all, they would have dealt with nobody except each other. Instead, look what happened. When Jill telephoned that Greek hotel, she was told that Wylie had never arrived. That was bad enough, but what should have been an overnight press sensation turned into a continuing drama. Livermore, who hoped to forget what he had done, was reminded of it every day—by television, by his fellow workers, by the other competitors for Noss Head. And then, on top of everything else, Cramer arrived in London."

"I suppose Livermore didn't like to be reminded that someone else was in the plot," Roberta Ore Simpson ventured.

"It was a good deal worse than that. Davidson Wylie had carved a genuine niche for himself at the department. Everyone found him congenial to work with, everyone had been his guest, everyone was in the habit of having a drink with him. Given the fact that the NDW and Macklin bids were evenly balanced, Livermore anticipated no surprise when the award would go to Wylie. Suddenly Macklin was represented by a stranger who ruffled people and with whom Livermore had no excuse to associate. Indeed, at their first meeting, Livermore had to assure Cramer he was going through with his part of the bargain, in front of a witness. By the time the award was finally made, everybody was astonished at Macklin's victory and both men were too nervous for safety. Cramer had already been stampeded into leaking a news item and sending himself a second ransom note. He was, of course, preparing to lay the blame for Wylie's continued absence at Engelhart's door. In many ways that cruel heat wave in London was a blessing to the conspirators. When we stopped over, Charlie Trinkam took one look and said that Livermore was so distracted he didn't know what he was doing. But with the entire English contingent wilting, that was not so remarkable."

Even Norris Upton was put off by this tale of botched timetables and lily-livered conspirators. "All right, Livermore didn't like pulling off this rope trick under a spotlight, But, as soon as Wylie turned up, everything was hunky-dory as far as Macklin was concerned."

"I am sorry to say that you and Cramer seem to think a good deal alike," Thatcher said dryly. "When he charged off to Ankara and found out about Wylie's accident, Cramer reacted with instinctive efficiency. He twisted everything that was said into an attack on Wylie's mental stability. At the time, he was inspired only by a desire to divert attention from Wylie's physical condition. When Davidson Wylie moved from that beach cottage to the Tidewater, he could plunge into a public swimming pool without his scars rousing curiosity. That was enough to satisfy Cramer."

If George Lancer had a fault, it was meeting trouble halfway. He could scarcely credit Hugo Cramer's insouciance. "But when he learned that Interpol was following them to Houston to find out about those missing three weeks, surely he must have started to worry then," he protested.

"Not really. Cramer has a tough hide and, if it had been him at the end of all those questions, he would have bluffed the whole thing through. It wouldn't have bothered him one single bit to have the police suspicious so long as they couldn't prove anything. But Wylie couldn't stand that kind of pressure. He suffered from the salesman's constitutional desire to be liked,"

Miss Simpson thought she had spied a weak spot. "If the man wanted to be liked, surely the last thing he would do is confess."

"You may find this hard to believe, Roberta," Thatcher said sympathetically, "but Davidson Wylie did not think he had done anything wrong. To his mind, he had simply evaded some pettifogging regulations so that Macklin money could be spent in Macklin's interest. He was genuinely horrified when it dawned on him that Interpol suspected him of diverting that money to his own use. Why, that would have made him a criminal! He wanted to clear up the misunderstanding. And, in order to appear as attractive as possible, he probably would have passed himself off as a zealous young man misled into exaggerated loyalty by a corrupt superior. I can almost see him doing it with that overdone earnest helpfulness."

"There's a word for that kind of behavior," Norris Upton pointed out.

"Yes," Thatcher agreed, "particularly when you consider the different consequences for the two men. Wylie was a virtual newcomer to Macklin. There was nothing to prevent him continuing his career in some other field. But Cramer's entire life had been Macklin, and he was now only one step removed from the top. Quite apart from the real possibility of criminal charges. When he saw the effect on Wylie of one round of Interpol questioning, he decided not to wait for the second."

"I suppose you could say that it was clever of him to use a bomb," Miss Simpson said with grudging appreciation. "That way, Cramer not only reinforced the terrorist motif, but he inflicted widespread damage on Wylie's body."

This point had not previously occurred to Upton who immediately subjected it to a critique all his own. "The damn fool should have known better than to rely on dynamite. If it had been me, I would have taken Wylie out into the middle of the Gulf on my cruiser and given him the old heave-ho."

It was too much to expect Roberta to break the habit of a lifetime and start admiring exercises in criminal ingenuity. Thatcher hastened into speech before she could deliver a blast. "Certainly the postmortem was a disappointment to Cramer," he said tactfully. "He had already done some spadework by telling Charlie that Wylie was terrified of his kidnappers. Now all Cramer could do was publicly bewail his folly in allowing Wylie to manipulate him."

"I don't see that he was so badly off." George Lancer hesitated for a moment before continuing. "Everyone decided that Wylie had been after the ransom for himself and a partner. Arthur Shute was following the police investigation closely, and he told me, in confidence, that the only serious suspect at Macklin was young Volpe. So I—"

But his fellow directors had both erupted into speech.

"I'll bet Shute didn't tell you if he was a suspect," Upton snapped.

"Why should Arthur Shute take you into his confidence, rather than me?" Roberta asked severely.

Lancer refused to be diverted. He continued to plow straight ahead. "So Hugo Cramer was still in a strong position. And what I want to know, John, is how you figured out he was the murderer."

"Mainly because of Francesca Wylie. She noticed a number of fallacies in the accepted view of her husband's activities and she kept mentioning them. I'm sorry to say that I did not take her objections seriously until after she was murdered. And I should have. After all, she was not a devoted wife saying that her David wouldn't do anything wrong. She was sufficiently disenchanted with him to divorce him, but she still had all the peculiar insights that a wife gains after years of marrage."

"Oh, for Christ's sake! That's what all these women claim. According to them, they can see right inside your skull. But what do they really know?"

Norris Upton was so heated that Thatcher felt a passing twinge of curiosity about Mrs. Upton. Nonetheless, he hurried on:

"I am not talking about sensitive perception, I am talking about money. A wife of any duration knows how her husband acts when he's feeling flush, how he acts when he's feeling poor, what his favorite petty economies are, what his extravagances are, and how far he will trust other people with his cash."

Norris Upton, caught with his mouth agape, paid this theory the tribute of silence. Roberta Ore Simpson cocked her head and apparently reviewed every married couple of her acquaintance. "On the whole, I am inclined to agree," she said at the conclusion of her deliberations.

Thatcher continued to punch home his argument. "Then look at the points that Francesca made the minute that suspicion centered on Davidson Wylie. First, she said that it was not his kind of money-making scheme. Second, fresh from a wrangle about real estate valuation, she said he was not feeling rich enough to stop trying to cheat her out of twenty thousand dollars. Finally she said that her husband would never, never have let a girlfriend hold the money. She felt so strongly about this last feature that she could even understand police distrust of her own role. In her view, a wife was the only woman who could reasonably have made the pickup. All of this was quite convincing, but Francesca did not add the last damning items until she was in London. Remember, she had been expecting machinations from Wylie on the property settlement, she had been keeping an eagle eye on his assets. Then after she had gone through his apartment and all his checkbooks, she arrived at two conclusions. Davidson Wylie had not paid the expenses for the fake kidnapping and, during the last months of his life, he had been thinking only of Noss Head and the approaching divorce. To her that meant one thing—Wylie had been acting as an employee. Unfortunately, when she tried to reach Arthur Shute, she got Hugo Cramer instead. Even worse, the second person she intended to confide in was Klaus Engelhart."

"Now, John," Lancer objected, "of course telling this all to Cramer was a fatal error. But why would going to Engelhart make it any worse?"

"Because the one person Cramer was afraid of was Engelhart. He would have preferred to have nothing to do with him. But Dave Wylie was convinced that NDW could be kept sweet with enough subcontracts. Nonetheless, every time Engelhart produced his famous sentence about Wylie's kidnapping being responsible for the Noss Head decision, he made Cramer's blood run cold. Basically, it was a character flaw that kept young Engelhart from divining the truth himself. He was contemptuous of the British for being sentimental about a human drama. He dismissed Francesca's stubbornness as unwillingness to recognize a younger woman in her husband's life. But Hugo Cramer knew full well that the day Francesca proved to Klaus there was Macklin involvement in the kidnapping, he would understand what had really happened. And if he was hell-bent on finding an older man in the toils of a young girl, he only had to look as far as Simon and Jill Livermore."

George Lancer liked everything crystal clear. "You mean that Engelhart and Mrs. Wylie separately were no threat. Engelhart could be suffering from sour grapes and she could be defending the memory of her husband. But if they pooled their knowledge, they would blow the lid off."

"Surely that is self-evident," said Roberta Ore Simpson with more acuteness than tact. "And we can all understand why that led Hugo Cramer to murder Mrs. Wylie. But the role of this senior civil servant is truly shocking. I am surprised that Davidson Wylie had the temerity ever to make the offer. The odds of its being accepted were against him, and a rejection would have left Macklin in an awkward position."

Thatcher shook his head gently. "The odds weren't as bad as you might expect. Wylie was relatively astute about people; it was his main stock in trade. When he began thinking of bribery, he stopped entertaining ministry officials alone and started asking their wives as well. He was looking for a couple that was hungry for money. The signs were not that difficult to read with the Livermores. Simon is not as expensively groomed as most of the administrative assistants he deals with, the Livermores take jaunts to exotic foreign resorts, but always as guests, Jill uses youth and beauty to sparkle in a scene where many of the women are using diamonds."

Miss Simpson accepted facts, however unpalatable. "I can see that they were in money difficulties, but why?"

"For two reasons. Livermore didn't have any inherited funds and the middle class is being squeezed hard in England these days. He would have had to retrench even if he hadn't changed his way of life. But just as the pressure came on, he started to support two households. He was trying to maintain traditional standards in his first ménage while catering to the needs of a young, expensive second wife."

"And doesn't that take a real bundle!" Norris

Upton exclaimed, with so much fellow-feeling that almost all questions about his current marital status were answered. "He could go into hock in a month paying for the things she dreamed up."

Thatcher was obliged to demur. "It was not simply a matter of bills to be met. Little by little, Jill was changing Simon's values."

"Ah!" As a college president, Roberta was quick to understand. "He was being exposed to the new morality."

"He wasn't so much exposed to it as assaulted by it. I expect that if Livermore had still been married to his first wife, she would have been shocked and appalled at the thought of his accepting a bribe. Jill, on the other hand, would have been shocked and appalled at his refusing it. Where was the harm, she must have argued. His technicians told him he had two evenly balanced bids by two equally competent firms. It would be preposterous not to benefit from the situation. And Wylie was clever in formulating his plan. Livermore had only to sit at his desk and sign on the dotted line. It was Jill and Wylie who engaged in all the histrionics."

George Lancer had been champing at the bit for some time. "This won't do, John. You're telling me what happened, not how it became clear to you."

Thus called to order, Thatcher proceeded in a more systematic fashion. "As I mentioned, Charlie and I began to think in terms of corporate involvement after Mrs. Wylie was murdered. We even considered the possibility that Engelhart used Macklin money to pay off Wylie. But that would have meant personal gain to Wylie, which Francesca had already barred. It was Arthur Shute who directed us from an unsuccessful bribe by NDW to a successful one by Macklin. But he failed to take the final step. In a complicated contest it is more efficient to bribe the referee than one of your rivals. When I remembered that, everything fell into place. The Livermores stood out like sore thumbs on the receiving end. To a lesser degree, Cramer stood out on the paying end. There had to be someone senior to Wylie who okayed the plan and funneled expense money to Europe. That meant it was Cramer or Shute. Cramer was the one who rushed to Wylie's side in Ankara, Cramer was the one who hid him away in a beach cottage, and, above all, Cramer was the one who forced the Livermores to give him an alibi for Francesca's murder."

"They must have loved that," muttered Upton.

"It broke their nerve," Thatcher agreed. "Geography insulated them from Wylie's murder. It was so far away, they could persuade themselves it had nothing to do with them. But they had a rude awakening when Cramer rushed into their living room, fresh from having killed Francesca, and told them they were all in the same boat. They reacted to the emergency by doing what they'd done once before. When Wylie failed to reappear after the ransom payment, Jill Livermore delayed her return to England. She stayed in Tangiers, sitting over her bank account like a hen, with Simon ready to flee to her side at a moment's notice. As soon as they'd given Cramer's alibi to Scotland Yard, Jill took off again. Simon intended to join her at the first hint that the police were closing in on Cramer. It never occurred to them that Jill would be the first one to be arrested."

Lancer was frowning harder than ever. "All right, John, you've told us how you solved it. But how in the world did you get Interpol to move against the wife of a high British official? They would have wanted more than your intuition."

Thatcher had been carefully leading up to this moment. Asparagus and lamb had been a celebration for everybody else. But he had been singing for his supper while the directors of Macklin felt free to pick holes, demand amplification, and air their own views. It was time to assert himself.

"I'm surprised at you, George," he said sorrowfully. "There was proof lying on the ground and you, of all people, should realize that. Wylie's scheme called for the employment of two drifters with a criminal background. In order to speed up the timetable as much as possible, it was necessary for them to hold the ransom note. A nightmare tormenting the conspirators was that the drifters might try to deal themselves into the payoff. Now, if you had been in this plot, what simple precaution would you have taken?"

The frown cleared as if by magic. "I would have given them the wrong account number," Lancer said, thereby justifying the Sloan's reputation.

"Which is why the note had to be addressed to Cramer, rather than to Shute. Cramer had a substitute note at the ready to show you. All I had to do was call the Istanbul police and ask for the number on the note delivered in the restaurant. Then I had solid proof against Cramer. Jill Livermore was even easier. Leopold Grimm identified her."

"I thought the woman in Zurich was disguised," Upton objected.

Thatcher cast his mind back to the night of the Arab party in Richmond. "Oh, she had nothing to fear from a casual encounter, though she took good care to avoid a face-to-face meeting. Her most outstanding characteristics were a very small-boned head and a peculiarly smooth, gliding walk. Well, six-pound mountain boots and a full wig took care of that. Once we found a close-up of her in a wig at her old modeling agency, Leopold was almost certain. Then there was the phone call made to Davidson Wylie's Greek hotel after the ransom was paid. As the call was not completed, the police could not trace it from the Greek end. But when I suggested that it might have originated from Jill's Tangiers hotel, they had no trouble at all. After that it was simple dogwork. In almost no time they lined up witnesses to her flights in and out of Switzerland. Then Interpol was ready to go forward with the arrest. And they caught Jill with two false passports and bank books in the same names. Livermore was arrested trying to board a flight to Tangiers. He caved in at once when he learned his wife was already in custody."

"And I suppose that Cramer caved in when he real-

238

ized that the Livermores had been caught," Lancer ventured.

"Good God, no." Thatcher wondered how to describe the stream of legal talent now circling around Hugo Cramer. "Faced with the evidence that he palmed the original ransom note, he has admitted to participation in the fake kidnapping. But he is still denying the two murders."

Lancer was aghast. "You don't think he'll get away with murdering Davidson Wylie?"

"I don't know whether they'll be able to find proof against him in the bombing, but they're building a very strong case that he killed Francesca. The Livermores will testify to his admission and his attempt to concoct an alibi. Then it turns out that Francesca's cleaning woman was in the room when she spoke to Cramer and asked him to drop by before she went out with Engelhart. And, of course, there's no difficulty about supplying the motive. Scotland Yard is putting forth a major effort, and they hope to find an eyewitness who can place Cramer in that apartment building at the time of the murder. However, Cramer seems determined to fight every inch of the way and turn it into a show trial."

At this vision of the headlines to come, the men relapsed into a somber silence. Only Roberta took action.

"Waiter!" she called, every bit as imperiously as Norris Upton. "We'll have brandy with our coffee. Remy Martin, please."

When the snifters arrived, Norris Upton stared sadly into the golden depths. "You're right, Roberta, we could all use a drink. God, what a mess. Macklin's lost its best men, it's going to lose the Noss Head contract, and Cramer will raise such a stench it will never get an award in Europe again. We may as well start the wake right now."

"Really, I have never heard such nonsense in my life." There was a steely glint in Miss Simpson's eye. "You make Macklin sound like a charitable institution. You're never going to get anywhere in the corporate world, Norris, unless you learn to be a little more hard-nosed. Macklin has to go where the money is, and that's North Sea oil. Losing Noss Head is out of the question. I admit that there have been certain unsavory aspects of Macklin's involvement to date. But the malefactors have been removed, Arthur Shute is as pure as the driven snow, and I understand that young Volpe is proving invaluable." A passing thought seized her fancy. "I wonder if that boy realizes that at the moment Macklin needs him more than he needs Macklin."

"He doesn't, but his wife does," Thatcher supplied obligingly.

"One would think we had never surmounted adversity before," Miss Simpson continued. "After what we three have been through, the problems of Macklin are a mere bagatelle. No government in the world can move as quickly as a construction crew. Our course is clear enough. By the time the British government can formulate a rescind order, the pipelines must be so far advanced that retreat is impossible. I personally look forward to a year-end at which Macklin is in unchallenged possession of Noss Head and has also retrieved its one and a half million dollars. Don't you agree?" She paused to look challengingly around the table.

Norris Upton was still shattered by the charge of being insufficiently swashbuckling. But John Thatcher and George Lancer knew there was only one reply.

"Oh, absolutely!" they chorused, raising their glasses on high.